a THORN in the HEART

Other books by Tim Stafford

a THORN *in the* HEART

TIM STAFFORD

ZondervanPublishingHouse

Grand Rapids, Michigan

A Division of HarperCollins*Publishers*

Requests for information should be addressed to:
Zondervan Publishing House
Grand Rapids, Michigan 49530

Library of Congress Cataloging-in-Publication Data

Stafford, Tim.
    A thorn in the heart / Tim Stafford.
      p. cm.
    ISBN 0-310-58061-7 (pbk.)
    I. Title.
  PS3569.T25T48   1992
  813'.54—dc20   91-44095 CIP

Edited by Harold Fickett
Interior designed by Kim Koning
Cover designed by The Puckett Group

Printed in the United States of America

92 93 94 95 96 97 / DH / 6 5 4 3 2 1

A
THORN
IN
THE
HEART

CHAPTER

1

FEBRUARY

It was raining the day that Robbie Hager turned up missing—a soaking, cold rain that swept in waves over the town of Oakdale. At the Hagers' house, young men and women clomped across the sodden lawn to and from the porch, carrying equipment that they futilely shaded with their hands and hunched-over bodies. Three large vans, each with its TV station logo, were parked at crazy angles on the gravel drive. To Frank Hager, who watched the TV people from his front door, it seemed a strange and intoxicating scene—unnaturally quiet, its colors deep and rich, like a movie's opening shot.

He would not let them come inside—he was particular about his home, and these were strangers—but he was glad the TV people distracted him. Frank Hager wore a tennis shirt and sweats. He was big, four inches over six feet, with rounded shoulders and long arms, an over-age basketball player.

In the middle of the porch stood Francis Balzeti, from the Fresno County Sheriff's Department. Short and broad, firm through the middle like a well-packed ham, he leaned against a post as though daring anyone to budge him. The TV guys would have ushered anybody else aside, but they were smart enough to let a uniform alone.

Balzeti had talked to Hager earlier—mostly questions like

what had Robbie been wearing, had there been any trouble at home, did Hager have a recent picture? Hager had tried to tell him more but had been brushed off. "I don't need to psychoanalyze him," Balzeti said. "Just find him."

The TV people seemed more interested, but they had work to do setting up. One of Channel 30's lights was shorting. Channel 24 was demanding that Channel 30 forfeit their turn. Channel 30 responded by pretending not to hear. Occasionally one of the TV people would ask Hager for something, which was the excuse he used to himself for staying nearby. Hager felt guilty about his interest—his son was missing, after all, might even be dead—but he was curious to see how they filmed the news.

He was the only one of the family watching. Lizzie had hung out with him for a while, until Carrie had taken her to Girl Scouts. He had tried to interest Carrie, his wife, in staying with him, but when the phone rang she had disappeared into the kitchen and had not come back. Stephen, his other son, had not yet come home from school.

Finally Channel 30 called Hager out and positioned him before the door, in the dazzling lights. Dan Conneraught shook his hand for a second time. Hager recognized Conneraught from TV, although it was like seeing an old friend at a fifteenth high school reunion: Once he made the connection, it was obvious, but until then he might have passed Conneraught on the street and never guessed.

People said that Dan had more talent than anybody else in Fresno. He had a problem, though: His lips did not move when he talked, making him look funny on TV, as though someone else was talking and the camera had accidentally pointed at Dan. He tried to overcome it, but at times he still forgot to lip sync with his own voice.

Dan talked to the camera. "Frank Hager, standing with me here at his Oakdale home, is a worried man. Last night four boys who had gone to a basketball game failed to come home. One of them is his son, Robert. Their car has been found on a back mountain road, deserted. No signs of a struggle have been detected.

"A high school prank? Probably not. The four boys are

what are sometimes called 'slow learners.' They have a slight mental handicap. They can care for themselves. They are not dangerous."

Dan turned his body sideways, into Hager. He spoke gently, as though they were old friends and his question was painful. "Frank, it's raining and cold here. Where do you think your son is?"

Hager had been fidgeting during Dan's warm-up, shifting his weight from one foot to the other, barely hearing. His face looked hurt and miserable. It took him a moment to understand that the question was aimed at him.

"Well, I just don't know. I hope to God somebody has them in a warm place, and I hope they let them go. They're just harmless kids."

"So you think they've been kidnapped. Has there been any indication, any ransom note?"

Hager shook his head.

"Why would anyone want to harm your son?"

Being interviewed, Hager looked like a young Lyndon Johnson: those big shoulders stooped over, those long arms. And something more: an unforced familiarity. Easy access to the emotions.

"Dan," he said, "a child like that doesn't have enemies. He's the sweetest kid. . . ." Here his voice twisted slightly. "All those kids are. They're so polite to everybody, and all they want is to be treated normally like any other kid. It would take a pretty sick person to want to hurt them."

The other conversations on the porch died out. Hager was coming across.

"In case he's seen by our viewers, would you describe your son for us?"

Suddenly Hager's voice began to flutter; he needed a deep breath to push words out of his throat. "He's a big kid, almost my size, with long hair, light brown. He usually wears a baseball cap. He had one on last night, and tennis shoes. Oh, and he wears glasses. He's just a really nice, polite kid. You wouldn't know he's slow."

"Frank, the Sheriff's Department and the Rescue Search

Group are out looking for your son and his three friends, as they have been all day. Have they found anything?"

Dan stuck the microphone too close into Hager's face, and Hager flinched back. For a moment he seemed to lose his bearings. "I don't think so. I guess they would have told me if they had."

"Meanwhile," Dan continued in the undertaker's tone that signaled he was closing out, "it is raining in Oakdale, and snowing heavily where the Hagers' car was found abandoned. Four boys are missing, and the search goes on in the hope that they are still alive."

Dan looked straight into the camera for several seconds, then said, "Got it?"

"Great," said the cameraman.

"Thank you, Mr. Hager," Dan said, and began rolling up his cord. Hager stood alone momentarily, as though expecting the conversation to continue, and then turned to go indoors. Before he reached the door, Channel 24 was talking to him.

Channel 24 had a new guy. Dark hair flopped over his forehead, he wore a bandit mustache, and he gripped Hager by the elbow, whether to steady himself or Hager was hard to say. "Do you have anything to show?" he asked, putting his face so close that Hager could smell the mouthwash. "A photo? Or some memento? Something that reminds you of your son?"

Hager went inside, to the family room where three large paintings hung by the fireplace. He carefully lifted down the one on the left, which showed a boy with a brown crewcut grinning broadly. Carrie watched him from the kitchen. Her friend Jane was with her; Hager had not seen her arrive.

"What's that for?" Carrie asked. She had cautious dark eyes and carefully managed black hair.

"Channel 24 wants to show it," Hager explained. "I told them it's an old picture, but they said it didn't matter."

"Don't let them keep it," Carrie said.

"I won't," he said. "Why don't you come out? I'm sure they'd like to interview you."

Carrie merely shook her head.

"The pastor called," she said. "He wants to come over."

"How'd he find out?" Hager asked.

"I don't know. Maybe it was on the radio."

"Is he coming over?"

"I told him you would call him back."

Hager set the picture on the floor, leaning it against his knees. "What do you think, honey? Do you want him to come?" Conscious that the TV people were waiting, he nonetheless restrained himself from hurrying. Carrie did not like it when he rushed off.

She said nothing, only stared at him, and for a moment he was afraid he had said something wrong. Then a quick sob shook her. He leaned the picture against a chair and went to her. Jane already had her arms wrapped around Carrie's shoulders. Hager took Carrie's hand, wet from brushing away tears.

"I think it would be good to have the pastor," he said. "I'll call him."

Carrie shook her head furiously, no.

"It's okay, Frank," Jane said. "You go finish up. I'll stay with her."

He hesitated, unsure what to do. "Honey, Robbie's only missing. There could be some explanation. They might find him any minute."

"Go on, Frank," Carrie said, her face buried in her hands. "I'll be all right. I love you."

Jane looked up at him and nodded, smiling her confidence that everything would be under control.

"Okay," he said. "I love you too. I won't be long."

One of the TV guys took the picture from Hager's arms as he went out the door, and before Hager could make sure they would return it the news guy had him by the elbow again and was lining him up for the camera. "All right, go," he said and put on his smile, which was wrong for the story.

"It's raining hard in Oakdale," he began. "At the higher elevations, snow is piling up. Somewhere, perhaps exposed to this rain and snow, are four mentally retarded boys who disappeared late last night on their way home from a basketball game. This morning their car was found deserted on a lonely mountain road."

Hager felt a slight jerk where the man's hand held his elbow, a tug like a fish on a line. Glancing up, Hager saw the newsman staring to one side, his face taut. The newsman looked back at the camera, then to the side again. "Hey! Hey!" he shouted, gesturing fiercely with the microphone. "Get out of here!" The camera crew from Channel 47, who were testing their lights, had broken his concentration.

One of the technicians looked up at him, smiled, and made an obscene gesture.

They started the film again, and ran through the introduction again just to be safe. "Here with me is the father of one of the boys, Frank Hager, a real-estate salesman here in Oakdale. Can you tell me, Mr. Hager, when you last saw your son?"

Hager hesitated. "I'm not really a real-estate salesman; I'm a developer. I do apartments. Small subdivisions." A flicker of pain shot through Channel 24's eyes, but he let the film run on. They were late. "I saw Robbie when he came home from school yesterday. Then he went off to the game."

"Did you notice anything unusual about his behavior?"

"Not really. He liked going to those basketball games, so I'd say he was really happy."

"Mr. Hager, did your son have any enemies that you know of?"

"No, not really, it was just as I was telling Dan, Robbie is a nice, polite . . ." He stopped because Channel 24 had dropped the microphone.

"Mr. Hager," he said, "please don't mention the other TV stations." After a moment's silence he lifted the microphone again. "All right," he said to his crew. "Can we pick it up at that question, or do we have to take it clear back to the beginning?"

They picked it up at the question, but the interruptions seemed to have shaken Hager. He kept his answers short, as though his mind was on something else.

"Can you think of any reason why someone would want to harm him or the other boys?"

"Not really. Sometimes other kids tease him, like kids do, you know, just to be mean. But not really to try to hurt him."

"Is there any possibility that this is a prank?"

Hager swallowed one time before he answered. "You know, these boys are slow learners. They might try a prank, but I never saw them get very far . . ." His voice trailed off.

The reporter hesitated, waiting for Hager to go on. He didn't.

"So the mystery is complete," Channel 24 said. "Four boys have disappeared—that much we know. But where they are, and whether someone intends them harm, we don't know. This is the face of Robert Hager." The camera panned to the painting, propped up by a young woman in jeans and white sneakers. "When last seen, he was wearing a baseball cap and tennis shoes. Anyone who sees this boy should contact the sheriff's office immediately." The newsman remained frozen and serious for a few seconds, although the camera was not on him but on the oil portrait. Then he barked, "Did you get it?" His cameraman did not bother to answer but began to pack things up. "You got it?" the reporter asked again, and again went unanswered. He left Hager abruptly, without saying thanks.

Hager had no chance to regret it. Already Channel 47 was on him. That is, Tom Bollinger had one arm around him, talking familiarly. Hager had seen him on the news for years, but never really liked him. Tom was round and soft, and anything he wore looked like a sweatsuit. He would never get out of Fresno.

While Bollinger chatted, seeming to have plenty of time, Channel 24 completed their packing, slammed the back of their van, and ground down the gravel driveway. Darkness was coming, and the porch was suddenly uncrowded. The TV guys lined them up in the pose that reminded Hager of baseball—cameraman pitching, reporter and subject huddled like batter and catcher. "Let's go," Tom said, and the technician brought a finger down to let them know the film was rolling. For a moment it was still; you could hear the rain sweep over the roof.

"Mr. Hager, where do you think your son Robert is tonight?"

It was too much for Hager. His emotions overwhelmed him. He tried to back away, but Tom's arm stretched out behind his back and held him. In a low voice Hager said, "Look, this is the third time I've been through this. Can't you think of some other question?"

Bollinger did not move. He kept the microphone steady in Hager's face.

"The point is," Hager said, "it doesn't really matter what I think. What matters is *him*." He struggled to take a deep breath.

He put a hand up to his face to brush his eyes, then dropped the hand and let the tears come. "It's incredible. Somebody must have him. Why, for God's sake? What do they want? We don't have that kind of money. He's just a kid who's no good to anyone in the world but me and God. He'll always be a kid. He'll never grow up and be able to act like an adult."

His big hands were loose and beginning to loop around. His voice was hurting, puzzled. "I've done my best. What I can't figure out is what anyone would want with him. We're the only ones who want him." He had lowered his face, and was almost mumbling; now he swung his head up to look into the camera, as though he could see through the lens to the people watching. "What do you want with him? What?"

He dropped his head again. "I'm sorry. But do you see? I miss him. I'm his father. To me it doesn't matter that he's—" He stopped as though he had forgotten his thought. Then he looked at Tom and half smiled.

"That was just fine," Tom said to him. "Good job. I'm sure they'll find him."

CHAPTER

2

Tears had come to Hager in front of the cameras, but after the TV people left he reverted to nervous, depressed loneliness. He went inside, suddenly remembering Carrie, but she had reverted to calm. She and Jane talked quietly, drinking coffee and leaning into the conversation at the kitchen counter. He interrupted for a minute, checking on her. She seemed to be fine. She reminded him about the pastor's call.

Hager telephoned the church. The perky voice of the secretary answered. The pastor had gone out, she said. She asked whether he wanted to be put on the prayer chain.

"Yeah, sure," he said. "That would be nice."

"It can't hurt," she said cheerfully.

"Just tell George not to worry about coming over just now. Jane Newman is here and we're doing okay. Just pray they find the kids."

He was restless, driving to his office but finding it deserted, then stopping by the coffee shop fifty yards down the highway. He hoped to run into some of his contractor friends, who often gathered there in the afternoon. In a corner booth he found a couple of younger guys he knew slightly. One did floors and the other did room additions and remodels; he could not think of their names but could visualize the floor guy's showroom. They invited him to join them. From the casual way they said it he could see that they had no idea what had happened, and he couldn't bring himself to tell the news. He said he had to get going and went home again.

Jane had gone. Carrie told him that she had talked to some of the other boys' parents. They were all worried, and Donnie's mother wanted to get them all together to share information. Hager started to phone the Aranians—he sometimes bought furniture through Richard Aranian, so he was a friend—but he put the receiver down before he had finished dialing. He didn't know if he could bear talking about it with Richard.

Now he stood awkwardly in the kitchen, wanting to make conversation while Carrie cooked but unsure whether talk was welcome.

"They're really sharp, those TV guys," he said. "They must have thought I was a real hick. I got all upset that they were asking me the same question about Robbie over and over. The different channels would each ask, you know."

He slipped up behind Carrie at the stove and put his arms around her, rocking her slightly. He usually liked her quietness and found it comforting that she didn't try to respond to everything he said. "Where do you think Robbie is right now?" he asked.

She didn't answer. Carrie was a rock. She kept on stirring her pot.

"I wish I knew," he said.

Still she made no response.

"You don't seem very upset," he said.

"Of course I'm upset. He's my son too, you know."

"Well, don't get mad. How am I supposed to know what you're thinking?"

He left Carrie without saying anything more and went into the den. He had designed the house himself, a spreading, comfortable ranch-style place, with a picture window overlooking the valley. He called the den his "signature" room. Carpeted in thick dark-blue shag, it had big modern leather chairs and an underdecorated sense of spaciousness. At one end he had designed a sunken fireplace, with carpeted bench seats around it. The television was built into the wall behind Spanish oak panels.

He had put in an intercom beside it; the TV salesman had talked him into it. He seldom used it because, though he liked it, Carrie didn't. Now he considered calling her in the kitchen but thought better of it. Instead he called Stephen in his room.

Stephen took a long time to answer. Hager had almost given up on him when a response came: a crackly "Yeah."

"What are you up to, Steve?"

"I'm reading."

"Reading what?"

"A book. Hemingway."

"*For Whom the Bell Tolls?*"

"*The Sun Also Rises.*"

"I've never read that. Is it good?"

"Yeah. Dad, what do you want?"

He was embarrassed. "Nothing, Steve. I just wanted to see whether this thing still works. I think dinner will be ready pretty soon."

"Okay."

"Over and out."

Hager thought he should be feeling something more traumatic, some dog-sick grief. He felt agitated, stirred up so he couldn't sit still. It was only when he tried to talk and his voice croaked that he knew how affected he was.

He made himself sit down in his big reclining leather chair; he crossed his size-thirteen feet. Each day he carefully powdered his shoes to avoid athlete's foot. Once, years ago, Robbie had, as a joke, literally filled them, so that when he had put them on his toes had been constricted, and white puffs of powder had appeared at each step. It had been the best joke poor Robbie had ever managed. Hager had played along with it to the extent of walking around in those shoes, leaking baby power, for most of the day. Robbie must have been about eight then.

Even if the kid was retarded, Hager felt closer to him than to anybody else. He had never tried to explain this to anyone except Carrie. To most people, a retarded individual was pitiful. Well, he had thought that way when they first began to suspect—when Robbie was tiny. He had lost sleep to the sense of horror. For a time he had even dreaded touching Robbie, as though he had a disease that could be contracted.

But that had passed. Now he thought the world might be better with more retarded people: too dumb to be really dangerous. The problem was, you had to protect them. But that was a problem a father should not mind so much. The truth was, Hager did not entirely like the idea that his children were growing up.

Some things he could not protect Robbie from, like when the neighborhood parents had said he could not play with the girls any longer. He couldn't stop the kids from teasing Robbie, and he couldn't stop his crying. But he could make sure Robbie didn't lack for food and clothes and even love, things that were just as important to a kid like Robbie as to any other kid—maybe more important, since his brain couldn't handle much beyond today and tomorrow.

When Lizzie came in, slamming the door, he called her over to him. She was eleven; she had braces and the figure of a newly planted tree, but she was going to be pretty. In her hand was a bright green plastic cassette player. "Give me a kiss," Hager said, and pulled her skinny body into the chair. He was glad she would still hug and that this closeness brought nothing more complicated than comfort between father and child. He felt the dampness of her dress through his own clothes; she had been out in the rain.

"What are you listening to these days?" he asked, picking the recorder out of her hand.

"*Crystal Wind*," she said.

He popped the cassette out and studied it. "Is this the latest thing?"

"Daddy," she said with mock disapproval, "they broke up a long time ago."

"Is that right? I need to keep up on this thing. Are those four guys with the long hair still together? The Beatles?"

"Are they some group from when you were a boy?"

"All right," he said. "Watch your manners."

"Aren't you going to watch TV?" she asked. "To see yourself?"

He looked at his watch. "Five more minutes."

They sat still. "Daddy, where do you think Robbie is?"

"I don't know, Lizzie. I can't begin to guess."

"Do you think someone might have kidnapped him?"

"That's possible," Hager admitted.

"And then they would want money, right?"

"They might."

"But if they wanted money, wouldn't they have kept the car?"

"Not necessarily. That old car isn't worth much. And a stolen car can be traced pretty easily."

"How much money do you think they would want?"

"I don't know. It couldn't be too much. None of us has much."

"I don't think they were kidnapped," Lizzie said firmly. "I think they've gone to a cabin up there and are just trying to scare us."

"What makes you think that?"

"Well, in the first place," Lizzie said, "why would somebody want to kidnap four retards? You just said we don't have any money."

Hager winced. "Retard" was not allowed; Hager never used it himself out loud.

"Who says that kidnappers have good reasons for what they do?"

"Well, I think they're just trying to scare us. I bet they snuck out to one of those cabins."

"Lizzie, they found the car on Tamarack Ridge. There aren't any cabins around there. Not for miles and miles."

"Somebody could have given them a ride. Or maybe they even hid a car up there."

Hager had a momentary vision of four ponderous man-children living it up in a remote, snow-covered cabin. What would they do with themselves? Maybe play hours of joyful football in the living room, knocking over anything they pleased, smashing out windows, then going outside and lying in the snow with no one to tell them they had to come inside. He hoped it was true. Of course, within an hour someone would be sulking, someone else would be screaming because the snow was down his shirt and he was cold.

"Let's turn on the TV," he said. "It's time."

Lizzie flipped back and forth between the channels. They stared at commercials, then the lead-in for channel 30 news. Hager was the first item. "Hey, everybody—Mom, Steve!—Dad's on TV! Come quick!" Stephen did not appear—possibly he could not hear—but Carrie came in, drying her hands on her apron.

"Look at that color," Hager said. "It's awful. Look. It's the shirt I've got on."

He was embarrassed at the way he sounded: nasal, slobby, as though he had a cold. He kept looking away from the camera too. They had switched to a shot of the station wagon, covered with snow. Lizzie changed over to 24 just in time to catch a final glimpse of Hager's interview and the shot of Robbie's portrait. The channel went to an interview with the Deputy County Sheriff, who looked fleshier on camera than in person. All he said was that they were doing everything they could to find those boys and would appreciate any information.

Stephen came in from his room and sat down on the floor. He had aviator glasses with a tint; Hager thought they made him look like a hood. "You missed Daddy twice," Lizzie said accusingly. She switched to 47. They showed the car and then the gym at Three Streams where the basketball game had been played. "The four boys left the gym about 9:15, while the game was still being played, after a scuffle with another spectator. Early this morning their car was found covered with snow on Tamarack Ridge, far off the route they should have followed home. Police say there was no sign of any mechanical trouble."

Then they put Hager on. This was the time he got emotional. He grew warm watching himself; he thought he looked ridiculous. But when it was over and he glanced shyly around at his family, he saw that Carrie was crying. He swung over the edge of the chair and went to put his arms around her. She did not respond but stood mechanically drying her hands on her apron.

"It's okay, babe," Hager said.

"I just don't know what's happening," she said. "I'm scared."

Lizzie started to weep too. The TV was talking about a farmworker's demonstration in Sacramento. "Steve, turn the TV off, would you?" Hager asked.

In the silence he thought he ought to make a short speech, to calm everybody down. "Look," he said. "Let's not get too upset until we have something to be upset about. Let's just keep our hopes up, and maybe Robbie will turn out to be fine. Okay?" He thought he sounded like a coach at halftime. "Let's just all stick together and help each other. You kids help your mom especially."

"Did you kids hear your dad?" Carrie asked, her voice cracking.

"Yeah," Lizzie said, and she began to sob. Carrie went to hold her.

"We're going to be all right," Hager said. "Let's not lose our cool." Then, as soon as the words came out of his mouth, he felt his guts heave and a sob escaped his lips. He put his arms out and leaned his weight on Stephen, who patted his back.

Finally they all stopped, lifted their heads, looked at each other. *It was good to cry together*, Hager thought, *though embarrassing*. Carrie shook her head and said she was all right; she went back to the kitchen. Lizzie asked if she could turn the television back on.

"Hey, Steve," Hager asked. "What was that about a scuffle in the gym? I didn't hear about that."

"It wasn't anything," Stephen said. "Paul dumped a whole coke on a guy sitting in front of him. The guy got mad and threatened to punch him out. So Paul started yelling and crying. They had to get him out of there, and Robbie and the other guys went with him."

"Did they go straight home?"

Stephen shrugged. His voice was soft, trailing toward silence at the ends of his sentences. "Obviously, no. I don't know where they went. But I told them to go straight home. I figured that if they hung around the school, they'd just get into trouble. And it was starting to snow a little too."

Hager was touched. From the time he was small, Stephen had been amazingly responsive to his brother's needs. "So you went outside to help them," Hager said. "You were the last person to see Robbie . . ." He'd started to say "alive"—but stopped himself.

Stephen seemed to consider it. "One of the last, anyway." Then he turned his head away and took off his glasses.

Hager put his hand on his son's shoulder. "Seems to be a pretty weepy family around here," he said. "And we haven't even got something to cry about yet."

The two of them stood that way for a few moments, Hager holding Stephen's shoulder softly, tentatively. Then Stephen seemed to pull himself out of the tears and put his head upright. "I probably shouldn't minimize that fight, Dad. I mean, at this point who knows what might have happened?"

"I'm sure the police will check everything out," Hager said.

CHAPTER

3

Frank Hager tapped on Stephen's door, then cautiously opened it. "Oh, there you are," he said. Stephen was standing over a bubbling salt-water aquarium, holding a small net. The storm had cleared overnight, and sun gleamed on the wet trees and grass outside, but only one bar of light broke through Stephen's curtains where they did not quite meet in the middle of the window.

Stephen glanced at his father and put his net down slowly. Watching the painstaking motion, Hager felt a surge of pity. He thought, *Isn't it strange? I have to talk, and he can't talk at all.* But Stephen was more like Carrie: a few close friends, careful words.

Hager had awakened feeling fine, full of atomic energy. Some fragment of a busy, sun-filled dream clung to his mind. Two steps out of the warm bed he had remembered Robbie and his agitation had returned.

"Steve, I got a call from the Sheriff's Department. They said we could come and get Robbie's car whenever we wanted to. I thought it might be kind of good to see where he disappeared. And anyway, we can't leave the car up there. Would you help me out? You can drive my new car if you want."

Stephen had picked up his net again and was gently dipping it into the water.

"What are you doing?" Hager asked.

"Feeding the wrasses," Stephen said. "Brine shrimp." He was leaning over, concentrating on the fish.

"You have to feed them by hand?"

"That's the best way."

"Can we go right now, Steve? I'd like to get up there."

"Just a minute, Dad." Stephen kept on dipping his net. Anxious to take off, Hager was momentarily annoyed and then sharply checked himself. Stephen was grieving, he realized, in his own solitary way.

Hager moved toward him and gingerly put a hand on his son's shoulder. "It's an awful time, isn't it, Steve?"

They stood together quietly for a moment. Stephen said, "Do you think you could get Mom to go?"

Again Hager felt annoyed, though he tried to keep it out of his voice. "It isn't going to take that long, Steve. The fish will survive for an hour, won't they?"

"It's not the fish. I just don't know if I want to go up there."

Hager was surprised, then moved. "Sure. I understand," he said, and gave his son's arm a squeeze. "I understand," he said again.

*   *   *

The road toward Tamarack left the Yosemite highway in town, dived into the valley and over the river, then switch-backed steeply up the ridge on the other side. Within fifteen minutes they saw the first slushy snow, and shortly they were driving hedged between three-foot banks of it. Carrie had insisted they eat lunch before going—she said she had it all ready—so it was already past one o'clock. A bright sun and brilliant sky cut the forest into one-colored shapes: sky and deep shadow, Crayola-colored forest-green trees, and stretches of snow as blank as typing paper.

Carrie was sitting with her head near the window, her legs tucked neatly underneath her. He could remember her sitting like that in high school. They seldom rode together any more; they were both too busy. Hager had been out with Robbie more than with Carrie until Robbie had gotten his license.

"I hate this," Hager said with sudden vehemence. "Carrie, I feel like he's gone. I don't know why, I just feel we've lost him. It's pointless to go up there."

"We're going to get the car," she reminded him.

Sometimes her common sense grated on him. Sometimes, fleetingly, he wondered how much she cared about Robbie. He knew the thought was nonsense; she was incredibly dedicated. She just wasn't a sentimental person. *Maybe*, he thought, *she acts like this to protect herself.* She took things hard, he knew. For months after Robbie's diagnosis she had been upset and uncommunicative, and he had worried about her. Only after Stephen's birth had she snapped out of it.

To Hager she never seemed terribly affectionate with Robbie. She said she was glad for the relationship he had with Robbie, but she never seemed to want to share it. Everything possible, she did for Robbie. She was a dedicated mother. Hager couldn't fault her, though her behavior seemed slightly mechanical.

"I know I'm making too much of this," he admitted. "I'm feeling pretty worked up. I don't know what I'm expecting."

"You know they're looking for him up there," she said. She had a harsh set to her face, as though seeing some invisible outrage.

"Yeah. I'm so afraid they'll find him. I don't want to be there to see him."

"You mean dead?"

He twitched from the word. "If he's alive I certainly want to see him."

"Well, don't give up hope. He might be."

"You don't sound very happy about it," he said, and then immediately was sorry he had said it.

They drove in silence, flashing in and out of sunlight, until they arrived at the turnoff for Tamarack Ridge. It required a hard turn back to the left almost 150 degrees. Their tires crunched onto the hard snow. From here the road was unplowed.

"You think we can make it up there without chains?" Hager asked, more of himself than Carrie. "I guess we can try. Hope we don't get stuck in a snowbank." He gunned the motor, and the tires spun, caught, spun again, grabbed traction, and pushed the heavy car up the packed ruts left by other cars before them.

Tamarack Ridge, named after the tall bush-crowned pines that grow on it, got a name only because of the road that runs along it on the way to a dammed lake. It lies in the mid-Sierra, where the bones of the hills are deeply padded with soil and humus, and mile upon mile of indifferent hills are covered with forest. A few scattered artificial lakes attract clusters of summer cabins, but away from these the mountains are empty of people, not because of inaccessibility but because of the absence of a defining detail—the peak, the deep river valley to attract the eye.

The road split the side of the ridge, ascending along it, and at a nameless spot Hager came on the place where Robbie's car had been found. At first, through the trees around a slight bend he saw a handful of cars, but when the road opened in front of him he realized that he had stumbled into a city of activity. He saw the big TV vans that yesterday had cluttered his driveway; then he saw the black-and-white police cars from the sheriff's. And there were other cars he did not recognize.

Only as he pulled up alongside did he see his own dark-green Chrysler station wagon, pillowed with snow. The snow had been marred on the hood and within an arm's length on the roof, by searching hands probably; but on the very top the snow lay deep and undisturbed.

No one seemed to notice him as he idled slowly along the row of parked cars. There were sheriff's deputies standing around, eying him. He recognized some of the TV people but they did not seem to see him. They were busy looking down the hill.

"Now what do we do?" he asked.

"Let's park," Carrie said.

Hager cut off the engine abruptly and got out of the car, leaving it in the middle of the road. One of the sheriff's men, a slender Mexican with a thin mustache, approached. "You need to move your car," he ordered. It's blocking traffic."

Hager was edgy, and he was used to blocking traffic.

Whenever he drove onto a construction site, he left his car wherever it stopped. "I won't be here long," he said. "I just want to get my car and go. What's going on?"

The little man, who had made detective after just three years on the force, was not going to be put off. "I don't care how long you're here," he shot back. "You're in the way. Move it out of here."

"Let me have the keys, Frank," Carrie said. "I'll move it."

But Hager's dander was up. "It's not bothering anybody," he retorted.

"Fine," the detective said and pulled a notebook out of his back pocket.

"You write that ticket and see what kind of hamburger the sheriff makes of you," Hager threatened. "Where's your boss? I came to get the car."

"What car?" The detective stopped, not quite sure of himself.

"That car."

"Are you the boy's father?"

"Yeah. Where's your boss?"

"I'll get him for you." The detective put away his notebook and walked briskly to one of the squad cars, where he opened the door, reached in and honked the horn.

Carrie looked up at Hager and smiled. He grinned back, sheepishly. He knew she loved this side of him. When they had been in high school she, the prim church-going girl, had given him those silent looks that egged him into doing all kinds of things. She was more sensible now—so was he—but it still amused her to see him get stirred up. Her reaction embarrassed and pleased him.

One of the TV guys came up, looking at their faces. "You're the boy's father, aren't you? We interviewed you yesterday."

When Hager said yes, the man turned and hurried off, returning in a few moments with Dan Conneraught, the Channel 30 reporter. "Did you come to identify the body?" was Dan's first question.

Before Hager had time to take that in, other TV people surrounded them, piling questions on top of each other. One of them put a hand on Carrie's arm, pulling at her to come aside for an interview. Hager swiped the hand away.

Then Balzeti arrived, having pushed his short body up the hill as fast as he could. He came charging across the snow with the stride of a rooster, head back, stomach out, pointing the toes on his boots out sideways as he thrust them forward. Before he reached the Hagers, he was already shouting at the reporters to get away. They ignored him, babbling questions more furiously. Balzeti pushed them aside. "Mr. Hager?" he said. "Mrs. Hager?" He looked around. "We need a more private place. Would you mind if we got into my car for a moment?"

Balzeti wore wrap-around Polaroids of a kind favored fifteen years before. He led the Hagers to his car. They got into the front, with Carrie in the middle. The TV people crowded around outside.

"Buzzards," Balzeti said, taking a deep breath and blowing it out. "Heartless." He shook his head. "Do you mind if I drive down the road a little bit?"

Hager said that he didn't mind. He was as aware of the reporters as he might have been of a fly buzzing around. He was barely aware of Balzeti, even of Carrie. She had reached out and taken his hand, which he noticed only when he looked down and found her fingers in his lap.

Balzeti turned on the ignition and drove, stopping a hundred yards down the road, leaving the engine sputtering. A plume of steam from the exhaust drifted over them. Ahead, the road, a pure ribbon of white, bisected the hill. Balzeti did not look at them while he talked. They all looked ahead.

"You probably know," Balzeti said, "that we've found a body. That's all the reporters know. I wanted to wait until you came to release the identity. It's your son." He waited a beat. "I'm sorry."

Hager had, of course, anticipated this moment, as every parent does. He had thought about what it would be like to lose a child—How he would feel, what thoughts would go through his mind. That was part of protecting them—anticipating possible failure.

But the expected reactions did not come. He did not feel

sick or sad. He felt nothing, as though he had been told about an airline crash in some small, far-off, God-forsaken country. And then he felt intense irritation with Balzeti for setting up this private moment. What was he supposed to say—thank you?

But it has to be accepted, because it is really true, Hager told himself. He squeezed Carrie's hand. She was crying without making a sound. He would not have known except for the wetness streaking her cheeks. Then she took in a sharp breath, almost a sob.

His son was dead. He couldn't say what he felt. He shouldn't shoot the messenger. He had to show that he appreciated the concern. Hager took a deep breath and managed to ask calmly where Robbie was.

"He's down at the bottom of the hill. As far as we can tell, he died painlessly in the cold."

Hager wanted out of the car. His body wanted to move, wanted motion as lungs want air. He tried to make himself stay still and his brain stay active. He wanted to remain rational. This was important. It had really happened: His son had died, and he needed to ask the right questions. Again he took a deep breath. "Somebody killed him, or what?"

"We can't tell yet. He doesn't seem to have any marks on him. We'll need an autopsy. But it could have been the cold."

"That's stupid." Hager lost control for a moment. "No, that's plain stupid. Robbie wouldn't stay out in the cold when he could get into the car. He knew what to do in the snow."

Carried squeezed his hand. "Don't," she whispered.

Hager ignored her. "You obviously don't know a thing about these kids," he said.

Balzeti didn't answer. He seemed embarrassed by Hager's reaction.

"I'm here to help," he stated quietly. "Just take all the time you need."

Which made Hager angrier. He had to get out of the car, but Balzeti sat as still as a stump, waiting for something.

"Put it in gear," Hager said. "Let's go look. That's okay, isn't it? I can see my kid?"

"Sure," Balzeti said. "I wanted to ask whether you would

mind making an identification. The body isn't in the best condition. I didn't know whether it would upset you." He punched the lever into reverse and looked up into the mirror while he backed toward the cluster of cars and people.

"I thought you said he died from the cold."

"He might have."

"But you said he didn't have any marks on him."

Balzeti nodded sagaciously. "No. Not that we can see. But the body has frozen, and it's in a strange position. It's hard to see the face at all. I'm just letting you know that it can be upsetting to look at. I'd suggest that Mrs. Hager just stay in the car. You don't both need to see it. But we would like an identification." Balzeti paused as they pulled to a stop and reporters began to come around the car. "And don't worry. If you need any relief, just let me know. Everyone understands. I'll try to keep these guys away." He indicated the reporters around them.

Hager grabbed for the door handle, but Balzeti reached across Carrie and put a hand on his arm, gripping it firmly, each finger pressing into his skin. "Just one more thing, Mr. Hager. I think it would be better if you didn't say anything to the reporters."

Hager did not ask why. He opened the door, swinging it out among the crowding reporters. His detachment had disappeared. He wanted to see Robbie.

"Frank." It was Carrie's voice, and he didn't want to stop for it, but he did, leaning back into the car. She put her hand up on his collar. "I love you, Frank."

"I love you too."

"Do you mind if I don't go down? I'd just as soon stay here."

"That's fine, honey. There's no need for you to go. Will you be all right here?"

"I'll be fine."

"I'll have my men keep the reporters away," Balzeti said.

Hager pushed blindly through the reporters, not hearing their questions, shoving one of them when he stepped in front of him.

Down the path they went. Hager had on tennis shoes;

there was slush and muck and needles underfoot in the thin trench that feet had worn in the snow. He had to watch his step.

"All the reporters have to stay on the road," Balzeti shouted from behind him. And then, to himself, "Vultures."

They came to the bottom of the hill. The reporters were gone, and it seemed as though the roaring of the sea had quieted. Only a few men in uniform were near, and they did not look at Hager. No one said a word.

At the center of a little mucky area was a dark-blue blanket, covering a knee-high lump. It was not long like a body; it had more the shape of a small boulder.

"Are you all right?" Balzeti asked, putting a hand on his shoulder.

"I'm fine," Hager answered, shrugging the hand away. "How did you find him down here?" Now that he was near, he was not in such a hurry to go nearer.

"To tell you the truth, we almost stumbled on him. It was like a needle in the haystack. One of my men had been searching through the snow down here, and later on I was looking down the hill and noticed something red showing in the snow. It was his parka. Ramirez had almost walked on him, and he didn't even know it."

"Oh. Pretty lucky," Hager said.

"You always need some luck," Balzeti said. "You try everything and you pray for luck."

"Right," Hager said, hardly hearing. The blue lump was making him queasy.

"Are you ready?" Balzeti asked, and when Hager nodded, Balzeti signaled his men to stand on the uphill side of the body, to shield the reporters' view. Then he lifted off the blanket, carefully folding it in his arms.

At first it was hard to see anything but a pile of clothes. The body did not make sense, for it was in a tight crouch, the back and behind raised up. The face was right down in the snow, and the arms shielded it.

"We could turn him over if it's necessary," Balzeti said. "But we were hoping that you could make an identification without that."

Hager put his hand out to the back. That was the hardest part: the first touch. As soon as he had done it his grief came, and he began to sob. This was not Robbie; it was hard, unyielding, a thing. Oh God, Robbie was gone. He ran his hand across the slippery red nylon of the parka.

"If you could identify these as your son's clothes, that might be enough," Balzeti said.

Hager could not catch his breath to look. He felt as though something had knocked his guts inside out.

"That's his parka," he managed to say.

"We found his wallet in the right-hand pocket," Balzeti answered softly.

"Not in his pants? He usually kept it in his pants," Hager said. "I know because I have back problems and a wallet gives me trouble if I sit on it." The trousers were blue jeans. They could belong to any kid.

"See if you recognize the shirt," Balzeti suggested.

Hager's hand reached out, pulling back the parka's collar. The shirt underneath was a red flannel, faded and soft. "I'm not sure," he mumbled. "His mother would know. I never remember clothes." His hand was pulling at the velvety fabric, trying to see more than a fragment.

"Maybe we should turn him," Balzeti said.

Hager noticed the hair, first as an odd detail, then as a sign he was fearful to read. A sound escaped his throat. It might have been a sob but was more like a low chortle. The hair was black. Robbie's hair was brown. Hager had his hand on the hair. No, it was not right, the texture was coarse. *It's not him,* he said to himself. He stood up straight with a wild happiness spreading over his face. "Thank God."

No one responded. Hager saw that they were looking at him with curiosity. He smiled. "Don't look at me like that," he said. "The hair is wrong. It's not him."

He bent over, his head touching the snow, and tried to see the face. "I think it's Petey. Sorry for smiling," he said when he looked around again and found them still staring.

One of the officers, the same short, slight man who had initially accosted him when he arrived, finally spoke. "Mr. Hager, we've already identified the body. He was carrying a driver's license. And other things. Photos. This is just a formality. But we can do it later. I realize this is a difficult time for you."

Hager felt impossibly happy. He smiled at the little man. "You can do whatever you want whenever you want. That's not my son."

The officer was not smart enough to quit. "Isn't your son Robert Hager?"

Hager had a temper. "Look, idiot, I know my son. I don't need a driver's license to recognize him." Suddenly Balzeti's hands were on him, pushing him back, and he realized he must have moved forward threateningly. He was embarrassed but all the while too relieved to care.

"I need to tell Carrie," he said. "Right now."

He started up the muddy path to the road, and as soon as he was going felt compelled to go faster, trying to run, slipping and falling in the snow, banging his knee down hard. Balzeti was calling for him, but he only glanced back and yelled, "I just need to tell her."

When he got to the road, he looked into the sheriff's car and found it empty, then looked wildly about. She was not in his car, either. Finally he spotted her in Robbie's old station wagon. She had started it, was warming the engine. He opened the passenger door and leaned in.

"Don't look so gloomy, Carrie," he said. "It's not him."

She did not seem to understand.

"Carrie, it's not him! I think it's Petey Aranian."

He felt a hand fall hard on his arm. Balzeti had a fierce expression. "Please, Mr. Hager," he said. "Talk all you want later on. But not in front of the press." Indeed, the reporters were now crowding around the car and asking questions, all at once.

Hager stayed after Carrie left with Robbie's car. He did not want to leave; he was happy in a place where his son had not been found. All through the afternoon he was a kind of celebrity. The TV people shouted questions at him, though Balzeti kept them off. The officers glanced at him and treated him with respect. He watched everything and went everywhere, while others were restricted.

Balzeti had staked off a rectangle fifty feet around the body. The officers swept clean the snow in a circle close to it, and the entire rectangle was systematically probed. They used six-foot dowels that Balzeti had sent an officer to buy from the nearest hardware store. The snow was flogged by searchers, but to no avail. In the vastness of the encircling woods, under the deep snow, a dozen bodies might be lying within a stone's throw, not to be found until the spring thaw.

Near dark one of the officers found, near the body, a set of keys. They were mud-covered when Hager saw them; he recognized them right away as Robbie's by the lump of quarters anchoring the keychain. Hager himself had welded them together. Robbie had a special love for quarters.

It was a painful discovery, because it reminded him that surely Robbie had been there.

Balzeti waited until dusk to put the body on a stretcher. By then it was too dark to take good pictures. The TV cameras were still there, and their lights glared on the snow and lit up the woods, but the TV people were not happy with the quality. That had been Balzeti's intention.

It might have been easier to carry the body without a stretcher. The limbs remained rigid in their curled position, and the body would not lie flat but teetered insecurely. The officers' boots slipped as they labored up the hill, and several times the body nearly toppled off. Even so, the stretcher seemed to offer the body some dignity. Except for muffled curses when someone slipped, they carried it in silence. An ambulance took it away, a procession of cars and TV vans following.

Hager and Balzeti were the last to leave.

"Why didn't you want them to get pictures?" Hager asked. He was freezing; the cold had come up through the soles of his shoes, which felt like slabs of steel.

"They're vultures," Balzeti said. "They would sleep in your bed if you would let them."

The sky overhead was violet; through the trees down the slope the horizon radiated a burning orange. The two men walked toward their cars, and the snow crunched underfoot like sugar.

"So what do you do tomorrow?" Hager asked, wrapping his arms around himself.

"What we do tomorrow is keep looking. I'm getting the Mountain Search people into this area. And we'll keep whipping up the snow, hoping to stumble on someone. Can't clear the whole woods, though."

"I can't figure it out," Hager said. "Petey wearing Robbie's jacket. Looked like he had Robbie's keys. But why didn't he get into the car? If he had the keys, why not drive home?"

"Well, if you do figure it out, let me know," Balzeti said. He shook hands and walked to where his car was running; he got in and jerked it into gear. The car spun crazily on the packed snow, then straightened out on the way to Fresno.

CHAPTER

4

Carrie met Hager at the door with an angry look, her make-up uncharacteristically smeared around the eyes. She announced that she was going out.

"What's the matter, honey?" he asked, feeling slightly afraid of her mood. She said that the telephone kept ringing with people wanting to hear news; he could answer it for a change. She swept out past him, started up the car that he had just parked, and was gone into the night. As though by a signal, the phone began ringing. Hager simply took it off the hook and wondered why Carrie couldn't do the same instead of getting mad.

But then he was lonely and wandered from den to kitchen and back again until deciding to go out back to shoot baskets. Illuminated by a single floodlight, he dribbled and shot, putting the ball up in a high arc that escaped the light and orbited into the darkness, then suddenly reappeared, thunking against the rim. He shot until he was soaked with sweat and worn out and ready to sit and watch the news and drink diet Pepsi.

Never had he watched so much news. When it was done he felt paralyzed, unable to move out of his reclining chair and turn off the TV. Thoughts barged in uninvited, out of sequence and distorted by anxiety, like one radio signal drifting in on another.

He kept reliving the moment when he had seen the body

that was not Robbie. Had he laughed? He did not know. He must have acted terribly for the cops to restrain him. He could feel those hands pushing him back; he could feel in his chest his own abundant anger. And he kept seeing that hair, the black, curly, bountiful, lustrous hair, mingled with snow.

How thankful he was that it had not been Robbie's. How thankful he was that he had realized it, that he had made the identification. At least he had done one thing right. The thankfulness welled up; he felt weak with it. He had thought that it would be better to know than to continue not knowing whether Robbie was dead or alive. But now he knew how grateful he was that he did not know. There was still hope.

Hager began thinking of Robbie, remembering something that had made him very proud and that had later acutely embarrassed him because he had been so proud. Robbie had been tiny, just walking and beginning to talk, when on a summer evening after the heat had let up, the family of three had gone for a stroll in the neighborhood. Robbie had let out a cry, calling their attention. It had sounded like "ball." Carrie had asked him where—had held him in her arms and said, "Ball where? Show us the ball." But he had pointed indefinitely into a yard where no ball could be seen.

"What are you saying, Robbie?" Hager had insisted. "What do you see?" But Robbie's face had shown blankness and confusion.

They had walked on, and he had said it again. This time they had not stopped. "Where is the ball?" Hager had asked.

Robbie had pointed very uncertainly.

"Funny," Carrie had said. "It sounds like ball."

"Do you want to play ball?" Hager had asked. "Play ball?" Robbie had smiled.

"Oh, you want to play! We'll do that when we get home, okay?"

"Frank, I'm not sure we can find his ball," Carrie had said. "He's lost it somewhere. Maybe that's what he's saying."

But as they reached home, Carrie had softly touched Hager's arm. "There it is," she said. He followed her eyes and saw nothing at all until she raised her finger to the perfect, delicate outline of a ghost moon.

He had been proud, Hager thought ruefully; he had told people about his sharp-eyed son, who saw and wondered over a day-moon that Hager had not noticed in years. It had seemed to put their fears to rest, for from Robbie's birth Carrie had worried about him, anxious that he was not right. The doctors reassured her that it was normal to worry about your first child, and Hager said the same, that all kids were different, that it was useless to compare. He used the moon as proof that there was nothing wrong. Then, only months later, Hager burned with shame when he remembered how he had talked. They learned that Robbie was retarded. In a single day the doctors changed from saying that nothing was wrong to saying that nothing could be done.

He and Carrie had been pushed out of their happiness into a waking dream: to long waits in doctors' offices, where they sat miserable, close to strangers, too distracted to read or talk, and never certain when they would be called. He could not now remember the doctors' names, nor what they had said, only the coming and going of people, the halls full of doorways, the gleaming, clattering floors, the endless low talk that left him feeling exhausted and hollow. Hager had given up trying to understand, but Carrie, growing bigger with Stephen, had gone to the library and ordered books and read everything she could find, as though she could outwit Robbie's slowness. She asked the questions; as far as Hager could remember, he always let the doctors talk to him in those earliest months. He made himself try to listen, which was like holding your mouth open so the dentist could drill. All the test results came out more or less the same. The doctors would say with a false kindliness (he felt they could barely wait to escape from the room) words he did not want to hear, and then he had to thank them.

One of the doctors had suggested that they send Robbie away to a home, as a kindness. To that he had been unable to speak; he had simply stared and wished that his eyes could light fires.

The process had worn and humiliated Hager, and the best he could say about it was that they had tried their best. It was a funny kind of pride, he thought, one he had probably picked up from football, where you got admired if you beat your head against the opposing lineman even though you trailed by thirty points. Nothing could be done, whatever truth the tests declared. No tests could speed up Robbie's brain.

Nevertheless, in a final burst of stubbornness Hager had taken him to UCLA for a week. Carrie had objected; Stephen's birth approached and she had wanted her husband near. Until then she had asked all the questions, and now she was willing to stop asking, to merely accept. But Hager grew angry at the passivity with which the doctors treated the mystery. Typically they asked Carrie a few questions about her pregnancy, then asked them both a few questions about past illness in the family, and then virtually shrugged their shoulders. They said it could be this and it could be that, but it was clearly irreversible. How did they know it was irreversible, if they didn't know what caused it? They never seemed to answer that question.

Hager had called Carrie from the motel every night while he was at UCLA; they talked in hurried, fretful spurts because long distance was expensive. So was the week. But nothing new came from it. It had been more of the same.

He and Robbie arrived home just in time for the birth. The delivery was entirely normal, though to Hager that had seemed an uncertain blessing. Robbie had seemed normal too.

Hager had been unable to help himself, he had looked at the tiny red bundle held by the nurse in the nursery window, and he had searched for flaws. He asked the nurses twice, three times, if everything had gone well. He wanted to be happy, as flushed with the grace of God as he had been at Robbie's birth, but that possibility had gone away. He had become too wary to trust in appearances.

After the birth, having been up all night, he had gone home and stood Robbie on the shiny kitchen table. He tried to tell him that he had a baby brother, while he squirmed and cried because he wanted down. Carrie's mother stood at the far end of the room, watching while Hager tried to communicate. Robbie was strong. He writhed against Hager's arms, so he had to grip him tightly to his chest if he wanted to hold him at all. Hager gave up and wept, while Robbie ran away into the living room. Later it occurred to Hager that perhaps he had told Robbie in a way that reminded him of the doctors' examinations.

Even when Stephen had come home from the hospital and Hager held him and counted his perfect fingers, burped him, and smelled the cottage cheese in his breath, Hager felt wary. He had told himself that Stephen was all right. Afterward, any number of times through the years as Stephen grew older, Hager had watched him or listened to him talk and thought to himself that Stephen was definitely all right. Yes, Stephen was all right physically, but there was something else. Hager had never felt Stephen's presence the way he felt Robbie's, or later on, Lizzie's. He felt guilty about it, but there it was.

Even as a baby, Stephen had been happy to play alone. He was more like Carrie: quiet, and altogether admirable, and somewhat beyond Hager. With her second child, Carrie seemed happy again. He let that be enough.

Robbie had been his comfort. Disinterested in Hager's gloom, he had been tactile, cheerful, soft, round, his body so gladly molded by a touch. He would put his arms open and come, not even waiting for an invitation. When a little child, his joy had seemed inexhaustible. Oddly, he was both the source of melancholy and its healing. Hager had developed the habit of finding Robbie when he was blue.

A happier scene pushed into Hager's mind. He and Robbie were in the car together in the late-March spring when the valley could be so beautiful. Robbie was almost twelve and had a soft crewcut and huge round glasses that made his eyes seem gigantic, like a June bug's. He sat as close to his dad as he could get, and Hager had his arm around him. They drove out on the farm roads, playing a guessing game with the crops just sprouting in the sodden fields. Black earth stretched out around them, and beyond, the icy dazzle of snow-covered mountains hung just over the telephone poles. The road was spotted with puddles. "What's that?" Hager would ask, pointing at the bare limbs of an orchard, and Robbie would tell him whether it was peach or nectarine or almond or walnut.

Everything in the world grew in the valley, and Robbie knew the look of each crop.

He loved the dials and switches in the car too. That was why Hager had started buying Chrysler; they went whole hog into gadgetry. Hager drove, and Robbie controlled the radio and the heater and the power windows. He searched for their favorite song on KYNO or KMAK, "Walk Like a Man," and they both pounded the dash in rhythm to its pounding bass and falsetto tremulo. And they talked. Hager talked expansively, for once knowing that the pleasure of his voice was all that really mattered.

They played the Encyclopedia Question game. "Dad, why is the sky blue?" Robbie asked, and Hager laughed and rubbed his palm in Robbie's soft crewcut. A salesman for *World Book Encyclopedia* had put the question to Hager years ago as proof that he was depriving his son of an education by not knowing the answer. He still did not know the answer, though out of admiration for the man's sales technique he had bought the books. Stephen had gotten some good out of them. All Robbie got was the question. He had been listening to the sales pitch, and the question had stuck with him. Now he asked it as a joke, and Hager always tried to think of a silly answer.

"The sky is blue to match the lakes."

"The earth is hung on a huge rainbow, so big we can only see the blue part."

"Blue goes with God's eyes."

Hager remembered trying to ask his own question. "You believe in God, don't you Rob?" He had gone on quickly, feeling nervous. "Why do you think God made you the way you are? You know, slow." Robbie would tell people, in a very serious, informational way, that he was slow.

Hager could not remember whether Robbie had answered. He remembered looking at Robbie as he asked the question, and seeing Robbie's blue eyes turn on him with complete, adoring trust. With pain he had thought that it did not matter that Robbie was slow. There was no punishment in it; a God of love had made a kid in his own image.

Once he had gone to his pastor and talked the question over; his pastor had given him a book that he had read all the way through but could not recall when he was done. He had raised the question once in a Sunday morning adults' class but had felt like a fool; people seemed embarrassed. Hager had never really minded that before; he had always taken a little pride in being the one who questioned the correct answer. But with Robbie he had felt otherwise, more private. He did not want to expose his feelings to the world.

That look of Robbie's had put those questions away, which was not quite the same as answering them. Hager did not feel that he knew why Robbie was slow or what God might want with a retarded person, but he knew that for him, personally, the question had stopped being really important. At least it was not important in the way it had been before he knew how "retarded" and Robbie would go together. When he thought of Robbie, as he was thinking now, he saw that soft crewcut and those goggle eyes. He would always think of Robbie that way, as eleven years old, before puberty.

Adolescence had thrown a shadow over Robbie, making him moody and shy. He had grown tall and had filled out. He had begun to shave. In addition, Hager had pulled away, though not willingly. The school psychologist, a nervous older man with a heavy beard, had recommended it. Robbie had to grow up and make his own friends, he said; Robbie had to learn some independence.

Just as his father had taught him, Hager had taught Robbie to drive, on the narrow, empty roads that cross-hatch the valley. It had been a melancholy experience: He kept thinking of how they had been over this ground together on earlier rides. Now he was teaching the skill that would separate them.

There had been times, after close calls, when Hager thought of giving it up. Not everybody considered that driving was a good idea for Robbie. The doctors had been ambivalent; they called Robbie "educably handicapped," which meant that he might someday hold a job and perhaps even live on his own. Some people in his category could learn to drive. Though it was unusual, they would not discourage trying, so long as he was very careful.

But Carrie had not been for it, and neither had the school.

They had thought he was unrealistic. They had as much as said that he did not know just how severe Robbie's handicap was. "All you do is play with him," Carrie had said once, with a coldness he had not forgotten.

She was wrong. He knew. Even if he had not known, he would have learned while teaching him to drive. Robbie would freeze and cry out while holding the steering wheel with all his strength and, sometimes, jamming down on the gas. He got scared, and it took all Hager's strength to break his grip. But he had taught him, first the mechanics of driving and then, when he was very confident, the harder task of the written exam. Hager had wanted Robbie to fly through on his first try; he wanted no suspicions raised by the Department of Motor Vehicles.

For all the scares, they had had only one small accident, when backing the car out of the garage. Robbie had put the car in drive instead of reverse and hit the front wall hard enough to crack a headlight and smash a work table. They had kept it a secret, going immediately to replace the headlight. When they came home again, Carrie asked if they had felt an earthquake earlier in the afternoon. Hager had explained the joke to Robbie later in private, and it had become one of their bonds. Sometimes he would ask Robbie whether he had felt an earthquake, and Robbie would laugh.

After Robbie had passed the drivers' test, he drove the old station wagon to his school every day. It was a tremendous status symbol. Then Robbie began driving a carful to local high school events. If Hager went—he always did if Stephen was competing—he went in his own car and sat somewhere else. Other parents, he knew, were doing the exact same thing, sitting apart from their kids. But he could not talk to them about it, because none of them had slow kids. He would not have liked their pity.

CHAPTER

5

Hager got up from his lounging chair and wandered down the long, wide hall. Blue, thick shag carpet was under his bare feet. In the hall were framed photographs of his wedding, of his parents and Carrie's when all were still alive, of Robbie and Stephen and Lizzie as babies.

He put his head into Robbie's room. It had not been picked up. The bed was messy and there were Fish cards and comic books on the floor. Hager straightened the cover on the bed and sat down on it. He felt something uncomfortable under him and when he reached beneath the covers pulled out a molded plastic Indian, such as children much younger than Robbie usually play with. He held it, seeing the soft, green tags of plastic that had leaked from the seams of the mold. For some reason it released the wave of grief that had been gathering in him, a surge of protest that seemed to rise through his chest and throat.

He was afraid. Afraid of what? He did not know. Frightened, perhaps, that he was losing control. Losing control of life. Of his emotions.

Then he knew it was too late to push it down; like a sneeze, it had to come.

He looked at the toy; the emotion expanded in his chest, stopped there, pressing on him, and then broke out through his head, wave after wave of grief. He cried and he cried and he cried. He could not stop. He heard himself saying, "Robbie,

Robbie." With one side of his mind he could listen to himself saying it and think what a useless sound, but another side could not stop.

Then it was done and the grief would not come any more. He was dry inside; he found a Kleenex and wiped his eyes. He was glad it had come; he wanted the emotional cleansing.

Hager looked around at Robbie's things, hoping they would bring the feeling back. When you want to cry, he thought, it will not come. Yet you can never quite forget that grief is in the background, waiting, until it catches you off guard and rolls over you and you have to sit down or hold on to something.

The room had plenty of material to launch a second wave. The bookshelves were covered with dusty plastic models of airplanes; hardened glue stood on them in globs. Stephen's junior high school letter, a purple T for Tenaya, was pinned to a cork bulletin board. When Stephen had been about to throw it away, Robbie had begged it from him.

Nearly covering one wall was an outsized poster of two rock climbers silhouetted against a cliff. At one time Robbie's whole desire had been to take lessons, and he had pleaded with them to allow it. They had said no, though Hager was still unsure whether that had been the right decision. They had wanted to protect him. That impulse surfaced so many times, like a drunk's desire for forgiveness. You never could do enough; you never could really fend off the world.

On the top shelf was a small plastic bank made to look like a safe. It had a combination lock, so the quarters stuffed inside would be safe.

They had been through a difficult time with him not long after he turned twelve. He had begun to sulk and balk and, if ignored, he would throw himself at them in a tantrum. He had been tall and heavy by then and hard to control. He had frightened Carrie sometimes, threatening her. Twice she had called Hager home from the office.

Robbie had always before been sensitive to a rebuke but suddenly had refused to accept punishment, whatever kind they tried. When they sent him to his room, he would wail and beat on the door; eventually he broke a hole in it. He learned to climb out the window and escape, and when Hager bought a lock for it, Robbie broke out the glass with a tennis racket. He would fight and kick hard whenever Hager tried to use force.

On a doctor's advice they had tried to ignore him completely. That had been the worst, actually: Robbie had followed Carrie around the house, whimpering, and had finally bit her to get her attention.

Hager had not known about the teasing until a neighbor lady, an older woman whose kids were grown, called to tell them. From her kitchen window she had seen a circle of kids dodging and feinting just out of reach of a tear-streaked boy who charged at them helplessly. Why Robbie himself had never told them Hager couldn't understand. He had thought Robbie was completely ingenuous.

They hadn't pressed Stephen to be a protector. He would have, Hager was sure: He always stuck up for his brother and never complained when Robbie tore up his room. The psychologist had warned them that Stephen needed his own life, independent of his brother's needs, so they left him out of it. Besides, he was only ten.

Hager had gone around to see all the parents in the neighborhood. For a time things improved, but kids can be cruel. Robbie wouldn't tell him and Carrie what happened, but they knew from his behavior that he was still getting it. Hager couldn't stop it, and he couldn't keep Robbie inside and away from it. It nearly drove Hager insane. Eventually they accepted defeat, building this house in Oakdale. The population was moving that way, and it was in the foothills and therefore cooler in the summer. There were development possibilities. That was the story they gave the kids. But it had really been to get Robbie away. Hager was a big civic booster now and said the move to Oakdale was the best decision he'd ever made, but the truth was that he missed Fresno and drove down thirty miles for lunch whenever he had a chance.

There was no more teasing, they were sure—they didn't really have any neighbors—but Robbie had remained moody. The doctor said he probably never would be quite the same again. "These kids change," he told Hager, "just like any other kid. Don't believe that stuff about their being perpetual children. They grow up. Robbie is an adolescent, and he has the same hormones every other kid around here has."

For his control problems another psychologist recommended positive reinforcement. That had not worked either, until after hugs, candy, and charts with gold stars, they had hit on quarters. Quarters, especially newly minted ones, could get Robbie to do almost anything.

He never spent them, except at Christmas. Hager had discovered that he kept them in a sock in a bottom drawer and gave him the bank.

Hager stood up to lift the bank down from the shelf and found to his surprise that it was empty, weightless. His first thought was that someone had stolen the money. But then he thought maybe Robbie had finally decided to spend the money. Maybe he had gone back to his sock. Until recently, Hager would have known. For so many years Hager had known everything in Robbie's life. The doctor had been right; Robbie was growing up. Who could say, maybe the quarters were not so important to him as they once had been.

That would not be all bad. Though they had helped with the discipline problems, they had also become a source of worry. Once, when they were playing golf, Stephen had bet Robbie a quarter he would miss a long putt; when Robbie made it, Stephen threw the quarter into a water hazard. In anguish Robbie went in after it and covered himself with mud, tearing at the bottom. After that, they made a rule about keeping quarters a family secret. They would not want kids using quarters to abuse Robbie.

Hager knocked on Stephen's door and, after hearing an answer, went in. Stephen was lying on his bed, propped on one elbow over a book. Only a small reading lamp was on, reaching over him like a crane from his desk, offering a small cone of light. Hager punched on the overhead light by twisting a dimmer switch that increases or decreases the amount of light. Hager was putting them in all his apartments now.

"That light's not good for your eyes," he said.

"Yeah," Stephen said. "Any news?"

"Nothing more." He tossed some reeking sweat clothes off a chair and sat down. "How was practice?"

"I didn't go. Remember? I didn't go to school today."

"Then how did these clothes get so wet?"

"I was out shooting baskets."

"Oh," Hager said. "Feeling bad?"

After a slight hesitation, Stephen said, "Yeah."

"You'd better give those clothes to your mother. They'll mildew like that."

Stephen went back to his book. He was an excellent student, straight A's generally, which Hager could never have imagined when he was in school. And Stephen was a good kid. Never once had they had a call from a principal.

Yet Hager found him hard to talk to. He broke into Stephen's reading apologetically. "Listen, Steve, I was wondering if you could explain to me a little more about what happened at the game. I haven't really heard all that yet."

"Sure. What do you want to know?"

"Can you tell me everything? I guess you told it all to the police."

Stephen put down his book, taking a deep breath. "There really isn't much to tell, Dad. I didn't see them when I first came in. The gym was packed. We had to sit down at floor level, right behind the scorer's table. I didn't even know they were there until the yelling started, and then everybody was looking at them."

"When was this?"

"In the second quarter. Everybody stood up trying to see. Paul began yelling. I recognized that sound. You know, the foghorn. So I pushed my way up there, and they were already leaving. I went along to make sure everything was all right."

"And the trouble was that Paul had spilled a drink on somebody?"

"Yeah, I think so. At least that was part of it. It was one of those guys who graduated last year. Laird Harris, a really big jerk. He was loaded, I think, and acting real tough. He followed them out, and he kept grabbing Robbie by the collar and yelling at him to fight."

Father and son sat in mutual silence. Hager knew who

Harris was, or at least knew his father. They had played golf together. Harris was a competitor, and Hager had little respect for the way he did business. But he had contacts with the county supervisors.

In a low voice Hager asked, "Steve, you told the police about all this?"

"Sure. But Dad, I didn't think it was too big a deal. Maybe it was." He stopped, seeming sad. "Who knows? But at the time, I thought it was funny. I started laughing. It was ludicrous. Harris is trying to make Robbie fight, and Robbie is backing away like a big, frightened sheep, and Paul is bellowing like a fire alarm. Everybody else is crowding around hoping to see a fight."

"You think that's funny?"

"Dad, that's high school. It happens all the time. Nobody murders anybody."

Hager felt stung. "So you tell me: what's happened to Robbie? How did Peter Aranian end up under three feet of snow?"

Stephen stared at him. "How should I know?"

"Well, you seem to be pretty sure that Harris didn't do anything."

"I didn't say that. I just didn't think that was anything to get too excited about. Not at the time."

"Well," Hager said weakly, "You told all this to the police, right? I hope they question Harris, anyway."

"I'm sure they will."

Hager glanced at the wall behind his back, which was covered with posters. They bothered him. They marked the walls, and one of them showed more of a girl than he thought was right for his son. She was smiling, standing in the surf, a wet shirt partly unbuttoned showing practically everything. Hager had never said anything about the poster. He had never been able to talk about such things with Stephen.

"Did you send them home right away?"

Stephen stared at him again, angrily Hager thought. "Dad, will you lay off?"

"I'm just asking questions, Steve. What's wrong with that?"

For a moment he thought that his son was going to cry. His face seemed to weaken, to crack. "Dad," Stephen said in what was almost a whisper, "this is a hard time."

"For me too, Steve," Hager said softly after a quiet moment. "It's hard for all of us. But I want to know what happened. I need to know."

He hated the contradictory feelings brought by the questioning, feelings so awfully typical of his relationship with Stephen. They were both grieving, and instead of the sadness softening them to each other it was making them antagonists.

"Just finish the story, Steve," he said. They would have to survive this bout of differentness. He had such a fierce desire to know. "After you left the gym with them, what did you do? Did they head out?"

Stephen seemed to resign himself to answering. "Not right away," he said slowly. "I took them across the street, to that chicken place, to calm them down. It was nearly halftime anyway. I bought them some chicken. Then I told them to go home."

"Did you see them go?"

"I saw them get in the car. I guess I saw them drive away. I can't remember."

"And where was Harris?"

"He was around. I think he was standing in front of the gym with his friends, smoking. I guess he knew that Robbie had left."

"Did he go back in to the game?"

Stephen smiled sadly. "He tried, but they wouldn't let him. He didn't have a ticket stub. He was swearing and he threatened the teacher who was taking the tickets."

"Threatened him with what?"

"I don't know. He was going to beat him up or something. Just big talk, I thought. Maybe I was wrong. I went inside, and I didn't see him again. He might have gotten in, but the place was jammed, and I didn't see him. So maybe he . . . who knows?"

"What about after the game?"

"After the game I didn't see anyone. I took Mary Ann home, and when I came in I thought the station wagon was in the garage, and I didn't think about it. When you told me in the morning, that was the first time I knew there was any trouble."

Another wave of grief swept over Hager, a small one. He was feeling very lonely, and he wanted to feel that somehow he and his son were kin. Hager thought of prayer as something that families ought to do together at a time like this. He looked at his son, who wrote poems, who was smart, who won awards, and he asked him hesitantly, "Do you believe in God? I've never asked you before."

"I do. Sort of."

"What do you mean, 'Sort of'? You either do or you don't."

"I believe in my own way. Not the way Mary Ann does."

He had met Mary Ann at a church camp. She had always impressed Hager as a dedicated Christian. She had no figure; she cut her hair very short and never wore make-up. And so serious. Sometimes Hager and Carrie talked about her when they were in bed at night, wondering what she and Stephen had between them. Carrie could not see it at all. It upset her. But Hager thought he could understand. She was not the kind of girl who attracted him, but she had her way of talking and moving, a strangeness that was interesting and could pique a man's interest. He tried to explain this to Carrie, and she said, "You mean you think she's sexy?" as though there were something wrong with that.

"I don't suppose you believe in a way that would involve praying, do you? I was thinking that we could pray for Robbie if you wanted to."

Stephen did not answer for several seconds, and Hager was ashamed to notice his own heart beating hard. "All right," Stephen finally said. "You pray and I'll think along with you."

Hager felt like an idiot. But prayer was sacred; once committed, he could not back out of it. He lowered his head, wondering whether Stephen would do the same, and began to pray. The words came out in clots. Nonetheless, he went on until he came to what seemed to be an ending. There he said, "Amen."

He looked up to see Stephen's eyes on him still. Was there

a trace of a smile? No, probably not. "Okay," Hager said, apropos of nothing. "Thanks for telling me about it. I appreciate it. I think we'd better start thinking about dinner." Then he escaped down the hall.

CHAPTER

6

In the late afternoon of the next day Hager's Chrysler Imperial appeared on Tamarack Ridge, poking along the line of cars and occasionally spinning its wheels on the ice before it parked in a space left vacant by a departed skier. Hager got out and surveyed the hillside, flapping his arms against his sides to battle the cold.

Nobody seemed interested in his arrival. One of the sheriff's deputies came walking gingerly down the snow-rutted road until he got close enough to recognize Hager; then he waved and walked back.

It had been a wasted day for Hager. In the morning he had gone to the office, where his secretary had handed him a pink stack of messages, most dealing with the business. He leafed through the stack twice without even understanding most of them. His pastor had called. They kept missing each other. Hager couldn't think of anything but Robbie.

Without returning a single call, without even telling Lila where he was going, he left to drive down to Fresno. Ostensibly he planned to see one of the Planning Commissioners, but when he found the man out it made no difference. Hager ate lunch at Kashians and talked briefly to some golfing buddies he found in the bar. They asked about the search, said it was too bad what had happened, and wished him luck. A few minutes into the conversation, Hager realized that he usually talked business with friends like these. He knew hardly anything about their personal lives. He didn't even know if they were still married to the same women.

While driving around town, Hager decided to go up to Tamarack Ridge. As soon as the car headed that way, his heart lifted.

Now that he had arrived, though, the familiar restless uselessness returned. He wandered around, said hello to Balzeti, and established that nothing had happened.

Overnight, Balzeti had called on the Mountain Rescue Team, which recruited back country skiers and Explorer scouts to search the woods. Their Volkswagens and station wagons made a ragged, unsightly line by the side of the road. It looked, from certain angles, like the parking lot at a ski slope.

The TV crews were there, inside their vans with the motors running while they watched for anything worth filming through holes rubbed in the steamed-up windows. None of the stations could afford to let the others get an advantage so they stayed, parked and leaking money. The sheriff's deputies thought this was amusing, and they joked about investigative reporters. The newspaper reporters, who were outnumbered, joined in the sarcasm. *The Fresno Bee* had sent two reporters and a photographer, and to everyone's surprise the *San Francisco Chronicle* had a good-looking woman reporter on the scene. The sheriff's deputies were giving her a hard time, speculating about how her paper would headline it. ICY KIDNAP FOR RETARDED CHILDREN. Or maybe, HIGH SIERRA HORROR. It might turn out to be the *Chronicle's* kind of story.

The deputies had expanded their rectangle where the body had been found, setting a larger perimeter and working through it with probes. One of the *Bee* reporters told Hager there had been several exciting moments in the morning when they thought they had found something, but by the afternoon they had become slower to jump to conclusions. The deputies looked cold. They were spending more time stamping and hugging themselves than probing and digging.

Hager hung around for a while, but there was nothing for him to do and no one to talk to. The police didn't want to send him away, but they didn't really want him there, he felt. Neither they nor the reporters seemed comfortable talking to him. He went back to his car, started the engine, and prepared to drive away. But why? Where would he go? He might as well stay, like the TV reporters. Something might happen here. Nothing was going to happen at home.

He turned on the radio and punched a mood-music station. It would be dark in an hour. The skiers were already beginning to come in, and the TV crews were stirring, getting out and stretching, and taking a few shots of the red-faced, bundled kids who were happily anxious to get their faces on TV. Something might happen. Someone might know something. Hager was not yet ready to be far from this place where his son had been.

By dusk, most of the Mountain Rescue Team had packed up their cars and gone, and the TV people had disappeared into the gloom, needing to reach Fresno to file a story. Balzeti had sent most of his deputies on the road home; there were only two black-and-whites left and just three civilian cars, including Hager's. The temperature was plummeting; the snow had crusted hard, and the remaining sheriff's officers moved with quick, compact, frozen steps. It was time to wrap it up.

Hager heard a shout. They all did. Balzeti was talking to the head of the Mountain Rescue just a few feet from Hager's car, and Hager saw them both look around in all directions, even up into the purpling sky. Then Balzeti pointed his stubby, bundled arm up the road. There was a figure on skis, still far off down the road, a dark silhouette only visible by the movement of his long strides. "That should be the last of your people," Balzeti said. "Look, do you think you could set a time limit on them tomorrow? We don't need anybody else getting lost out here."

The skier came up a minute later, out of breath, practically shouting his news. "I got it, man, I got it!" he said jubilantly. "I found one of the kids!"

Balzeti quickly faced the skier. "Where?" he asked.

"Up there, five, ten miles. It was just a chance in a million, but I found him."

"Alive?"

The skier guffawed. "No, man, he's a popsicle."

Hager heard these last words—he had rolled down his window to miss nothing—and the lethargy of his heart instantly vanished, replaced by the spread of anguish like ink in a glass of water. He knew, he seemed always to have known, that it must be Robbie.

And yet the conversation continued, and he could listen to the discussion in an almost scientific manner as though he had been accidentally connected to someone else's telephone conversation. He heard Balzeti make arrangements for the officers to get snowmobiles and a sled and a body bag. He heard the Mountain Rescue chief suggest they wait for the morning. He heard Balzeti's curt dismissal of this strategy. "We go in now," he said. "Nobody would sleep anyway."

In a matter of minutes one black-and-white had crunched off to get equipment, and Balzeti had taken the skier into his car to question him. It was that time after dusk when the snow seems far brighter than the sky overhead, when sizes and distances are deceptive, when the cold seems to bite doubly hard. Hager wished he could get in the car with them and learn more about what the skier had found, but he did not have a question to ask, merely an emptiness, an aching for knowledge.

Previously he had thought it out this way: Either the boys were all lying dead and under snow not far from where Petey had been found, or they were far away, somewhere down the road out of the snow where someone for some reason had taken them. But why and how would they have gone toward nowhere, traveling miles in a snowstorm on an unplowed road?

There were horrible people everywhere, people even willing to harm the harmless. Perhaps the somebody who did it had taken them purposefully there, to dump them, thinking they could not be found before spring. Hager found himself shaking as he thought of it.

He had tried so hard. He had tried to protect his son, his first-born son, and all his love had been unable to shield the kid from the worst. What more could he have done?

He waited for over an hour, thinking and sometimes trembling, before he saw wavering yellow headlights appear in the trees. He heard the heavy rumble of a truck. Hager watched while it passed him, pulling a trailer with three snowmobiles. Then he turned off his engine, got out, and slammed the door of his car. The cold gripped him even though he was warmly dressed, and he went back to get his gloves.

A huddle of officers conferred over a map in the headlights of the truck. Hager saw Balzeti peer at him suspiciously, leaning his body forward and seeming to puff up like a blowfish. Then, recognizing him, Balzeti relaxed. "This is Frank Hager, everybody. The father of one of the boys who's missing." Everyone murmured something.

The skier edged around the others and stuck out his hand to introduce himself. "Memphis Purcell. Yeah, nice to meet you," he said. He had a stringy little beard and looked, in the shadows cast by the headlights, like a televised demon. "Unbelievable, isn't it?"

Purcell was eager to talk, oblivious to Hager's silence. He put a hand on Hager's elbow. "You want to hear how I found it?"

Surprised by the man's forwardness, Hager said, "Sure."

"I'd been out there all day, and didn't see a thing. I was coming in, skiing along, not even looking hard any more, and I ran right over him. His arm comes up like this, like *heil Hitler.* I thought I was flashing. I almost fell on top of him. Wouldn't that have been something?"

Hager turned slightly away, not wanting to be rude, even wanting to hear, but not feeling able to bear this. Purcell said no more, but he stayed by Hager's side as though they were friends. Balzeti was studying the map, making plans. A few minutes later, Purcell nudged Hager's side.

"This is quite a military trip, isn't it?" Purcell said, indicating the uniforms.

Balzeti began to swear violently. He had discovered that only one of his men had ever driven a snowmobile. No one responded to his curses. When he ran out of outrage, the only sound was the muttering of the truck's engine.

"I can drive one," Hager said quietly.

"Who's that?" Balzeti said, squinting. "Oh, yeah." He

impatiently blew out a cloud of steam. "Okay," he said, and hesitated. "Maybe you can help with the identity. Why don't you come then."

The snowmobiles broke the quiet, coughing into their obscene whine. The party took forever to get organized, partly because no one could hear while the snowmobiles were running. Finally, with a sound like multiple chain saws, they left. Balzeti led, with the skier mounted behind him; he was followed by another officer pulling the stretcher sled; and Hager and Ramirez brought up the rear. Ramirez was Balzeti's sidekick, the little man Hager had nearly flattened.

They snarled into the darkness, up the road. The machine humped through deep drifts, its small engine biting into heavy snow and then screaming when it bobbed over the top and wallowed into another hole. A thick frosting of snow soon covered Hager's jacket; it flew from the snowmobiles in front as well as from the soft drifts that buried them to their waists.

After a mile or two they left the road abruptly, charging up an embankment and onto a narrow, steep track. Pine boughs brushed them; the path was hard to follow in the dim, bobbing light. Hager fell behind; they were soon out of sight of the other snowmobiles.

"What's the matter?" Ramirez shouted in his ear. "Can't you speed it up?"

"It's not as easy as it looks," Hager shouted back.

"I thought you knew how to do this."

"I lied."

Ramirez laughed in Hager's ears, which were in fiery pain from the cold. "The man is going to love that, huh?" Ramirez shouted.

Fortunately the second snowmobile stopped to wait for them, and then the trail leveled out. They seemed to be in a valley. The moon was low, broken into a thousand splinters by the dense trees. Hager tried to think of where they were, but could not locate it in his mind. They had hiked in this area when headed into the high country. But it was so featureless, the ridges, rocks, streams furred over with the trees.

They fell into a rhythm in which the scream of the motor

stopped hurting their ears, in which the fragments of moon-light and shadow grew redundant and tedious. Hager lost any sense of how long it had been. Then without warning they came up on the others and slid to a stop. "This is it," someone shouted.

Snowmobiles were switched off, and silence rushed in. Ramirez and Hager joined the other three men, visible more by the bobbing yellow beams of their flashlights than by the dark bulk of their bodies. They stood clustered together, shining their lights on the body.

Hager had not prepared himself for this moment; while they rode, he had needed all his attention concentrated on the snowmobile. Now he could not bear to look. Yet he was compelled to look, almost to the point of pushing the others aside. How slow they seemed!

The body lay on its side, half covered with snow. The face was turned up; in their lights it did not appear human. The eyes were huge shadows, caves. A series of reactions washed through Hager, one after another: dread certainty that it was Robbie, then a corresponding sureness it could not be, then mere horror at the unhumanness of the face. For a moment he felt sick: A soft tumbling of his stomach took him by surprise. He had seen bodies beside the road after an accident, the orange lights of police cars whipping savagely over them. But those bodies had been a hub of official activity; here, now, the simplicity and silence of the woods distracted nothing from the strangeness of the body.

Regardless of the identification, this thing was not Robbie.

"How far are we from the cars?" Balzeti asked.

"It must be ten miles," someone said.

"About six," said the skier.

"How did he get all the way out here?" Balzeti asked. "In the snow."

The men talked about making an identification. Hager listened to them, barely able to stand the sound of their idle voices. Their speech dragged through his mind like a damaged tape, slurred, distorted, patchy, off-time. How could they talk with such sickening calm? Is it this one? Is it that one?

Balzeti, suddenly remembering that Hager was there,

asked in a sober, thoughtful voice if he could tell which of the boys it was.

"I don't know," Hager said. He was surprised at hearing the calmness of his own voice. "It doesn't look like any of them."

They held three flashlights on the face, one from the top and two from the sides, to try to make the light more normal, but it did not help. By flashlight they could not even tell hair color. Hager was shaking violently from the cold.

"How tall is he?" Balzeti asked.

One of the cops had a tape measure and they ran it along the spine. Hager knelt and held the end to an ice-crusted heel.

"Sixty four inches," Balzeti read from the head. "Which kid is short? There's a short one, isn't there?"

"Dan Smithson," Ramirez said. "Five-foot-six."

"Must be him."

"Dan," thought Hager. "This is Dan." But for some reason he felt none of the relief that had overwhelmed him when he had identified the first body as Pete, not Robbie.

It was very cold, so much so that he needed real effort to do the simplest task. For the most part he watched while the three officers worked. He tried not to hear the skier's prattling voice. The moon sank below the trees, leaving a soft glow on the horizon and a sky lush with diamonds overhead. Their flashlight beams jigged chaotically over the deep, soft snow, which sifted softly into everyone's boots. The officers pounded in stakes close to the body, then another set five yards out. They dusted snow from the body, then zipped it into a bag and strapped it to the stretcher. No one talked more than necessary. To talk, air had to be let into your mouth.

When they were done, they stood for a few minutes, stamping their feet and somehow reluctant to go.

Balzeti walked over to Hager, seeming to think about something as he came. He put a mittened hand on Hager's elbow. "Mr. Hager," he said quietly, "We didn't quite think this thing through. I need to leave one of my men here at the site, and I was wondering . . ."

"I'd like to stay here with him," Hager said. It just came out of him; he had not been thinking it.

Balzeti stopped short. "That wasn't what I was going to say. I was just thinking that you could ride behind me."

"Wouldn't it be easier to pull the sled without a passenger?" Hager asked.

"Yes, "Balzeti said. "But we could manage it, I'm sure."

"Whoever is staying here could use some company. Why don't you let me stay? I'd like to, and it would be easier on everybody. If anything happened, I could drive out and get help. Your guys can't drive these things." Again he was surprised to hear his voice, to hear the words spoken so clearly, rationally.

"All right," Balzeti said, hesitantly. "You can stay. If you're sure."

"Call my wife, would you?" Hager asked.

CHAPTER
7

The gray light finally appeared, as though rising from the snow-covered ground, pale, denatured, seeming colder than even the darkness. The columns of the trees took shape. Ramirez had gotten up and stamped a flat place in the snow. Hager watched from his sleeping bag while he began dragging pieces of rotten wood to the site.

"Come on, man, can't you help me with this?" Ramirez was struggling with the weight of a large hunk of log.

"Sure, I'll help. Just leave it there. You've already got enough wood to burn for three days."

"I want a big fire, man."

"Don't worry, it'll be a big fire. What you need are some sticks to get it started. Didn't you ever try out for Boy Scouts?"

"Where I grew up scouts were the little kids who watched for cops."

Hager managed to laugh and got up to help. With Ramirez's cigarette lighter they started a smoky fire. In the freckles of sunshine that spit through the trees, they could hardly see a flame. The pile of soggy wood emitted a cloud of smoke. It partly warmed and thoroughly choked them both, and soon Ramirez was working hard with the heel of his boot, digging out channels for the melted snow to run away in.

"That was quite a night," Hager said.

Ramirez agreed. "This thing is getting stranger every minute," he said. "How on earth did that kid get back here?

This could be one of the great cases, you know? I mean, it is going to take some brains."

This perspective was so utterly different from Hager's that it took a few moments for him to grasp what Ramirez had said. For Hager the strangeness had to do with snow, darkness, silence, with his own loss and grieving.

He felt better, calmer in the morning light. "Why did we come in at night, anyway?" Hager asked.

Ramirez stopped digging and tilted his head to one side. "That's easy. So the reporters couldn't get any good film of the body. Just like the other day when we found the first body, and Balzeti waited all day to take it out. He acts like they're his personal treasures, and he has to protect them from the press."

"Yeah, well," Hager said, and stopped.

"What?"

"Well, you have to like his sincerity. Don't you?"

Ramirez laughed. "Sincerity? What are you talking about?"

"Well, I mean, think how you would feel if they were your kids."

Ramirez snorted.

"You don't agree?"

"Don't get me wrong, Mr. Hager, but as a cop the best way you show respect for the dead is by finding out who killed them."

Hager was kicking the fire with his toe. "Is this a big enough fire for you?" he asked. "See, it doesn't take so much wood. We've got enough for all day." He paused, looked around him, over at the trampled spot where they had found the body. "Hey, no one told me. Did you get the lab reports on Pete?"

Ramirez looked blank. "Pete?"

"The first kid. The boy we found on Tamarack Ridge."

Ramirez was immediately careful. "It's supposed to be a secret." He looked at Hager impersonally. "I guess I can tell you. Only don't say anything."

"Why not?"

"It's good not to make public everything you know. Then

if you have a suspect, you can see whether he really knows what happened."

Ramirez dug his heel into the snow and splashed icy slush up onto his pantleg. "The kid died of asphyxiation. There were bruises on his neck."

When he was warm, Hager left the fire and poked around in the snow near the red stakes. Not even an impression of the body was left, only the scuffle of tracks from the night. Without tools to dig there seemed no hope of finding anything. The snow was deeper here than on Tamarack, and it was entirely possible that they were walking over more bodies without knowing it.

Ramirez stayed by the fire, looking at a topographical map. Soon Hager gave up on the search and joined him. He had become curious to know where they were.

The quadrant was green all over; only in the northeast corner did a cluster of mountains emerge white and gray above the forest. They were far from those peaks. Tamarack Road made a clean black line across the lower left corner of the map, and after some study Hager thought he had located the trail they had followed—a dotted black line that crossed the road and ran nearly parallel to it, going east. He had hiked this trail with Robbie, he realized.

Up the trail farther east, the map showed a pothole lake and a tiny black box marking some kind of building. The topographic lines were broadly spaced, waving gently over the nondescript forest. Toward the south, the lines packed close together; the thin blue line of the Kern River ran at the bottom of a deep, close canyon.

Hager pointed out the building to Ramirez. "What do you think could be up there? I mean, there's no road."

Ramirez didn't know and didn't seem terribly interested. He said he was only interested in keeping warm. A set of thin clouds had drifted over the sun. Hager kept thinking about it, trying to remember what was on the trail. His memory was hazy for this part of the forest; all he recalled were trees.

"There's a cabin up there," he said suddenly. "It belongs to some doctor. I remember passing it."

*   *   *

Hager could not help but go looking; hope had sprung up again. Robbie had always been a strong hiker; perhaps he had remembered the cabin and gone there. Maybe Lizzie was right. Maybe they were hiding out.

Ramirez had seemed disinterested and said he had to stay at the site. But he did not mind Hager's exploring on the snowmobile. Hager was surprised by how careless he seemed.

The trail led through expanses of foot-thick yellow-trunked pine trees. The way was marked with blazes, old scars in the shape of exclamation points nearly overgrown by the oozing, spreading bark. In the deep stands of trees the light was somber and blue, with snow still heavy on the boughs and pressed into the bark like moss.

At first the trail stayed nearly level in the broad valley; then it began to climb. The lay of the land revealed itself in a gradual slope to the right. Screaming and scraping over concealed rocks, the snowmobile sometimes plunged down hard through soft drifts, making Hager grunt.

He had no special love for this country or even for the high mountains, which Stephen so loved. Hager's best memories of Robbie were of driving in the car or wrestling in the dining room. But they had spent many days on trails like this, sometimes even in the snow.

The family had first gone camping at Dinkey Creek with a group of families from the school. Robbie had loved it and so had Stephen, but Carrie had found it oppressive. "A whole week with people who can't talk about anything but handicaps," she had said. So they had given that up.

Regular camping was out, because too many people stared at them, or at least Hager thought they did. But when Robbie was twelve, Hager had begun backpacking with him. Carrie thought Hager was pushing too hard, but Robbie proved to be a good hiker. His balance was poor, but he would go anywhere that Hager led; he never seemed afraid. In the back country they saw few people; and Robbie loved it. Hager had never learned to really care for it, but he loved to watch Robbie so happy, unfrustrated by an environment that conspired against him. Robbie could keep up with the wilderness.

Thinking of this so captured Hager's thoughts that the cabin took him by surprise. He caught it out of the corner of his eye and immediately stopped his machine. The small building, almost a shed, stood old and sway-backed; its planks were worn to colorlessness. Standing on nearly level ground at the end of a clearing, it was sheltered on the left by a thick stand of firs. Beyond, the ground dropped away into the canyon, vast and gray.

Hager suddenly wished that he had come quietly. There is no sneaking up by snowmobile. He punched the throttle and rode across the clean sweep of pillowy white, stopping near the narrow porch. Again he let his eyes sweep across the building, thinking that he might have to describe what he saw. He listened but heard nothing, no response to the engine's whine. Then he saw the paths in the snow, running along the front of the cabin all the way to its corner. His heart jumped. The edges of the track were soft from blowing snow, but they had been made by human feet.

Should he call out? He did once, tentatively, then again with more determination, but he heard nothing. He got off his machine and walked to the front door. No tracks were there. The wind had piled snow against the door. A rickety screen door, it would have to open outward. He pulled on it until it jammed against the snow; when he pulled harder, he heard wood crack. The hinge was breaking away from its rotten wood moorings.

Working with his feet, huffing as he kicked back snow, Hager was able to scrape the door open, but when he tried the inner door he found it locked. He hammered on it, crying out. No answer.

Should he break in? Destruction did not come easily to Hager; he had been raised to respect others' property. Instead, he backed off the porch and looked again at the cabin. The tracks in the snow went around the corner, and he followed them—staying off them so as not to spoil any evidence. On the side of the cabin they had not been shielded from blowing snow and were nearly obliterated. But enough was left so that he could see: They followed the wall as far as a window.

The window was high, up over his head. The glass had been broken out, and he could see something dark—dried blood?—on one long shard of glass that remained stuck in a corner. Running his hands in the snow beneath, he found no glass. It must have broken inward, struck from outside.

They might be there.

He plunged around to the back of the cabin, but found no other entrance—not even another window. He proceeded on around, all the way to the door again. Hager decided to break it down.

He gave two hard kicks where the lock was, but the door did not yield. He applied his shoulder, and thought he heard a slight crack. But when he repeated the shove, nothing gave way. Hager stood panting and rubbing his arm.

The porch was not big enough to take a run at the door. He tried kicking again, planting his left foot firmly in the snow and giving all his strength to it. This time the cracking was unmistakable. The door was giving. He braced himself again and kicked, lost his balance and fell backward, painfully, on the porch steps. Swearing, he got up and kicked again. Now the door frame was visibly breaking around the lock. It finally gave way with a splintering screech, and the door burst open.

It was so dark inside that Hager could see practically nothing at first. No blood or bodies met his eyes. On his left was a stone fireplace, with a small nest of kindling in it and a few sticks of wood. Pieces of old, overstuffed and exhausted furniture circled it. In the back of the room a wooden ladder led up to a small loft, and under this loft, which made a very low wooden ceiling, was a small kitchen with a sink and an array of worn porcelain pans hanging on hooks. There were no cupboards, only nearly bare shelves. A few cans of food lay scattered on the floor.

On the right was the small broken window, offering the only light in the room. Hager knelt below it. On the cracked linoleum were fragments of glass, as he had expected, and some drops of dried blood. He touched one lightly; it was still gummy.

Hager's eyes shifted to the loft. Breathing shallowly, he climbed the ladder and poked his head over the edge. It was quite dark there, nestled under the tin sheet of the roof. He saw a mattress, its black and white stripes mostly covered by a rumpled quilt. A kerosene lantern stood on a small dressing table. Hager climbed two more steps, and then could see quite clearly that someone was under the quilt.

He shut his eyes for a moment, dizzy, before climbing up onto the platform. The plyboard yielded spongily under his weight. He could only see a head, half covered by the quilt. Stooping to avoid the roof, he pulled the cover back, and the person—it was a boy—did not stir. Putting his hand to the cheek Hager found it cold as ice, and as hard. He carefully pulled the quilt back to expose the whole body. It lay on its side, curled tightly into a fetal position, fully dressed.

He saw no wounds, not even on the hands. Not a visible scratch. The hands were tucked up close to the chest, as though to keep warm.

The boy had on jeans and a padded jacket. His hair was long and tangled together. It was Donnie Gilbert. *He must have died of the cold,* Hager thought. *The position is so natural. No one could have laid him out that way.*

He backed down the ladder and stood looking around the room. How could he have died of the cold? There was wood for a fire.

Hager walked slowly from one end of the room to the other, like a man trying to remember something. He sat in one of the chairs and looked carefully at the wood near the fireplace. One piece was a crooked stick with a string tied to it, a sort of bow. A kitchen knife also lay there, and another piece of wood with a small hole gouged in it. There were scraps of wadded paper. Somebody had tried to start a fire Indian style, whirling a stick with the bow to make friction. Hager muttered to himself. "No matches."

Then he got up to look at the cans on the kitchen floor. Some were dented, and their paper wrappers were torn where something sharp had struck them. One had been smashed into the shape of an egg, but it had not opened. *They couldn't find the can opener either,* he said to himself.

CHAPTER

8

Taking off his sunglasses just inside the church foyer, Frank Hager picked up one of the small printed cards the funeral home had provided. He was carefully dressed for the occasion, a handsome man who made his dark blue suit look good. Carrie, beside him, was small and neat. Her suit, with its high neck and trim cut, seemed designed to hide her from notice. Stephen walked slightly ahead; Lizzie curled against her mother's side.

Five days had gone by since the three boys' bodies had been found. Although it was awkward for the Hagers, the other families had decided on a joint ceremony. As Mrs. Gilbert said, they couldn't wait forever.

Frank was very conscious that Carrie was with him unwillingly. Perhaps he imagined it, but her clasp on his elbow seemed stiff in protest. He had insisted they come, to put in an appearance.

This was their church, the First Presbyterian Church of Oakdale, and its normal sound on Sunday morning was chatter. Today the sound was a low mutter—nothing in the higher registers. Hager recognized many of the faces. He saw them in the grocery store or on the golf course. They were people who lived side-by-side in a small community, knowing each other to nod. Their faces were not grieved: They looked anesthetized, masked, with a hint of impatience underneath.

Hager wondered why they had come. Then he thought they had come for the same reason he had: to put in an appearance.

The church was a modern A-frame building. Light issued from illuminated plastic panels on the walls, strips of bright color in swirling imitation of stained glass. Bright orange foam cushions on the pews and a light gray carpet gave the room a jaunty look. It had been new when they moved to Oakdale; time had not made it comfortable. People seemed to hurry in and out, as though reminded of appointments elsewhere.

Hager started to slip into a pew near the back, but Carrie pulled his arm. The caskets were in the front of the church, their tops propped open.

Stephen had already seated himself. Hager called his name softly, and then, when Stephen did not respond, reached out to touch his shoulder. Stephen shrugged him away. Hager slipped down next to him and said in his ear, "I want you to come with us."

"It's not necessary, Dad," Stephen said.

"Stephen, there are certain things you have to do."

Stephen sat unmoved, and Hager felt his fury rising. But Carrie was on his arm. "Frank, it doesn't matter," she whispered.

Hager happened to notice Stephen's hand, which was holding the back of the pew in front of him. Its color was marbled, spots of red swirled into creamy bloodless tissue. He was gripping the pew so hard it might break off in his hand. Hager took a deep breath, relaxed his grip on his son's shoulder and left him.

If Stephen would only say what he was feeling, would say that he didn't know if he could face a funeral. If he would do anything to let other people know his heartache, then everything would be easier. But Stephen didn't do that.

But then, Hager thought, that was a poor excuse. Stephen made it hard, but if you're a father you break through that.

He remembered vividly, as though it were yesterday, the day Stephen had passed his brother. He must have been three or so, and Robbie five, when Hager found them nose to nose screaming at each other, until Robbie began to lash out, to hit. After Hager broke them apart and stopped both their crying, he learned that Stephen had made an awful discovery: that he could put plastic animal shapes through cut-out holes in a plastic ball much faster than Robbie. And Stephen crowed about his triumph. Hager did not remember what he had said to Stephen, but he remembered the heavy heart that had come with the knowledge of what Robbie could not do, would never do.

It was not Stephen's fault, of course. Hager told himself to go easy on the kid, and with that thought his bruised feelings surfaced, his sense that he had been beaten and was wounded yet had to stand and take still more. Like now, being at this funeral.

They stood at the tail of a short line of people paying respects; Hager had an arm wrapped around Lizzie. The mourning families flanked them in the front pews. Hager looked toward them and tried to smile sympathetically. But no one seemed to see him.

Lizzie clutched his waist when they came to the front of the line. Hager looked down at her, into her eyes, and saw that she was afraid. He leaned over. "You don't have to look if you don't want to," he said. "But if you do, I think you'll be glad." He could remember very clearly the first open-casket funeral he ever attended, his grandmother's, when he was perhaps Lizzie's age. It was never so bad as you expected.

The boys had been put in identical caskets and were dressed in suits. Hager had often seen these boys with Robbie, but had not studied their faces as he did now. Peter was in the first casket, cushioned in white satin, seemingly asleep. Hager saw no lingering evidence of the awful, crouched figure on the mountain. Peter's Asiatic face looked abnormally pale but nonetheless, in its thick construction and overhanging eyebrows, the strong, stubborn Armenian feeling came through. He looked unbendable, almost imperial.

Hager wondered how it would be to touch that face, or to take the hand. Nobody did that. You would not want to muss them. Already a distance had been opened from the living.

Hager realized that Lizzie was straining away. He let her go to her mother. He looked also at Dan and Donnie. His eyes focused on their suits, on the smooth, never-worn gray fabric, on the pearl-gray buttons. For some reason he could not keep his eyes on their faces; his gaze kept drifting off to the suits. He began seeing Robbie, goggle-eyed, buzz-cut Robbie. With an effort he turned and walked back to his seat. Waves of memory, almost hallucination, rolled through him. He could see Robbie, really see him, with depth, with movement. Perhaps he was alive, perhaps dead, but at least he was not yet in one of those caskets.

As Hager sat next to Stephen, Robbie's nearness evaporated; Hager could not hold it. He put out his hand and wrapped his arm around Stephen. "I'm sorry," he said softly in Stephen's ear. Stephen nodded—stiffly, he thought. At least it was an acknowledgement. And at least he, Hager, had said the words.

He became aware of Stephen turning his neck, looking in at the center aisle. A crowd of children, the Lambs School, had come in. They must have hired a bus, for there were at least thirty of them. Teachers were moving rapidly, keeping the children in line, hurrying into the pews those who wanted to linger. Most of the children looked ordinary, though some had a slow, hulking way of moving, more like sheep than lambs. If their minds did not grow old, their bodies seemed to hurry that way: They took the slumping shape and shuffling movements of the elderly while they were still young.

The adults who shepherded the children were middle-aged women, except one: Mary Ann. Today she had come to the funeral in a tight black pullover and stretch blue jeans. Every other woman in the church, surely, had worn a dress. She had graduated last year and gone to work as an aide at Robbie's school. Robbie adored her. Whenever Stephen brought her over, Robbie would go and sit next to her and talk loudly to her. Maybe that was why Stephen so seldom brought her around.

She was very thin and flat, without the long angles to make that attractive. Hager could never get her to say much, and when she did talk she tended to stop conversation. For instance, she was the only vegetarian he had ever known. She had once asked him, truly curious, not hostile, whether he thought about the animals when he ate meat. He had told that to Carrie, and she had laughed in her private way and said that it fit.

Mary Ann might have been kidding him, Hager realized, but he couldn't tell. She seemed very serious.

Hager was called to attention by the quietness. The organ had stopped. After a long silence punctuated by coughs and the low rustles of people settling in, the Hagers' pastor rose to the podium. He was a spare, older man, blessed with hair as white as linen. Hager liked him; everybody did, he was so kind, though not really easy to know. He welcomed them gravely and read a few lines from a poem, then sat down to allow Donnie's sister Allison to play a laborious, breathy piece on her flute.

The service was a production, patched together out of the various temperaments and beliefs of the families involved. Three pastors took part—Presbyterian, Assemblies of God, Unitarian—as well as a rabbi even though none of the families was Jewish. That would be Mrs. Gilbert's touch. The Presbyterian choir sang, wearing purple robes. The principal of the Lambs School, a large, broad, energetic woman, read a piece about the right of every person to live up to his or her potential. Then it was time for reflections.

The Assemblies pastor stood, a gentle-spoken young man with a peach complexion and glory in his eyes, looking barely older than the three boys in the caskets. He gave a short remembrance of Peter Aranian. When Peter had first come to the church, he said, and he realized that Peter's parents usually brought him, he had wondered how it would work out. But he had come to like having Peter in the service, and—he said quite seriously, without a smile—if a Pentecostal pastor couldn't live with the unpredictable he must be in the wrong business.

He had asked Peter once how one gets to heaven, and Peter had said—here the pastor smiled broadly—"By Jesus." "And Peter," he had asked, "do you have any doubt where you're going to go when you die?" Peter had said, with a shout, "To heaven!"

It seemed to Hager that people were holding their breath, wondering whether the pastor would embarrass them. He seemed to hesitate, and the happy glow on his face grew fuller as he surveyed his audience. Was he conscious that he made them squirm? Hager thought he would go on, but he didn't. He said simply that he knew Peter was now celebrating his new life in heaven, because Peter had been very sure of his salvation by faith in the Lord Jesus Christ. He stopped short of inviting them all to an on-the-spot conversion. Hager thought that people relaxed and lifted their heads when he sat down.

The other two pastors, dressed in their ceremonial robes, gave more polished oratorical memorials, which had perhaps a better effectiveness in making the mourners feel that the boys' lives were celebrated transcendently, that the gathering had summoned God and the angels into the process. The Hagers' pastor went out of his way to talk about the dignity of all people. Without mentioning mental retardation he made them all feel sorry for it, talking about God's love for each and every last living thing, regardless of race, creed, ability, or success. The rabbi read a prayer, dryly, in a deep, rasping voice: an Old Testament prayer, somber with the stillness of the desert. Then with the organ dripping notes, they filed out.

A warm wind blew up the slopes from the south. There was no receiving line, for which Hager was thankful. Some refreshments had been set up in the social hall opposite the sanctuary, but most people stopped short of there, clustering in the patio's sweet sunshine. Soon their shyness wore off and Hager heard laughter as at any garden party. He shook a few hands of people emerging quickly from the church on their way to the parking lot.

Stephen had gone off, presumably after Mary Ann. The three remaining Hagers picked a corner behind a planter. Lizzie was squirming, saying she wanted to go home.

"I certainly don't feel like talking to anyone," Carrie said.

"I don't think anyone feels like talking to us, either," Frank replied. "But we need to stay for a short time." He would rather have been any place on earth. He felt wounded and edgy, and he did not know whether he could stand people's sympathy.

He caught the shifting eyes of a few people, but no one approached, nor did he and Carrie stand as though they wanted anyone to do so. They huddled with their heads close together, talking softly. What could anyone say to them? No one knew whether Robbie was dead or alive, whether to offer condolences or hope. Nonetheless it made a bitter feeling to be on the margins, grieving yet with nothing to be grieved about.

Hager was relieved when he saw Mary Ann coming, pulling Stephen by the hand. "Wasn't that a beautiful service?" she said to them. "So moving." She stood very close, looking unflinchingly into their eyes. Her face would never be called beautiful, though Hager saw in a way he never had before that it was an interesting face, long and thin, with pronounced parentheses around her eyes and mouth. She wore no make-up and looked older than she was. She might have been any age.

Carrie asked her what she had found "moving." She said that it had been the music, to which there seemed no possible reply except, "The flute solo?"

"Oh, that was lovely too, but I meant the organ," Mary Ann said. "I don't know when I've heard it so beautiful. Who was the organist?"

Hager had no idea who the organist was, except that she was a stern-looking woman who played every Sunday as though she were punishing the keys.

Mary Ann seemed to have exhausted her store of conversational openers and stood looking brightly back and forth between the two Hagers, as though she had put in a quarter and was expecting something. Finally Carrie asked how the Lambs School was reacting to the deaths, and Mary Ann told them the students were extremely excited. All of them had wanted to come to the funeral, but the principal had limited it to the upper grades.

While Mary Ann was talking, Mrs. Gilbert swept up. She was a short, big-boned woman wearing a dark tweed suit. "Oh!" she said, "this must be misery for you. How awful to have to stand around at our boys' funeral when your own is missing. Do you feel all right? Wouldn't you like to go home? Because that would be fine, you know—we all understand and appreciate that you've come."

Hager took a breath but before he managed to say

anything, Carrie said, softly, that they had wanted to show their concern for her and the other families.

"Oh, you're very kind," Mrs. Gilbert said. "How did you feel about the service? Was it misery?" When they didn't respond she went on. "Wasn't that Pentecostal man just awful? Could you believe that he would do that here? I thought he would, I warned Dr. Gillespie, but they all said it would be fine."

Mary Ann made the mistake of asking what she meant. Mrs. Gilbert lifted her eyes toward the sky. "I mean bringing in the Lord Jesus Christ and going to heaven. Honestly, do you think a man like that, probably not very well educated, do you think he just didn't know that there were Jews and agnostics here today? Is that possible, that he just didn't know? And talking as though the boys were complete babies. Can you imagine? 'How do you get to heaven, Peter?'" She mimicked the pastor's gentle voice.

Hager felt himself growing more tense as Mrs. Gilbert talked. He disliked her and felt guilty for it. She taught at the Lambs School; she had taught Robbie. People said she was a superb teacher, and whether or not that was so, she was certainly very dedicated. She had given her life to the school.

But he did not like her, nonetheless. And while he too had been embarrassed by the Pentecostal pastor's words, he did not like to hear them mocked. The man was, after all, a pastor. Hager could never talk about his beliefs as the man had done, and he was certainly not prepared to argue about them. But at a foundational, emotional level he considered himself a Christian and did not want his faith mocked.

Which meant, he couldn't help thinking, reproving himself, that he should love Mrs. Gilbert. God knew she needed love from somewhere. Two years ago she had tried to kill herself by jumping off the bridge in town with two heavy lead weights tied to her feet. The creek had been up so high with spring thaw that the rush of water had pushed her into a log jam where the water only came up to her armpits. Someone had fished her out, but not before she passed out from hypothermia and nearly died of that. Carrie had volunteered to take Donnie for the weekend. He had seemed like a nice kid, nicer than his mother. But that wasn't fair, Hager knew; these kids put a lot of stress on their parents. As he knew.

He felt a touch on his elbow and was glad to divert his attention from Mrs. Gilbert's raving. Now that the ice was broken, others were coming over to greet them. Francis Balzeti, out of uniform and dressed in a black suit—who has a black suit any more?—thrust out a hand, a doleful expression on his face. "I don't know whether you remember me," he said. "Balzeti, from the sheriff's department. I just wanted you to know how sorry I am."

"Well thanks," Hager said. "We're still hoping, of course. Have you met my son Steve?"

Stephen was looking away, into the distance. On being introduced he put out his hand. "Stephen," he said, and glanced testily at Hager. Hager often forgot that was what he wanted to be called.

"Yeah, we met, didn't we?" Balzeti seemed vague.

"And you know Margaret Gilbert?"

But Mrs. Gilbert had already seen him. "I was just asking Carrie," she said a trifle too loudly, "when do you suppose the police will start working on this case? How nice to see that you've begun now."

"We're doing our best," Balzeti murmured. He had put his finger into his collar, as though letting pressure escape. He twisted his neck. "I just wanted you to know how sorry I am," he said.

"Your best? It's very nice to know that. I feel better. Do you have some leads? Any ideas?"

"Margaret," said Carrie reproachfully, raising her eyebrows. "It doesn't help."

Balzeti's eyes shifted. He could not fight back with a woman, especially at her son's funeral. "We're trying, ma'am," he said.

"Well, how would I know?" Mrs. Gilbert said. "I went to Columbia but I don't suppose that qualifies me to know, really. I would have thought you would talk to family members, and that kind of thing. Just to see whether they have any ideas."

"We're planning on that," Balzeti said. "We don't have unlimited people."

"No, I suppose not. After all, you have to keep a certain number out in the snow."

Balzeti looked up sharply, as though he had just recognized an object through the gloom. "We found your son, ma'am. There's still a boy missing. That's our priority."

Hager realized that, except for a few brief questions asked the day Robbie had turned up missing, no one had talked to him, nor to Stephen so far as he knew. It had not occurred to him, until now, that the police were failing to do enough.

Balzeti had turned a deep plum color, and he stood unmoving, looking at Mrs. Gilbert as she talked on as though addressing Carrie. At the first possible moment, Balzeti excused himself, saying to Mrs. Gilbert that he would be in touch.

Mrs. Gilbert continued, but Hager was not listening. He heard Carrie's voice, then Mrs. Gilbert's. He was looking down at the patio pavement, seeing the gray and brown pebbles of the exposed aggregate, as sharp as a photograph. Why had it never occurred to him that the police should come and ask questions? He wondered whether he ought to do something—ask some questions himself, maybe. He might find out more than the police.

Then for just a moment he saw Robbie again, the crewcut. It was so painful, so awfully, delectably painful.

CHAPTER

9

"She had a point, don't you think?" Hager said to Carrie, standing in the kitchen, with his long fingers wrapped around the warmth of a mug of tea. "Margaret Gilbert, I mean. When she went after the sheriff. It does seem strange that they haven't talked to anybody. Not even Stephen, and he was the last to see the boys."

"You know what she said to me?" Carrie asked. She was mechanically putting the dinner dishes into the dishwasher as though her body operated from memory and her soul were far off. "She said, 'Isn't it a relief?'"

"Isn't what a relief?"

"She meant not having the boys any more to look after. She said she'd had the most peaceful week she could ever remember."

Hager was truly shocked. "What did you say?" he asked.

"What do you think I said? I told her I couldn't imagine what she was talking about." Carrie's voice did not seem to carry authentic indignation. It sounded as though it came from under a heavy mantle of dust.

"It was hard when he was young," Hager said. "Remember?"

"Not just then. You have no idea all that I do. But it's not a relief to lose your son." She spoke firmly as though these were the final words, the end of the subject.

Hager was not willing to let it drop yet. "Do you miss him

as much as I do, Carrie?" he asked wistfully. He was troubled by her weary attitude. "And we haven't lost him yet. I wish that darn sheriff would get to work."

"Do you think he can bring Robbie back?"

She seemed to always take this impotent, fatalistic attitude when they talked about Robbie. Hager, watching her speak, tried not to let the sadness conquer him. He loved this woman. It seemed to be a long time since their hearts had met, but he loved her.

"I guess not," Hager said gloomily, sitting down on one of the slat-backed stools and putting his elbows on the counter. "Probably not. But I can't just leave it alone. I keep on hoping. I wish I could just stop thinking about it."

Hager had Rotary the next day. He felt nervous as he parked and walked into the Rustler, the steak place where they always met. It was hard enough to carry the emotions of loss with him constantly, and harder yet to join with others who had no such grief. If he was silent, the thorn in his heart burrowed deeper; but if he spoke, it was hard to make a connection, and he felt how alien he had become.

The room was crowded with men talking loudly, laughing, and calling to each other. A lot of them Hager knew and considered his friends; he played golf with some of them, did business with others, and knew nearly all by name. A middle-aged waitress in white stockings was pushing through with her cart, setting out pear-and-mayonnaise salads. "Excuse me, honey," she said to Hager in a smoke-scratched alto, her eyes locked onto the table she was serving.

Bob Castaneda, his insurance man, came over to shake hands. He looked at Hager with a sorrowful look, saying something about being sorry he had missed the funeral. Gene Shepherd and Carlo Dravecky, lawyers Hager liked to play golf with, joined them with serious faces. Soon Hager relaxed, realizing that nobody was going to ask him anything too personal. He was glad to be with men, on safe ground. It eased the burden a little.

He saw Harris across the room—Harris, the father of the kid who had given Robbie a hard time on the night he had disappeared. Hager thought about going over to talk to him then discarded the idea.

But a few minutes later Harris sat down across from him. "Hi there, Frank," he said, reaching out over the table to shake hands. "No news about your boy? Well, no news is good news, I guess. I understand that you've been pretty actively involved in the search."

"Well, not intentionally," Hager said. "I've just been hanging around."

"The way I heard it, you went through all kinds of heroics, sleeping out in the snow and breaking into that cabin."

Hager was conscious of people's listening. "You kind of surprise yourself sometimes," he said and then hesitated, wondering whether to go on. "Say, I'm not criticizing the sheriff's department, but I'm just curious. Have they been to talk to your son yet?"

"Which one? Laird?"

"Is he the one who graduated last year?"

"Yeah. Why would they want to talk to Laird?"

"Maybe you didn't hear. Apparently he got into some kind of fight with the kids the night they disappeared. That's why they left the game."

Harris laughed humorlessly. "I guess I did hear that he'd been acting like a jerk that night. That's certainly nothing new." He looked around as though others would see the humor of it. "No, as far as I know nobody has talked to him about it. Why should they?"

Hager made an effort to calm himself before he spoke. "Your boy was one of the last to see those kids. My Stephen was there too, and they haven't talked to him either."

Harris was looking toward the podium, impatiently twirling his fork between his palms. He flicked his eyes toward Hager. "Well, Frank, I'm sure it's been exciting to be in the chase. My experience has been that the police end up doing a pretty good job, if you give them time."

The gavel began beating, and the meeting was called to order. Hager heard nothing of the invocation and the introductions. He was burning inside, and a series of possible rebukes ran through his mind. He ate his meal in silence. When the meeting was over, he got up quickly to leave.

"Frank."

It was Harris. "Frank, come on by the office and talk to Laird if you want to. I'll make sure he's available. He's working for me now. Got a lot of business going these days and we're busy as hell. But I'd make sure he talked to you."

Hager drove home, burdened, and found Carrie in the laundry room, folding sheets. He helped her, stretching his arms out full so that the room was filled with billowing white.

"The pastor came by," she said.

"Oh?" His voice was muffled because he had his chin down on a sheet as he folded it.

"He just wanted to see how we're doing. He said to say hello."

"That was nice of him," Hager said mechanically. "I've tried to return his calls. I keep missing." He told her about what Harris had said. She was impatient. She did not even let him finish. "Frank, I'm tired of this topic. I don't know why the police haven't talked to everybody but I'm not going to spend the rest of the year talking about it. I really don't think it makes any difference."

"What does that mean?" Hager asked. "It doesn't make any difference whether they look for Robbie?"

"No, if you want to put it that way, I think it probably doesn't. I don't think Robbie's alive." She broke into tears, dropping her hands while still clutching the sheet and then throwing it in frustration to the floor. Hager could not get to her without stepping on it; he pulled the clean sheet into his arms and tossed it onto a chair. Then he held her, caressing her temples, trying to rub the anger away where the white skin showed through her black roots of hair. She let him, but he could feel that her body was tight. She was holding herself like a fist.

"We can't give up," he said. "Babe, we have to keep on. I know it's hard."

But she would not be pacified. "Don't tell me that any more, Frank. If you want to talk about it, go and talk to that sheriff. Don't talk to me about it anymore."

*   *   *

"Could you tell me whether you have any clues to follow?"

Feeling foolish and weak, Hager looked wishfully at Balzeti. He had driven into Fresno to talk to the man, but he was not getting anywhere. Balzeti acted attentive and unhurried, his little round-packed body sitting at attention in his gray government chair. He said their priority had been the search; they would follow up with Stephen and Laird Harris, but it might be a few more days.

"Well, unfortunately we don't have very many clues, Mr. Hager. You understand that I can't tell you everything about our investigation, but right now we don't have a lot to go on. We've got just that one witness who saw them after they left the high school." A man who owned a cabin in the area, Balzeti had explained, remembered passing two cars pulled over to the side of the road not far from Three Streams on the crucial night. He thought one car might have been the Hager's green Chrysler. The snow had been falling heavily, and the man had pushed on, thinking that one car had stopped to help the other. Balzeti had spent hours with him, had tried everything but torture to make him remember, but to no effect.

"That's not much to go on, Mr. Hager. We've dusted the car and the cabin for fingerprints, but we haven't really got anything. The blood from the glass is the same as Robbie's but also a few million other people's. It wasn't the Gilbert boy's. He didn't have a cut on him. Whoever cut himself left the same way he came, and disappeared."

"It could have been Robbie," Hager said miserably.

"It could have been," Balzeti said. "And there could have been others involved anywhere along the way."

"Why would he go and Donnie stay behind?"

Balzeti made a barely perceptible shrug of his shoulders. "Donnie's mother told me that he hated the snow. He would never go out in the cold if he could avoid it. That's what she said."

Hager briefly buried his head in his hands, then remembered what he was doing and sat up straight. It was true that the police had not talked to everybody yet, but it was also true that doing so would be just fishing—casting about with the hope of stumbling on something, much as they were casting about in the reaches of snow looking for one last body.

"Do you think," Hager said, "do you think that it might have been just a fight between the boys? Maybe just a prank that went wrong?"

Balzeti shrugged again. He stood and walked around his desk, putting a small hand on Hager's shoulder. "Anything is possible," he said. "At this point I don't have any idea what got them that far out in the woods. But there was violence. There was a murder."

The telephone rang, and Balzeti slowly removed his hand from Hager. With surprising agility he circled his desk and picked up the receiver.

"Balzeti," he said, and then listened in silence. "I have somebody here right now," he said, and listened some more.

"Tell me how to get there," he said, and began scribbling on a pad of paper. "I'll be there," he said. "Bye."

He tore the top sheet off his pad of paper, then looked up. He seemed almost to jiggle with the desire to move. "Well, there may be something happening at last," he said. "I can't tell you anything yet, but we may have something, Mr. Hager."

CHAPTER
10

Hager did what he always did when he was confused and upset: He got in his car and drove around. A dense fog had settled just overhead throughout the valley, so that the tops of the telephone poles were slightly blurred. The sky was a featureless smear, and the ground and everything on it dulled by the shadowless monochromatic light.

He did not want to go home to rattle around there. Carrie had as much as told him to stop talking about Robbie. He did not want to go in to his office or to the coffee shop.

So he took the road out of Fresno toward Three Streams, a narrow, winding country road that dated back before better highways, probably to a wagon road and to the loggers who had first cut the big trees. It was a good road to take because it required all his concentration to push the big car through the turns. When he reached the foothills, the sun began to punch through holes in the fog, and wisps of gray blew past him until, looking up, he saw overhead the perfect robin's egg blue of the mountain sky. Then, in a moment, he was dazzled by the sun and could look back into the valley to see a white layer of fog lapping softly at the mountains like an inland sea. His spirits lifted. He received that common, comforting illusion of travel—that he was getting somewhere.

Three Streams was a smaller town than Oakdale. The lack of a good road had left it stranded, without the new restaurants and sporting goods stores and real estate offices that were sprouting up along the highway in other mountain towns. Hager drove up the main road and back down the only side street, noticing with the eye of a developer that the few stores still lacked paved parking, that their windows were small and cluttered and offered no opening to a stranger. He turned the car back onto the main road, driving up the hill again. Above the town was the high school, just past where the road came in from Oakdale. The school was the newest building in the town, the fruit of a school unification bond issue of fifteen years before, done when Three Streams still had a population comparable to Oakdale's and was able to influence the choice of location by siding with smaller roadside towns.

Hager pulled into the parking lot and slowly toured it, marveling at the cars kids drove. He saw Stephen's car, an aging Gremlin, parked in the senior section. *If I were in high school*, Hager thought, *I would work my tail off to get a better car.* Stephen said he was happy with it, that he did not care about driving fast but just enjoyed making the most of what he had, which, in the Gremlin, was not much.

Across the street was the chicken place where Robbie and his friends had eaten with Stephen the night they had disappeared. It was a small white building with a red door and a new molded plastic sign outside: The Chicken Shack. Nobody was there, but the smell of fried food permeated the air. In a short time the high school would spill kids out for lunch and the place would be jammed full.

Hager was not sure what he was looking for, but he was not finding it. All he found were mute reminders of what he did not have, did not know, could not find. The brief lift he had received from sun and movement was gone. He turned his car out of the parking lot and back down the main road, past the road junction for Oakdale. He was still not ready to go home.

When he passed the Copper Kitchen, he saw two police cars parked in front. It was unusual to see anyone from the sheriff's department here. Perhaps they had come down from the search on Tamarack Ridge. There were still search parties out there though their numbers had dwindled.

Hager pulled over just past the restaurant, where a muddy

roadside plot served for parking. The Copper Kitchen was an aging pancake house that had lured a series of hopeful owners into partial facelifts. The latest owner had kept the name intact but put money into plants and cedar shingles on the inside walls; the only copper left was in the name. A large trout remained mounted over the grill, a fish with an origin no one could remember. People joked that it was the original owner of the place.

In the entryway Hager rubbed his feet on a rubberized mat and peered into the gloom of the windowless main room. The place had once been a bar. Why the owner had decorated it with plants was anyone's guess; nothing would grow.

He located the cops in the back, sitting across from each other in a booth. One was Balzeti. Remembering the telephone call that had ended his conference with Balzeti, Hager began to feel stirred. Balzeti was talking to Ramirez, the little Mexican with the mustache. Balzeti was leaning over his cup of coffee wolfishly.

Hager walked over and stood by them. It took a moment before they realized that the shape at their elbows was not a waitress. Hager heard Ramirez say, ". . . he came in wearing this hat, right up on top of all this hair . . ." Ramirez stopped his sentence at a gesture from Balzeti.

Balzeti was not glad to see him. He started to rise to his feet and was stopped by the impossibility of standing in the booth. "You followed me?" he asked, glaring.

"Follow you?"

"Mr. Hager, I've tried to be helpful. But that's enough. You're interfering with police work."

"Look," Hager said, trying to gather his wits, "you don't understand. I was just driving by."

Balzeti looked at him balefully. "Just driving by."

"Yeah, just driving by. My boy Stephen goes to school here."

Ramirez smirked.

"Okay," Balzeti said slowly. "Sorry if I jumped to conclusions. We're in a very sensitive part of the investigation." He held out his hand to shake Hager's. "Sorry about that. Now, we need some privacy."

Hager shrugged his shoulders, turned, and walked out. By the time he got in the car, his agitation and excitement were boiling. He started up the engine, put it into reverse, and then as the big weight began to rock into motion, stomped his foot suddenly on the brake. He sat for a moment, poised in indecision, then put the car back into park and turned off the engine. He wasn't bothering the sheriff, and he had every right to watch.

He walked up to the porch of the Copper Kitchen and bought a newspaper. Taking it back to his car, he tried to read it though his mind would not follow the words. Soon another black-and-white came driving up the road, fast, then slowed sharply just past the Copper Kitchen. There was no place to park along the street, so the driver stopped completely, blocking the road while he looked for a spot. After a long hesitation he backed up to enter the dirt lot where Hager was waiting. Just as he was entering the lot, another police car came up the road and followed him in. The first car stopped; the second car pulled up alongside and conferred. Hager tuned his ears but could not hear what they said.

Then lumbering slowly up the road came one of the TV vans, hesitating when it came opposite the two police cars, then entering the pot-holed lot with the slow grace of a pregnant woman. *Something is really up*, Hager thought. A second TV van, going faster than the first, passed by on the road, shuddered suddenly to a stop, backed up to the parking lot, and turned to enter.

At the Copper Kitchen's entrance a small cluster of locals had stopped to stare, wondering what was going to happen and whether it would be worth waiting to see. Hager saw Balzeti come out the door. His reaction was slapstick; you could see it across a football field. He stopped, did a double take, and exploded with rage. Then Balzeti came toward the parking lot on the double, his chest and belly leading the way, his head back, his boots kicking out in front of him. He was shouting at the TV people, ordering them out of the lot.

Balzeti went to the Channel 24 driver's window and rapped on it. The man rolled it down a few inches. Balzeti's voice got very high when he was shouting. "Get out! Get out of here! Police investigation." The man said a few words that Hager could not hear, Balzeti shouted something, then the man rolled the window up again. Balzeti continued yelling and then suddenly stopped, standing speechless for a moment before he walked quickly over to the two police cars.

Two officers got out of one of the cars, stretching. They, along with Balzeti and Ramirez, squeezed into the other black-and-white. A few minutes later the doors opened and they emerged again and trotted to their cars. Balzeti was parked on the street and started up, gunned the engine, and pulled out in the lead; Ramirez, parked just in front of him, followed; then the two other black-and-whites squealed out of the dirt lot. The two TV vans lumbered slowly to follow. Lastly, Hager started his engine and brought up the rear. When he passed the Copper Kitchen, he saw a knot of men in quilted jackets, boots, and blue jeans, watching silently as though it were a funeral.

The procession went up the road, turned left at the Oakdale Road and rapidly picked up speed, flashing in and out of sunlight among thick pines. The TV vans could not keep up. Soon Hager could not see the squad cars even on curves where the bulk of the vans did not block his sight.

The sheriffs were flying, without sirens. They passed one old rusted pickup, which the TV vans could not get around on the narrow, curving road. Hager watched the vans veer in and out, gunning their motors in hopes of a chance to pass. The road was lined with a strip of dirty snow; all buildings were left behind.

The police were far out of sight by the time they reached a long straightaway. The TV vans pulled out simultaneously to pass the pickup, with Hager right behind them, blind to whatever lay ahead. Suddenly their brake lights came on and he too had to jam his foot on the brake pedal. He swung the car over behind the pickup so he could see.

The police cars were just ahead, slowing to a stop. Ramirez's car pulled alongside Balzeti's and stopped in the left lane, blocking the road. The third car stopped behind, and the fourth car pulled to the right, to the edge of the shoulder, then backed in an arc, throwing gravel, so that it stopped perpendicular to the road, blocking both lanes. The deputies got out, slammed their doors and stood, hands on hips, guarding each shoulder.

The two TV vans pulled slowly up behind. So did Hager. So did the pickup. While they watched, the first three squad cars took off again, going fast down the straight, around a curve and out of sight.

Hager had seen enough of Balzeti's methods not to be surprised. Keeping reporters away was high on his list of priorities. Perhaps, too, they were expecting trouble.

Hager tried to think of what lay ahead down the road. A mile or two farther was an old deserted barn, he remembered. Off the road from there, down the hill, was a creek and a section of logging flume where kids went to drink beer in the summer. Nobody would be around at this time of year.

There was, Hager remembered, another way in. Back a couple of miles from where they were stopped, an old overgrown logging road ran into the woods. Hager had been on it a few years before, looking over a plot of land as a courtesy for a friend who had wanted to build a cabin. They had driven the road in a jeep, but he thought his car would make it. He remembered that it had cut around to the right, paralleling the highway as it worked along a dried-up, sandy stream.

As soon as he thought of it, he was tempted to try it. All Balzeti could do was shout at him. Roads belong to everybody.

Hager put his car in reverse, sawed the steering wheel back and forth and finally got the big car turned around. He might get stuck, certainly. The creek would be full of water now. But Hager had his blood up—he wanted to see what the sheriffs were doing. He wanted movement.

Backtracking, he missed the logging road the first time, discovering that he had gone too far only after he came to a culvert where the stream bubbled under the road. He had the same laborious time turning the car again, all the while thinking that a vehicle coming fast from Three Streams might take him out broadside. He wrestled the car around and drove back more slowly, looking at every space in the trees until he found the spot. He had forgotten how steeply it dropped off the embankment. There were young trees, knee-high, growing in the roadway. In another year it would be gone.

He pulled left over the edge, scraping the oil pan hard on the embankment as his front wheels went down, sliding in the small rocks and muddy clay. The Imperial came to rest gracelessly at the bottom. Hager smiled to himself. No going back—he would not be able to get up that grade.

But once down, the road was not difficult. No one had driven it for years, it appeared; vegetation had grown almost to eye level. The trees were dense and old, their trunks choked with dead, gray branches, and the path of the road between them was obvious. He charged ahead and did not worry about what he ran over. Sometimes he felt muck underneath or heard the splash of a puddle he had run through. He kept the car rolling so as not to take a chance on sticking. The big car smashed over small trees, brown corn lilies, mats of dead fern. On his left was the creek; sometimes he was in its damp, gravelly borders.

Hager had no reason for what he was doing and no idea of how long he would need to continue, but he felt a manic happiness in his chest. How he loved to plunge.

Then, finally, a dirt road came in from the right, and the vegetation vanished from his path. This part of the old road was traveled. It hooked to the left, down. Before descending the slope, he stopped the car. He thought he knew where he was now. This was the road leading down to the old flume, where the kids hung out. Going farther would lead him away from the main road. He backed the car to the road juncture and turned uphill.

He did not get far. A hundred yards up a log had fallen across the road. He turned off the car and got out. The tree was too big to move, and there was no way around it on this part of the hill.

He weighed the possibilities. He could get a chain saw and cut out this log. That would be the surest. Or he could backtrack and try to find some other way back up to the road. That might be possible, but it might also get him absolutely stuck.

In the meantime, he decided, he would walk up to the

road and see whether he could see anything of Balzeti and his crew. It couldn't hurt. Maybe he would get lucky and come across somebody with a chain saw.

The road was a track here, two ruts with a ridge of small rocks shoved in the middle. Hager whistled to himself as he started up it. His brown wingtips were not the best for walking, but he did not have far to go.

The ground leveled out, and he saw signs of habitation—a pile of rusted cans, a split-open moldy mattress. The track forked into two, both ways seeming recently used. Then, ahead in the woods, he heard a dull pounding. He heard a distant voice: "Anybody home?" The voice was Balzeti's.

He heard nothing more and so went slowly forward, taking the left fork of the track. Within twenty yards he saw a roofline appear through the trees. Stepping off the road, he eased up onto some rock shelves that ran alongside. They enabled him to shelter in manzanita as he worked his way slowly toward the house. Again he heard Balzeti pound on the door and ask, "Anybody home?" From the muffled sound it seemed he was around the front.

The cabin must have been here all these years; Hager could not imagine how he had been ignorant of it. It was neat, dark green with white shutters, and there were curtains in the windows. A cut-out Santa face had been taped in one. Below the back steps a summer garden had grown in raised beds; now, with the snow so recently gone, it lay in tangles of burst tomatoes and dark stalks. An old Ford Falcon was parked to the side of the cabin.

Hager stopped and listened intently. All he heard was a steady dripping somewhere, the drops striking with metallic explosions.

Hager kept a good distance and a screen of bushes between himself and the cabin. The rock shelf grew higher and more exposed, so he circled behind it and came out in some leather-leafed bushes in front of the house. He saw Balzeti leaning up against the house, peering in a window. The sill was at chin level, and he was standing on tiptoe to see over it.

The presence of the car suggested someone might be inside, someone who did not answer the door. Hager surveyed the Falcon, noticing that there were no pine needles on its roof or hood. It had not been parked there too long.

Then he noticed that Balzeti was not moving. He was standing stock still as though he saw something through the glass. For a moment he was frozen, and then, suddenly, he whirled and ran straight at Hager, stooping, zigzagging, pulling his pistol, yelling, "Drop it! Drop it!"

Hager stood rooted in horror. For a moment he thought there must be someone behind him, whom Balzeti had seen. He did not know what to do—run or shout. In seconds Balzeti had reached the brush and charged into it. Hager left his crouched position and stood up, half to identify himself, half to defend himself. Balzeti did not stop. He ran straight over the bush into Hager, locking his arms around Hager's waist. His packed-ham body knocked Hager to the ground. Hager gave a grunt of pain and lay still, not struggling.

"It's me," Hager said.

Balzeti struggled to extricate his legs, then propped himself up to see whom he had straddled. His face expanded with astonished rage. He lifted his arm and slammed his pistol butt into Hager's ribs. Hager's mouth opened in bewilderment and pain.

"What's going on? Did you get him?" Ramirez was standing fifty yards off with his pistol out, covering the cabin from the side.

"Stay there," Balzeti said, panting to catch his breath. "We got some volunteer help."

Standing, he yanked Hager's arm to drag him to his feet. "How'd you get here?"

Hager tried to back away. "I walked."

"You walked through the roadblock?"

"I took a back road. My car's down there." Hager gestured, and winced when he felt his ribs where the pistol had hit him.

"Then somebody told you how to get here."

Hager, who felt understandably humiliated at being caught, began to get his bearings. "Nobody needed to tell me. I figured this was the only place you could be going."

"So you tell me, Mr. Hager. What in the devil do you think you're doing here?"

A man who has dealt with plumbing contractors is not so easily faced down. Hager's anger surfaced easily. "I have a perfect right to be here."

"You're interfering with a police investigation, and that's a crime, Mr. Hager. And you can get hurt."

"I did get hurt," Hager said with a threatening tone in his voice. The two stared at each other for a moment.

"All right." Balzeti returned to the business at hand. "Since you're here, you're going to help us." He grabbed both of Hager's arms from behind and roughly whirled him about so he faced the cabin. "Watch the door," he said. "If anyone comes out, yell bloody murder. And don't do anything else. I wouldn't particularly want to have to report that I accidentally shot you."

He walked to where Ramirez was standing, holding his pistol. "Put that thing away and listen. We're going to need a search warrant. But if somebody's in there he could get away. Frank there is going to watch the front. You stay on the back. I'll go to the car and radio for help."

Ramirez had a crooked little wise-guy grin on his face. "What does Frank think he's doing here?"

"He's helping. If the black guy takes him hostage, don't bother to save his life. He wants to help."

"Right, Chief." Then, gesturing toward the cabin, he asked in a low voice, "You really think there's somebody in there?"

Balzeti shrugged. "I don't know. But we don't take chances in this business. You have to learn to cover every angle."

Ramirez smiled and said, "Right, Chief."

Balzeti walked up the dirt track, disappearing into the pines. When he was gone, Hager moved gingerly out into the clearing, feeling his ribs. They would be very sore tomorrow, he was sure. And for what? He did not know why he found it so hard to stay away. This would turn out to be just one more frustrating, fruitless search, probings in the snow. Balzeti had said it: covering every angle.

He looked at the cabin. Balzeti had said something about a black guy, but this neat little place looked like *Goldilocks and the Three Bears*. Balzeti wasn't going to find anything in there.

A distant sound caught his ear, a scraping, sliding noise like a dump truck delivering itself of a load of gravel.

Then he heard Balzeti's shout. "Stop!" A pause. "Stop, or I'll shoot!"

Hager waited for the sound of a gun. He heard, instead, breaking branches in the trees toward the road.

"Ramirez! Ramirez!" Balzeti sounded out of breath. "He's going your way! Head him off! We've got him!"

Hager glanced toward the side of the cabin and saw that Ramirez was standing there with his pistol out, his eyes darting around. Then on the other side of the house, out of Ramirez's sight, a tall, broadly built black man in a gray wool overcoat lumbered out of the trees and crossed the clearing. As quickly as he had appeared he disappeared into the trees again, running like a bear. Without thinking, without a sound, Hager turned and ran after him.

He followed the sound of breaking branches. The old trees grew thick here, sprouting numberless dead sticks at chest and eye level. Hager had his arms up high as he bulled his way through them. He saw a flash of gray ahead. Then he struck a tree. Something sharp gouged his arm.

Suddenly he was, without warning, in the stream bed. His right foot went deep into the water and he fell sprawling face first into a shallow pool. "Get him!" he screamed, his legs pumping the water even before he was vertical again. "He's down here! Get him!"

He ran on blindly down the stream bed, thinking that he had lost the man. He could hear nothing over the sound of his own panting. His ribs jabbed like a knife at every step, and he was about to stop when he caught another glimpse of gray ahead and found the strength for a burst of speed.

The ground was dry now; they were headed back uphill. Hager heard branches breaking behind him and for a moment was completely confused. Were there two fugitives? A trap? "Ramirez!" he yelled hoarsely, with barely any breath, and then stepped on a rock, lost his balance, and for a suspended moment was running sideways. He hit something he did not see, and his body spun. Then everything stopped moving and he was on the ground. Ramirez came running up, clutching his gun. Hager had no breath to speak; he waved Ramirez on, urgently. "Put the gun away," he gasped hoarsely as Ramirez disappeared, crashing ahead. "It's dangerous!" he yelled after him. Then Balzeti also ran past, red in the face, gasping and asking, "Are you all right?" and not waiting for an answer.

Sense began to return to Hager's brain. He heard them scrambling, at what seemed a long remove. Getting to his feet, steadying himself, he tried to run toward the sound and immediately clutched his side and stopped. His ribs must be cracked, not just bruised. He limped a few steps and then managed to break into a slow lope. He had lost the lust that could force his body on.

The crashing still went on. He heard Ramirez shout. A gun fired once, then again. Ramirez's voice, sharp and high, reached him: "Stop! You crazy fool, you're going to get killed. Stop!"

Then he heard no sound at all, and he began to care again. He picked up speed, his left arm strapped around his ribs.

They had run through a copse of small, intensely green trees, leaving deep depressions underfoot in cream-colored sand. Hager pushed through a close-standing clump of trees and came into a dry clearing twenty yards across littered with stumps. At the far side was Ramirez, crouched, extending his gun with both hands. Balzeti stood behind him, holding out his hands as though to stop a bullet. Hager stopped plunging through the thick branches and slowed to a walk. Then he saw the man twenty yards beyond Ramirez, among the trees. He was leaning over, one hand holding a slim sapling to steady himself, the other hand on his knees. As Hager came closer he could hear breath exploding in and out of the man's mouth.

"Just keep holding him, Ramirez," Balzeti said. "Don't move!" he said to the black man. "I'm coming, but don't move or you'll get shot." He strolled past Ramirez and circled behind the man, putting his gun in its holster when he had verified that the man had no weapon.

"Stand up slowly now," he said, "so I can search you."
The man did not respond.

"Stand up!" Balzeti said fiercely. Slowly the man unfurled
his body to its full height. He was a giant. His face showed no
expression. On his head he wore a baseball cap, which looked
ridiculous because of the huge ball of hair that was under it.
His eyeballs were half shaded under drooping lids, flaccid as a
lizard's. Balzeti slapped his hands over his body, searching for
a weapon. "You're under arrest," Balzeti said, as he snapped
handcuffs onto his wrists. "For murder."

Hager saw that the baseball cap had an orange B on a deep
blue field. B for Brixley, Michigan, where Carrie's brother
lived. It was the hat Robbie had been wearing when he
disappeared.

CHAPTER

11

Frank Hager told the story of the arrest to Carrie when he got home, expecting her to be proud of him. She listened in silence, her dark eyes lowered. Her friend Lorraine was there, and Carrie didn't say anything until she'd sent her friend off. Then she started right in on Hager, wanting to know what had prompted him to go around the police roadblock.

"You could have been killed, Frank."

"I don't think so, honey. There were three of us, and he didn't have a gun."

"You didn't know that."

They were standing close together in the kitchen, automatically lowering their voices so the children would not hear them disagree. Hager saw that tears were forming in Carrie's eyes. Nothing could make him feel more helpless.

"You have no business acting this way," Carrie said, in a stubborn won't-give-it-up voice he knew well. "You have other children. You have responsibilities. You can't keep acting as though the world has stopped on account of Robbie." Her voice had been invaded by panic.

He reached out and took one of her hands. She hesitated before she let him clasp it.

"Honey, I think you're overreacting," he said. He was thinking, miserably, that she reacted this way because she didn't care about Robbie heart and soul, but he could never say that. "What has it been, just over a week? And now they've got the guy. I thought you'd be so glad to know that we caught him, and here you're making me feel like I should be ashamed of myself."

Carrie pulled her hand away, snatched a Kleenex from the top of the refrigerator, and dabbed her eyes. "It seems like it's been going on forever," she said.

"It's just a week. We're finally getting somewhere. Carrie, do you realize, it's not impossible we might see him today!" He wanted to believe it and was determined to stay upbeat, but he felt her pessimism dragging him down.

She smiled at him enigmatically. "That's so unrealistic," she said, shaking her head.

"It's possible," he said vehemently. "Anything is possible. It's not right to give up hoping."

"I don't see that it makes any difference whether we hope or don't. He's either alive or he's not."

"No!" Hager said, saying it more loudly than he had meant to. He stopped short, unable to think what to say. The two of them stared at each other.

Finally Carrie extended two fingers toward Hager. He took them. "I just don't want you to get hurt," she said. "Please."

"'Let the police take the chances,'" he said hollowly. "'That's what they get paid for.' All right. I don't think any more chase scenes are going to come my way, anyway."

A half hour later Stephen Hager lay on the thick den carpet, his head propped on one elbow. His father got up to change channels although the news had not yet started. Carrie's reminder that he had other children had pricked Hager's conscience, and when Stephen had come in from school, Hager had made a beeline for him, telling him the good news about the arrest. He did not seem to be reaching Stephen though. Stephen's emotions, never tropical, seemed pressed down; his speech, rehearsed. Hager tried, but he grew tired of trying. He wished that Stephen would make it easier.

"How's Mary Ann? I haven't seen her since the funeral," Hager asked in an absentminded way while staring at a commercial. He didn't wait to hear an answer. "I think there should be some film of the guy. If there's anything it'll be Channel 30, I bet," Hager said.

Carrie came in from the kitchen, drying a roasting pan. "You're watching the news?" she asked disapprovingly.

Hager twisted his neck toward her, frowning. "I thought they might have a picture of the guy. Maybe news of Robbie. It's normal to want to keep up with the news when it involves your own flesh and blood."

"I just want it to be over," she said, looking down at her hands. "It's probably not right, but I feel that way."

"They aren't going to find Robbie, Dad," Stephen said. "Not alive."

"No?" Hager sank back in his seat. "How can you know that? You don't know that. Anything is possible."

The news came on with its familiar theme—the announcer's first words told them there had been a break, a suspect arrested near Three Streams.

"Dan Conneraught was on the scene for the suspect's pursuit and capture at gunpoint late this afternoon. We'll get Dan's firsthand report right after these messages." They went to a commercial.

The phone rang, and Carrie went to answer it in the kitchen. "It's for you, Frank," she called.

"Who is it?"

"Margaret Gilbert. Donnie's mom."

"Tell her to call back. Then come out here and listen to the news."

"That's what she wants to talk to you about."

"Tell her I'll call her back." Then, to Stephen, "Did they say that Conneraught was part of the chase? That's a lot of baloney."

"Maybe they mean when the TV vans were following the cops out of Three Streams," Stephen said.

'Well, that was nothing. You might as well say that the fry cook at the restaurant was involved."

Dan Conneraught came on the television screen and told about the arrest of the suspect, whose name, he said, was Wallace Reid. Dan was growing a light-brown mustache, but it did not help with his lip-sync problem—his mouth seemed to move even less than before. He said that one of the youngest members of the Sheriff's department had not only made the arrest but done the investigation that led to Reid. "Louis Ramirez, a detective for just eight months and a criminal justice graduate of Fresno City College and Fresno State College, learned that a baseball cap Reid wore belonged to Robbie Hager, the boy still missing in the tragic Tamarack Ridge slayings." They showed the oil painting of Robbie, even though he didn't look like that any more.

"Sheriff's department officials aren't saying anything more," Conneraught said. "Neighbors describe Reid as quiet and unsociable. They believe him to be unemployed."

The picture changed to the news studio, and an item about rats at the city dump. Hager had not been mentioned.

"No picture?" Frank Hager said and got out of his chair to switch to Channel 24.

Carrie, still holding her pan, said, "They called me about that baseball cap this morning."

"What did they say?" Frank started, and then, as he found the channel, said, "Shhh. There he is." The television showed a black man in a long gray coat walking up a forest road toward the camera, his arms behind his back. Surrounded by police, he came closer until his face practically filled the screen. It was an impassive and unfriendly face, full and jowly, with hooded eyes. He dipped to get into a car, and another shot showed the car driving off. The news voice was giving the details about Wallace Reid.

Looking at the picture, Hager had felt an odd welling up of emotion, of sadness and hatred. This was the man who, probably, had killed his son. He had not felt much emotion toward him after the chase, but now he thought to himself that he could quite calmly kill the man.

"That's the guy," Hager said. "Cold as ice, did you notice?"

"What did you want him to do? Smile?" Stephen asked.

"No, I expect him to look just like he does. Mean as a wolf."

"You're pretty quick to assume that he's guilty."

Hager was taken aback. "Yeah, I guess I do think that."

"Because he's black?"

"Stevie, the police for heaven's sake, are the ones who arrested him, not me. I just don't like the way he looks." Annoyed, he shifted his body to face his wife, who stood with the roasting pan, still staring at the television. "Hey, Carrie, what were you saying about that cap?"

"They called today. I think it was that Ramirez. He wanted to know what the colors were on Robbie's hat and what team it came from. So I told him that it had belonged to Uncle Paul back in Michigan. He was real interested in that. He asked me if I knew of anyone else who would have a hat like that."

Hager shook his head, almost happily. "Isn't that amazing. Imagine that guy walking around with that cap on his head, and he never guesses that of all the things he could choose to wear that's the one thing that gives him away. Can you believe how stupid that is? He marked himself. There can't be another hat like that in the entire state of California!"

All three of them stared at the television for a moment. Lizzie came in, slamming the front door. "Lizzie," Hager said excitedly, "you just missed the news."

"Were you on it again, Dad?" she asked, coming over near him, where he took her hand. Lizzie found considerable excitement in the fact that her father had been on television.

"No, but I was right there when it all happened. They've arrested a guy. A huge, mean-looking guy."

"A black guy," Stephen interjected.

"It doesn't matter if he's black or yellow or green. He had on the hat that Robbie was wearing. And he ran when he saw the sheriff. We had to chase him through the woods."

"Did you chase him, Dad?" Lizzie was wide-eyed.

"Yeah, I did. Of course if it had been up to me he would probably still be running. I fell down."

"Oh, Daddy! Were you hurt?"

"Not really. Just the wind knocked out of me. I'm a little sore."

Lizzie leaned over and hugged his head. "Oh, Dad, I'm glad you're all right," she said. It entered Hager's mind that it was the first friendly word anyone had said to him since he returned home.

"Oh, it wasn't really dangerous," Hager said. "I was just glad to be there. I think we'll be hearing some news about Robbie soon. I'd imagine they're questioning that guy right now."

"Dad," Stephen said, "did you ever think he just might have found that cap somewhere on the side of the road?"

"Oh, yeah? Like what road? Tamarack Ridge? Steve, use your head. Robbie hasn't been on the kind of roads that people just wander along. Besides, they've been searched up and down for a week."

"Dad, nobody knows where Robbie has been. You use your head. The guy just happened to be black, so the police assumed he must be the murderer. He's probably the only black guy within fifty miles of Three Streams."

"Good grief, Steve. You assume that because the man is black he couldn't have done anything. If he wasn't guilty, why did he run?"

"Maybe he ran because he was scared. You might be scared too if you were a black guy and a bunch of cops with guns showed up at your house."

"Stephen, sane people do not run away from the police. They might be scared but when the police yell, 'Stop, or I'll shoot,' they stop."

"I want you two to stop," Carrie said in a low voice, and they did. The television blared on. Then the telephone rang, and Stephen got up slowly to get it. It was Mrs. Gilbert again. She confused his voice with Hager's. Stephen interrupted her and said he would get him.

Stephen took Hager's chair and sat staring at the TV while his father talked to Mrs. Gilbert. Carrie came up quietly behind him and put her hands on his shoulders. She began massaging them.

Finally Hager hung up the telephone. "That is quite a woman," he said. "She thinks just the way you do, Stephen. She just assumes that the sheriff arrested Reid because he's black."

"I hope he has a good alibi," Stephen said.

"Well, I hope he doesn't. I hope he fries."

Stephen merely shrugged, and Hager felt his emotions beginning to rise again. "Stephen, why do you have to be so negative? If Robbie's alive and that's the guy responsible, he can tell us where Robbie is."

"Don't get your hopes up, Dad."

"Thanks a lot. Let me finish. I was going to say, if Robbie's dead and he's the guy responsible, I want him to pay for it. I don't care if he's black or green or whether he came from a negative family experience. I want him to burn."

Stephen got up and left the room without a word, leaving Hager with a gut full of frustration.

CHAPTER

12

All day Friday Hager stayed around the house waiting for the phone to ring. He assumed that the police were working on Reid, extracting a confession and discovering what he had done with Robbie. Yet he heard nothing. Late Friday afternoon he even put in a call to Balzeti. The receptionist took his number. No one called back.

Perhaps, Hager thought, they were too busy to communicate with him; perhaps they were taking turns with Reid, good cop, bad cop in a small room, and had no time for the telephone; or perhaps they might even be off on a search. Perhaps, who could say, they were combing some landscape for Robbie this moment.

Hager kicked around his garden, watched a little TV, cleaned in the garage. Every object he saw, every voice he heard seemed overstated. The sounds seemed to come out of speakers, the objects—tools and bags of fertilizer—to jump out from their surroundings. The material world seemed staged. Hager wanted to know what lay behind the scenery: what was happening with his son.

He was a rational man; he knew that he had no part in the investigation. Yet it chafed him that he must be shut out from an affair so personal to him. Like every victim, he felt that his wounds should concern everyone as much as they did him, and yet the officers showed scant interest. Balzeti tried to demonstrate respect but was concerned mainly with law and process. In a strange way it was the press, the bloodthirsty ambulance-chasing press, that had Hager's heart most in mind even if their interest was in cutting open his chest for all to see on the six o'clock news. Their attention, however, had apparently flagged. Hager would have been more than willing to give an interview, but no one called.

He felt that it was impossible to talk about these feelings with Carrie. He had always relied on her and on her wordless comfort but now felt that they were at odds. She would not say much to him. From her manner he felt she was angry. And she was in league with Stephen. Both of them treated him like a child whose tantrums must be ignored.

On Saturday morning Carrie made him go to the office, telling him he needed to get out of the house, that she had things to do and he was in her way at home. He found the office deserted and freezing inside. Turning up the thermostat, he wondered what he should do with himself. On his desk was a stack of pink messages held down by a ceramic trout; he could not bear to lift a single note or even to sit at his desk. While standing, he called the sheriff's office. The phone rang ten, twelve times before someone answered. Hager explained who he was and asked if Deputy Sheriff Balzeti was in.

"I think he's around here somewhere, but I can't connect you. The switchboard doesn't work on weekends." The man, whoever he was, said Hager should call back Monday.

Hager sat down at his desk. The little A-frame office of which he had once been so proud looked cheap and flimsy to him. It had been designed like a snug mountain cabin. The exposed beams were solid wood, yet today they looked like fakes you would see in a new mobile-home park community center. And why had he wanted orange carpet? He could not imagine. He tried to think what could be done to give the office the look of solidity and wealth he had intended, but he found himself unable to concentrate on such things. He couldn't care.

For just a moment a thrill of fear ran over him. If a developer couldn't stand to think about such things, he was in the wrong business. Perhaps everything would be lost, his work as well as his son.

He walked briskly to the wall, turned off the thermostat, and went out the door. Getting into his still-warm car he drove fifty yards, maneuvering through the parking lots rather than entering the highway. He was surprised to find the coffee shop bustling. He had not known that so many people went out to breakfast on Saturday. He bought a *Chronicle*, took a seat at the counter, and tried to read. The woman reporter hadn't written anything about his case.

Sunday was more of the same. They went to church, and after the service Hager felt a powerful urge to escape, to get away as soon as possible from people who might pity him. Carrie, however, was supposed to discuss the Presbyterian Women's schedule of speakers, so he was forced to wait for her. He, Stephen, and Lizzie went into the fellowship hall, where coffee and doughnuts were served; he gave Stephen money to buy doughnuts for them all and waited, holding Lizzie around the waist, hoping to be left alone and dreading it. Several men stopped and shook hands and asked how he was. They seemed to have forgotten all about Robbie. Someone Hager knew only as Roy, an affable, talkative character with a balding head and the walk of a cowboy, a man who did not quite fit into the ordinary way of conversation, came over and stayed, talking about the city council. It was not too bad. Finally Carrie reappeared and they fled. Hager spent the rest of the day reading the paper, watching a basketball game, washing the car.

By Monday morning he felt he could barely stand another day of limbo. The sharp memories of Robbie would not come any longer; he could no longer see the crewcut and the June-bug eyes. Half a dozen times he looked at the painting on the den wall, hoping to make the pain come back, but for now, at least, it had gone. Perhaps, he thought, the terrible, suspended detachment would fade too, in time.

Carrie went out shopping for groceries—as she did every Monday morning, she informed him as though making some kind of point. He had almost made up his mind to try going in to the office again when the telephone rang. It was Ramirez, seeming in a hurry. Balzeti had asked him to call and say that he had something to give Hager whenever he could stop by.

"Where are you?" Hager asked, reaching eagerly for a pad of paper and a pencil.

"Down at the county annex. There's no hurry."

"I'll be right down," Hager said.

"It's nothing urgent," Ramirez said.

"Can't you tell me over the phone?"

Ramirez paused for a moment. "Sure, why not. He's got that baseball cap for you."

"The baseball cap?"

"Reid wanted you to have it."

Hager was at a loss. "Isn't it evidence?" he asked.

"Oh, we had the forensics people go over the cap. But they didn't find anything. We figured you could have it back. We're releasing him this afternoon."

He did not immediately understand. "You're letting him out?"

"Yeah, there's not enough to charge him. All we had was the hat."

"You couldn't get him to talk?"

"Oh, yeah, he talked after we worked on him a while. He talked."

"But no confession."

"No, no confession."

"What did he say?"

For a moment he heard nothing, then Ramirez said, "You know, I really am not supposed to divulge this kind of information to the public."

"I'm not the public!"

Again a pause. "Yeah, I know, Mr. Hager, but the law doesn't quite see it that way. Why don't you come down sometime and talk to Balzeti. He might be able to tell you more."

"He's going to be around this afternoon?"

"Yeah, unless something comes up."

"Could you tell him I'll be down right away? I need to talk to him."

Ramirez hesitated again. "Okay, but you might want to take your time. He usually goes out to lunch, and I don't know when he's going to get back."

* * *

Hager found Stephen in his French class, his earphones on and his head down on the table. Hager stood in the doorway, watching for a moment. Stephen was a handsome kid, dark-featured with his mother's heart-shaped face.

The teacher looked at Hager questioningly. Hager pointed at Stephen, who, seeing his teacher's face, turned toward the door. Hager beckoned him.

"Hi, Steve," he said just outside the door. "How would you like to cut class today? I talked to Mr. Walker and he said it would be fine."

"What's going on?" Stephen said cautiously.

"The sheriff's office called and asked me to come down. I thought maybe you'd like to go with me. Do you need to get a jacket?"

In the car Hager opened the window to feel the air, but it was too brisk; he pushed the button that made the window hum back up and closed the last crack. On an impulse he had decided to come for Stephen. He felt he needed someone with him. Besides, for some time he had been feeling that he ought to try again with Stephen.

Hager ventured to speak. "You've been pretty quiet lately, Steve."

"Yeah," Stephen said.

"What are you thinking about?"

"Nothing, really. Just thinking. Sometimes I like to be alone."

"You think about Robbie a lot?"

"Yeah. That's one of the things I think about, anyway." Stephen looked carefully at his father's face. "Why are we going down there, Dad?"

Hager took a deep breath and blew it out. "They called a little while ago to say I could have Robbie's baseball cap back. The one they found on Reid. They're letting him out."

Stephen did not say anything, so Hager went on. "They said the hat wasn't enough evidence to keep him. They couldn't get him to confess."

"So we're going down to get the hat?"

"Well, I want to talk to find out what's going on. Nobody tells me anything. I don't even know if they're looking for Robbie."

"So why do you want me?" Stephen asked.

"I just thought it would be a good chance to be together. I can use the company. And you don't need to worry about your grades, that's for sure." They entered the curviest section of the road then and were both silent for a time, bracing their way through the bends. "I hope you don't mind coming," Hager added.

"No, I don't mind," Stephen said. "I'm glad to hear that they let him out."

"Oh, I forgot. I guess that makes you right," Hager said. He had forgotten their argument after the arrest. Then he was sorry he had said something sarcastic.

"So how are you doing, Steve?" Hager asked. "I mean *really*, how are you getting along?"

"Okay, I guess. I resigned from the student council."

"When?" Hager asked.

"This week."

"Why? What made you decide to quit?"

"I don't know. My heart just wasn't in it, I guess. I only did it to look good on my college applications. So I decided, screw it."

Hager automatically reacted, not only to the decision; the words "screw it" gave a little jolt.

"Steve, don't you feel responsible to finish the year?" Hager regretted saying it as soon as he had. He looked over to see that Stephen had turned his head away and was staring out the window.

"Look, I'm sorry," Hager said. "The last thing you need from me is a lecture on responsibility. I should be as responsible as you." Hager glanced over at Stephen, who did not respond. "I'm glad you told me, and it's fine with me. We just have to get through this time as best we can, I guess."

They left the conifers and entered the large, greening sweep of the foothills punctuated with single oaks. It was country that opened Hager's spirit, giving a sense of space and hope.

"You know," he said, trying again, "I remember that first day when we found out Robbie was missing and we all got together in the evening and I made a little speech about us helping each other. That seems like an age ago, doesn't it? Today it struck me that I haven't been doing what I said. I've been in my own world. I wanted to say that I'm sorry."

"You really loved him, Dad," Stephen said softly.

Hager was taken aback by this short, quiet sentence.

"Yeah, that's true," Hager said. "I loved him. I still do. And I'm sure we all love him very much in different ways. A father loves his children in a way that isn't quite like any other love."

"Yes," Stephen said with a note of quietly stubborn assertion, "but you loved him more than most. It was amazing how you loved him."

"And I love you too," Hager said. "Just as much. Though for some reason it's harder for me to express it with you." Stephen did not answer. Hager could not help wondering whether Stephen believed him. Not that Stephen had ever said he felt unloved, but his silences often seemed to convey it.

"Hey, that reminds me, I noticed something interesting in Robbie's room the other day. You know the bank where Robbie kept all his quarters? Well, it's empty. Nothing in it. Do you know anything about that?"

"Maybe Lizzie took them," Stephen said.

"Yeah, maybe. I'll have to ask her. I thought it was strange because as far as I ever knew, Robbie would never take them all out. I wonder what was going on with him? Was there anything funny that you know of?"

Stephen said, "No, not that I knew of. But if you don't know, nobody would. He told you everything."

The Fresno County courthouse was a plate-glass box. A large clean expanse of linoleum tile in the lobby echoed the squeaks of rubber soles. Hager went there often.

"You don't remember the old courthouse, do you?" Hager asked.

As a boy, Hager had often wandered through the old courthouse's underlighted hallways, half believing that he might stumble on some antique and forgotten marvel, half afraid some adult authority would ask what he was doing there. The lofty central space under the dome had been his favorite shrine: still and dim, with WPA murals of California history high up on its walls. For a boy like Hager to whom church was a room with sheetrock walls and a cross stuck up front, the old courthouse had offered a feeling of the holy never encountered elsewhere.

But Stephen would not understand that, Hager felt sure. Stephen had grown up in a different era, after the real estate people owned the town. They had torn down the old courthouse. The picture of the dome frozen halfway to the ground had appeared in *Life* magazine, with a caption announcing that they would use the space for a parking lot. That had not been strictly true; the new courthouse had been built on the spot. But Hager thought of it as true enough. The fall of that dome—Hager still remembered clearly the photo of it hanging sideways, a split second from decimation—had killed the old town. The new town had the soul of a parking lot.

He, Hager, had helped do it. He didn't know whether Stephen could understand all that or whether the new town had, for him, some other kind of soul.

"Do you like this building?" Hager asked.

Stephen looked around. "It's okay," he said.

Hager smiled apologetically. "I was just feeling nostalgic for the old courthouse. You know, old things have their charm. I was thinking that maybe someday you and your friends will be feeling nostalgic about these new things you're growing up with, just the way people my age feel about the old things. Do you think so?"

Stephen looked down at his loafers. "I suppose so, Dad." He had a look of boredom on his face that backed Hager right out of the past.

Hager led them to the Sheriff's Annex, through a set of glass doors with crash bars. Stephen did not want to go in, but Hager pulled him along. He was suddenly extremely nervous and wanted Stephen's company. He wanted Robbie back and equally he wanted somehow to break through to Stephen. Neither seemed very likely.

"You're in real estate, aren't you?" Balzeti asked when he had ushered them into a sizeable, drab room full of government-issue gray metal desks. Occasionally a detective walked through on his way somewhere. "Some kind of development?" They were seated beside his cluttered desk.

"I bought some land up your way last year," Balzeti continued, looking as though he had missed some sleep. "Nothing very big, just two half-acre lots. Do you think that area is going to develop? I'm not looking for any big return but I thought that sooner or later that area might do something."

"Where did you buy?" Hager asked politely. The subject did not surprise him. People brought up real estate with him the way they discussed symptoms with doctors.

"Sonoma Estates. It's up on top of the old Sonoma Ridge Road."

"Yeah, I know where it is," Hager said. "Fisher Investments. That's a nice area. Real private." He turned to Stephen. "It's up past Woodleaf."

"I know," Stephen said.

Balzeti took a sip of his coffee. "So you think that's a good buy?" he asked.

Ordinarily Hager enjoyed talking about real estate; now he was especially glad for the topic, for he had a kind of dread of what they would discuss. "Oh, I would think so. Of course I don't know what you paid. I'm sure you're planning on holding on for a while. That place is a little out of the way for most people."

"I paid $17,000 for the two lots," Balzeti said, a little anxiously.

Hager pursed his lips. "That's not bad. I would have thought a little lower, but when you're looking at a long-term investment, that doesn't make so much difference." Balzeti looked sunk, Hager noticed. "Of course I haven't seen the property," he added. "The view makes quite a difference, the trees, whether it has a stream on it, and so forth."

"It has quite a few trees on it," Balzeti said. "The two lots are side by side, up at the back of the development."

"You just give it some time," Hager said. "Don't be in a hurry. It'll develop, it's bound to develop. That whole foothill area is going to be like San Francisco some day, and the whole valley is going to be Los Angeles. You just have to wait long enough. Nobody ever grew poor buying property."

For a few moments of silence Balzeti seemed lost in his dreams. Then he reached down and opened a drawer in his desk. He pulled out the baseball cap, deep blue with an orange B, and tossed it on the desk. "Reid asked me to give it to you," he said.

Hager looked at the cap as though it were a small and deadly bomb.

"We're letting him out this afternoon," Balzeti said. "We don't have the evidence to hold him." He continued, as though Reid were a distasteful subject. "I don't really think we're done with Mr. Reid yet. But you have to have evidence to charge somebody. The D.A. said the hat wasn't enough."

"But you've been questioning him?" Hager asked cautiously, unsure of what he would be allowed to know.

"You bet we've been questioning him. Day and night. He says he found the hat by the side of the road."

"Then why did he run?"

"He's not so clear on that." Balzeti spoke in a mocking tone. "He gets very disturbed when we ask that question. He tries to give us the impression that he felt responsible for the whole thing. He felt guilty because he didn't help the boys. Maybe nothing would have happened if he had helped them like he should have. That's what he says."

"Help them?" Hager's tension spilled quickly into his voice. "How could he help them if he never saw them? Did you ask him how he could feel responsible if he never saw them?" Hager spoke rapidly, one word jumping on the next.

"Yeah, I asked him." Balzeti was leaning back in his chair, full of lethargy and disgust, a complete contradiction to Hager's hurry. "He did see them. He says that he saw them changing a tire, right there by his cabin when it was snowing. So why didn't he help them? The man seems confused by that question."

"He's holding out," Hager said. He was sitting forward.

Balzeti closed his eyes for a moment. "That's occurred to me, Mr. Hager. At any rate, so far as I can understand what Reid is trying to say, he claims that he didn't help them at all. He just watched from the trees. They didn't even know he was there, he says. He says that he was too frightened to do anything."

"Frightened of what? That big guy? Frightened?"

Before Balzeti could answer Hager went on, talking quickly. "I remember reading about that case in Illinois where they got the guy because of the bite on the girl's leg. Is there something like that? Something we could trace to this guy? A thread from his clothes or something? What did you find when you searched his house? Did he have a lot of guns in there?"

"No. No guns, but the kids weren't killed with guns."

"No, that's right." Hager tried to concentrate for a moment. Not knowing what to say or think, he glanced at Stephen for a clue. But Stephen had his eyes trained on Balzeti.

"How were they killed, anyway?" Hager asked. "I never heard what the autopsy found." He remembered not to mention what Ramirez had told him about Pete.

"Mr. Hager, that is something I cannot tell the public."

Hager, who had grown excited thinking of ways to catch Reid, came back to earth. A flame of anger licked up and he leaned forward making his voice stay under control. "You think I'm the public?" he asked. "We're talking about my son."

Balzeti started to respond, then shut his mouth. He looked Hager and Stephen over before slowly speaking again. "Okay, but look, both of you, this information must stay in your family. We can't have it broadcast. The way we interrogate suspects is by making sure that we know more than they do. You understand?"

They nodded. He still looked at them sternly. "I'm sure you want to catch the guy who did this as much as we do, so you'll keep these facts to yourself. I don't even want the other parents told. Please."

"We won't even see the other parents," Hager said.

"Fine," Balzeti said. Then he leaned back in his chair. "The first boy died of asphyxiation. That's the one we thought was your son, Mr. Hager. We aren't quite sure how. He wasn't strangled; he had bruises on the back of his neck but not the front.

"And the other two boys died of the cold. Froze to death. Hypothermia. Simple as that. No signs of any violence at all."

"So," Hager said slowly, "the guy forced them to go up the Tamarack Ridge road, killed one, somehow got the others to go back on that trail, then dumped them there to die of the cold."

Balzeti smiled grimly. "We don't know they were forced to go up there. The way up Tamarack Ridge makes a Y off the main road." With his hands he showed the two roads diverging. "If the road wasn't plowed, you could make a mistake in the dark and drive right up, thinking you were on the regular road."

"But what if the road had been plowed?"

"I don't think it had been."

"You don't know?"

"Not yet."

"Well can't you find out?"

"We may be able to," Balzeti said. "If the man who did the road can remember."

"But you haven't checked on that?"

Balzeti leaned back in his chair again, looking at the ceiling. "Mr. Hager, do you have any idea how many details there are to follow up?"

"No," Hager said slowly. "Have you had a chance to talk to the Harris kid who threatened the boys that night?"

"Yeah, I know about him." Balzeti sighed. "In fact, I think it was Steve there who told us about that, wasn't it? We checked on him. Harris is kind of a mean kid. The local police know him pretty well, though he's never been in any kind of serious trouble. And that fracas didn't amount to anything."

"Did you talk to him?"

"No, but we talked to others who were there."

"Well what about afterward? What happened after they left the game?"

"I don't think the Harris kid was involved in any other activity that night."

"He definitely came out of the game. Didn't he, Steve?"
Stephen nodded.

"Look," Hager said, "I certainly don't know how to do
your job for you. But I don't understand. You let your only
suspect go. He might be halfway to Mexico by tonight. And it
doesn't sound like you've gone after anybody who knew
anything about what happened that night. Don't you want to
talk to these people?"

"The answer is yes, Mr. Hager. But frankly, we just don't
have enough detectives to do everything right away. This isn't
the only crime in Fresno County, you know. And the search
has taken a gigantic amount of time. It still does."

"What about that cabin? How did they find that cabin in
the middle of nowhere? Do you know whose cabin it is?"

"It belongs to a doctor," Balzeti said, seeming relieved to
know the answer. "A fellow way up in Turlock. And you told
us, as I recall, that you had led the boys right by there on a
hike."

"Have you talked to the doctor?"

Balzeti just stared.

"Well, I don't think those kids got up there just for the fun
of a walk in the woods even if they did remember where the
cabin was. Which I doubt. Those kids weren't exactly Ein-
steins, you know. Somebody must have known where that
cabin was. Maybe the doctor can give you an idea who it might
be. At least he might know if Reid knew the place."

Balzeti was growing visibly uneasy; he pulled on his
mustache. "That's one of the things we're doing, by the way.
We're keeping a close eye on Reid."

"You have him staked out?" Hager asked. "How do you do
that? I mean, out in the woods a police car is pretty visible.
You don't have to tell me—I was just curious."

"No, that's all right," Balzeti said. "You're absolutely right.
We don't actually watch him all the time; we just keep a close
eye on him."

Hager said, "Oh."

"We're also continuing the search for your son. We've still
got men up on Tamarack."

"Anything else turn up?" Hager asked. "Clothing?"

"No, nothing," said Balzeti with a sigh. "Nothing yet."

"So actually," Hager said, and then he paused. Who cares, he thought, he would say it. His temper had been lit. "Actually you are keeping an eye on things so that if the murderer comes along and wants to confess, you'll be available."

"I wouldn't say that," Balzeti said, beginning to touch his mustache as though it had been glued on and was coming unstuck.

"What would you say, then? Just what are you doing?"

"Mr. Hager," Balzeti said with dignity, "We're doing our best with limited resources."

Hager took some time to calm down. He slammed the car door and waited while Stephen got in more slowly. Then he drove methodically through the empty, wide, downtown streets. The sun shone off the dirty windows of stores deserted for the shopping malls.

"Dad, where are you going?" Stephen asked.

"Nowhere," Hager said. "I used to hang out here when I was a kid."

"It must have changed."

"It looks about the same to me." He turned the car in a wide, looping U-turn. His anger flickered out like a candle, replaced by a deep well of sadness.

"Can you believe that guy? 'We're keeping a close eye on him.' When they're not doing a thing. They're doing nothing, but he wants to talk about the price he paid for some lots."

They drove through some of the smaller residential streets, passing old, sleepy houses with rundown lawns and graying oleanders that swamped the windows with fountains of leathery leaves.

"I know he must be dead," Hager said. "Somebody had to get them to go off into the snow that way. I think we'd trained Rob pretty well to stay with the car. And they all hated snow so, especially Donnie. I'm sure they didn't just get lost out there. But if somebody got them to go back there, I don't know how he did it. Can you imagine it, Stephen? I don't know how you could force them to do it even with a gun." He shrugged his big shoulders.

"And why?" he continued. "That's the other thing I can't figure out. Maybe it was a real pervert, but then you have to remember that he hardly touched them." Hager's face looked tired and heavy as he talked and he seemed to have drifted into his own world.

"Well, it's all over now, Dad," Stephen said.

Hager glanced over to see his son's withdrawn sadness and put a hand out to his shoulder, gripping it with strong fingers. "Yeah, I know. You're right. It's a shame that they couldn't get anything on Reid. If he's the one who did it."

Hager had stopped at a stop sign and become so lost in his thoughts that he forgot to go on. Finally he realized that he should move and took his foot off the brake. They rolled slowly through the intersection.

"I miss him, you know," Hager said. "Do you really think we should just forget him?"

"Not forget him, Dad. Just forget what happened. Because you're never going to know. That's what that guy was trying to say, except he couldn't quite say it."

"You think he should have just told me, 'I'm sorry, Mr. Hager, but we don't have anything to go on, and finding your son's body under some tree isn't going to help.'"

"I think," Stephen said, "that you have to face the facts and then go on with life. The best thing is to forget about it. He lived his life and now he's gone, and it's probably for the best anyway."

"For the best?" Hager asked.

"The longer he lived the more of a problem he would be. Maybe that wasn't a problem to you, but it was for other people."

"Like who?" Hager tried to control his voice, but he was enraged. This kind of talk always got him, like when someone said that it was a mercy that retarded children didn't live long.

But what Stephen said diffused his anger. "Like Mom, for instance. The point is, we should put it all behind us now."

Hager considered this in silence. "I don't know if I can do that," he said. "I suppose I'll have to." The pain was not going away. Hager did not even want the pain to go away.

They drove on, leaving the old houses and entering the

horizontal landscape of a post-war housing development. "Hey," Hager said, "do you want to see the first apartments I built?" He turned off the main street and drove two blocks, then parked in front of a modest two-story stucco box, with a wide, empty lawn in front of it.

"It doesn't look like much now, but it was really something new then," Hager said. "Come on, let's get out and I'll show you." The car doors sounded loud as they slammed them; it was a quiet, chilly day with a weak sun, the kind of day when you can hear a dog bark from blocks away.

"You see those planters? I had seen those in Hollywood, and these were the first ones built in Fresno. And this was one of the first apartment complexes that had a pool. Within a few years they all had them."

In a central courtyard a small garden cupped a tiny kidney-shaped pool. Hager leaned against a wrought-iron gate painted blue. "I was really proud of this place," he said. "You just can't believe what it was for me. I thought I was famous. I expected people to be talking about it for years. I was real young to be putting any kind of package together, especially in those days. The apartments filled up in about a week, which was unheard of.

"I built Tahiti Gardens after this one. That was really a new concept. Now it seems old, doesn't it?"

"I didn't know you built those," Stephen said.

"Yeah, all those banana trees. And the curving stucco. I had to show the plasterers how to do it. Nobody had ever seen anything like it." Hager took his eyes off the gardens and looked at Stephen, who seemed to hover just out of reach. Hager could not read his eyes, whether he despised him or whether he wanted to be closer but couldn't quite say it.

"I guess we better go," Hager said. "Sorry to bore you with all this stuff. I think you have to be a builder to understand."

"No, it's interesting, Dad."

In the car again, after they had left town and were among the streaking aisles of the orchards, Stephen asked his father how he had gotten into his work, about what had interested him in buildings. Hager started out rather sternly—Stephen had never asked such questions—but he soon lost himself telling stories about the Wild West days of developing property in the fifties. Finally that topic petered out. This was different, talking to Stephen personally. He asked Stephen about his plans for college and then, shyly, about his plans with Mary Ann. He was nervous asking it.

"I've broken up with her," Stephen said. "I thought you knew."

"How would I know? If you don't tell me, I don't know. You know what, Stephen? I wish we could talk like this all the time."

Hager put his hand onto Stephen's shoulder and massaged it with his strong fingers. "So what happened with Mary Ann? You just didn't have much in common?"

"She's moved away, Dad. She's up in Madera now." Stephen's voice seemed to well with emotion.

"She was the one to call it quits?"

"Not exactly, Dad. It was mutual. It was time, that's all."

CHAPTER

13

When Hager told Carrie about his conversation with Balzeti, his anger flared up again. It was after dinner; he was helping her with the dishes. He kept his voice calm, he thought, but he could feel the outrage in his body.

"But you took Stephen with you?" Carrie asked.

"Yeah. I'd been thinking about him." Hager paced in the kitchen. "We really hadn't had a talk in a long time. Did you know that he and Mary Ann have broken up?"

Carrie looked surprised. "No, I didn't."

"He says it was mutual. She's moved away, somewhere up the valley."

"I'm surprised," Carrie said. She had stopped washing the dishes and turned to face him. "I'm sure it's for the best. It would have happened when he started college, anyway."

"Yeah, I suppose so." The topic seemed to interest Carrie, but Hager could not keep his attention on it. He wanted to talk about Balzeti. "Carrie, do you think I'm wrong? I know you don't like to talk about it, but doesn't it sound as though the police aren't doing a blessed thing? I couldn't believe that guy's attitude. It was like we were sitting around drinking a couple of beers. No big deal, just a few kids murdered and another one missing." He felt his own anger and desperation rise and he moved to re-stack the dinner dishes beside the sink.

"Well?" he asked. "Don't look at me like I'm crazy. Doesn't it sound to you like they're messing up?"

She pressed her lips together. "I don't know," she said. "They found three of the boys. I think if we were parents of the other kids, we would think they were doing a lot."

"Hey, I found one of those boys. They might not have located that cabin yet."

"What are you saying?" Carrie asked. Hager could tell that she was biting her lower lip, because it was slightly indented. She did that when she was upset. Sometimes she bit down hard enough to make it bleed.

"I don't know what I'm saying, Carrie." He wanted her to stop looking at him so skeptically. "I'm saying that I've done as much as the sheriffs have, and I haven't tried. They just don't give a care."

That night he lay listening to Carrie's deep, slow breathing and thought obsessively over what had happened, numbering the ways in which the police had failed to follow up on even the most elementary clues. He considered talking to Ramirez. He, at least, had discovered the cap on Reid's head. But when he remembered how Ramirez had acted when he proposed going off in search of the cabin—he had shown no interest either way—Hager thought the cap must have been a fluke.

Hager knew he would not sleep thinking these thoughts, so he got out of bed and made himself hot chocolate, scalding the milk in a saucepan and pouring it into a blue aluminum tumbler, then dribbling a thin string of Hershey's syrup on top, making loops, and watching them cling to the surface before they plummeted out of sight. It was chilly in the kitchen, and he wrapped his large fingers around the warm glass. The milk seemed to settle him down. Long ago, when he was a boy and could not sleep, his father had made him chocolate milk like this.

Suddenly he smelled smoke and jumped up, looked wildly around, and snatched the pan off the stove. He had forgotten to turn off the burner. The residue of milk had turned a crinkled black, giving off an acrid stink. Hager ran water into the pan, shutting his eyes at the steam cloud that rose from the first explosion of water, then sat down again much less calm.

He realized then that he had made up his mind. He was going to find out what had happened to Robbie. At least he would try. Maybe he would find him. It was possible. More likely he would simply embarrass himself. At least he would know that he had done all he could.

He had not known that he was considering this, but once he had made the decision it seemed to calm him. Hager could not let Robbie go, could never forget him and go on with life while so much was left undone, so many loose threads remained. He owed it to Robbie to look for him, to find him, or if not him—his killer.

When Hager awoke the next morning, he did not immediately remember his resolution. Carrie was already up and gone from the bed, and he lay under the warmth of the covers assembling himself for the day. First he realized that he felt more energetic than he had in many days. Then, with a start, he recalled why. He got up humming, showered and shaved, then stood in front of his closet, pondering what to wear. *Somehow*, he thought, *the day deserves different clothes*.

"Where are you going?" Carrie asked when he came into the kitchen in a coat and tie.

"I'm not sure yet," he said. He told her what he had decided. "Where are the kids?"

"They've gone to school. What are you going to do?" Carrie stood across the kitchen in that pose he knew so well, intent and still, absolutely focused on his face and his words. He wanted to go to her that moment to clasp and hold her, yet he did not want to break into that wonderful stillness.

She went on. "Frank, you've done what you can. There's a time to say enough."

"I haven't even tried," he said. "I was counting on the sheriffs. Not anymore, though." He shook his head, feeling the power of his decision.

But she was looking at him with that confused, doubting stubbornness in her eyes and her mouth. He could not resist her any longer; he went to her and held her, his body absorbing her slender shape. And she let him. So many times through their marriage this physical bond had carried them.

"It will be all right," he said, rubbing the small of her back. "It will be fine."

"You always say that," she said, pulling away and looking at him. "Frank, I don't want any more. I want to stop thinking about it and hearing about it and dreaming about it." He felt trembling in the hands that gripped his wrists.

"All right, then I won't talk to you about it." He had his jaw set. He could not afford to lose what he had decided in the night.

He ate his breakfast in silence, starting to talk on several occasions but then, remembering what Carrie had said, shutting his mouth. If she did not want to hear about it anymore, then he would not tell her any more. She certainly had a right to her peace, but he had a right to his too. That would not come, he was convinced, until he knew. He had never been good at giving up. He could not stop, could not close his mind.

An hour later he parked alongside a muddy field where a backhoe was trenching for sewer lines. The slope had been crudely denuded, with clots of mud and the oversized tracks of work machines congealing on its surface. Hager carefully picked his way through the muck to a point where the backhoe operator could see him. He waved him to a stop and then tiptoed over to boost himself up on the machine.

The operator was a beefy red-faced kid growing a beard. "Are you Laird?" Hager shouted over the engine. The kid nodded. Hager held out a hand to him. "Frank Hager. Your dad said it would be all right for me to come by and talk to you. Do you mind?"

Laird Harris reached out and turned off the backhoe, and the raw hillside was enveloped by a foggy silence. Without a word he swung out of his seat and clomped through the mud to a construction shack. Inside was a desk cluttered with invoices, a couple of chairs, and several cardboard boxes of miscellaneous tools. Harris leaned over and plugged a portable electric heater into the wall. Its fan began a tinny rattle. Harris took the chair behind the desk, then got up again to move a notebook from the other chair so that Hager could sit down.

"What's up?" he asked after sitting down again.

Hager was excited, too excited to have thought about the

right approach. But in business he had never had much use for buttering people up or trying to establish the right atmosphere. He always went right at it. "I don't know if you know who I am," he began.

"Sure," Harris said. "Hager Construction. I've seen you around."

"Well, I want to talk about something else. Your father said it would be all right if I came up here and asked you a few questions."

"You said that. I don't need to know what my father said about it. Talk."

Hager recognized a jerk when he saw one; working with subcontractors gave him plenty of experience. Usually, though, he talked with them over a dollars-and-cents deal, where he had some control.

"You know my son was one of those boys that disappeared a couple of weeks ago. They still haven't located him, and I'm trying to learn anything I can about what happened. I understand you got into some kind of a scuffle with them that night."

A smile slid onto Harris's face, as though he were letting Hager know that this was amusing to him. After allowing enough time for the point to be made, he said, "Yeah, I guess you could say that."

"There was some pushing and yelling?"

"Yeah."

"What happened afterward? Did you see them any more?"

"I sure did. I took them all out in the snow and beat them to death." Harris waited a beat and then roared with artificial laughter. He stopped as suddenly as he had begun.

"No, really," Hager said.

"Yes, really," Harris replied and snorted again, a short hiccough of a laugh.

Hager had an impulse to turn the desk over and walk out. He restrained himself. For a few moments he and Harris looked at each other. Harris smirked.

"Look, I don't want to waste your time," Hager finally said. "I'm just trying to find out any bit of information that might give me a clue what happened that night. I figured that since you were there, you might remember something."

"You know what I remember?" Harris said. "I remember thinking, 'These retards have no business being out of their cages. They need somebody to take care of them.' And just then who should appear but little brother Steve and his virgin girlfriend, just the people they needed."

Hager made himself go on, ignoring everything but his point. "Did you go back into the game?" he asked.

"No," Harris said.

"So where did you go?"

"I told you. I took them out in the snow and beat their brains out."

"Come on, Harris."

"You really want to know?"

"Yeah."

"You don't believe I killed them?"

"I don't know who killed them. If you did, you wouldn't tell me like that."

"Then why are you asking me?"

"You were one of the last people to see them. I thought you might tell me something that would be worth following up. Some clue. Anything you might remember."

Harris had rocked back in his chair and put his feet up on the desk. He now tipped forward again, coming to the floor with a bang. "I don't know why I should tell you anything," he said. "I probably wouldn't if I knew anything. But I don't. I took my girlfriend home to her apartment."

"Who's that?" Hager asked.

"Ruthie," Harris said. "Ruth Quintrell. Ask Stevie-boy. He knows her."

"So you took her home. Then what?"

Harris smiled. "You want the details?"

"Sure."

"That's pretty low. Why should I tell you the details about me and my girlfriend?" He winked.

Hager was embarrassed and disgusted. "I mean where did you go after you took her home."

"I didn't go anywhere. I stayed with her."

Hager required a few seconds to realize that his line of questioning had reached an end. "So after you left the high school, you went straight to her place? And you were with her all night?"

"You're very intelligent."

"Did you ever hear anything about what happened to Robbie and the other kids?"

"Sure, I heard what was on the news. And what people said."

"What did people say?"

"People said it must have been some pervert."

Hager asked him if he meant anybody particular. "Nah," Harris said. "I don't hang around with perverts."

Hager sat for a moment looking out the small, dirty window, watching the gray light. He said thanks, got up, and left. He heard the door slam behind him, and it took all his self-control not to turn and look. He got to his car, and by the time he had it turned around, he heard the roar of the backhoe starting up again. Then he looked over his shoulder. Harris waved at him. Hager turned his head forward and drove.

CHAPTER

14

Frank Hager turned off the highway a few miles below Oakdale, where a faded wooden sign read, THE LAMBS SCHOOL. Beyond, up the hill, the drive turned from muck to gravel under his tires. White-painted rocks marked the border of the road as Hager reached the school grounds.

It was a pretty place, an old apple farm with shaggy, bull-necked trees. A two-story frame house stood at the end of the drive, and below it on the hill were three pre-fab classrooms and a battered Quonset hut. Hager had been here many times for work parties and parents' nights. He had built shelves and closets in classrooms, working alongside other fathers, none of whom ever mentioned their children beyond their names. The women could talk to each other, but the men—it was as though someone had jammed a two-by-four down their throats. Hager himself, he realized, knew very little about what went on at the school during regular hours. He had never consciously chosen not to know. The knowledge had simply escaped him.

When Hager got out of the car, he stood for a moment in the silence, considering why he had come. His conversation with the Harris kid had taken the excitement out of him. Hager understood now that the truth might never come out, that this might all be futility. And so he felt a sadness in place of yesterday's energy and excitement. Nevertheless he had come.

As he strolled slowly toward the house, two boys appeared

on the walk. One, a towhead, stood just ahead of the other. His companion was smaller, with bristling dark hair. They both watched Hager intently. When Hager reached them the blond boy said, "My name is Peter. What is your name?"

Hager told him.

"I am taking Ray to the bathroom," Peter said, and jerked his hand forward, holding it out as though he had recently acquired it. The hand felt moist and warm when Hager shook it. Ray also shook hands and seemed to try to speak in a choked gurgle. His small black eyes were set deep into his head, enfolded in lines of skin like the eyesockets of a carrion bird. But it was not their appearance that struck Hager; it was the intensity with which they watched.

"I'm looking for Mrs. Gilbert," Hager said. "One of your teachers."

The words did not seem at first to register. Then Peter said as though Hager's voice had just reached him after a long delay, "Mrs. Gilbert teaches the little kids and the new ones."

"Where is she?"

Again there was a pause. Peter turned and, taking Ray's hand, walked down the path toward one of the pre-fabs. Hager followed, unsure whether Peter meant to lead him. As they were walking, Peter waited and slipped his hand into Hager's. Hager nearly jumped.

"I earn money in the workshop now," Peter said.

"Oh? What work do you do?"

"I am a stamper. Ray is a porter. He doesn't get paid, but I get thirty-five cents for every one hundred envelopes."

"You put stamps on letters?"

The question required consideration. "It's a rubber stamp," Peter finally answered. "The postman licks stamps. She gets fifty cents."

They had reached the doorway of the classroom and could hear the drone of a class repeating after a teacher. Peter pulled Hager to a stop. He looked up into his face but did not speak. "What is it?" Hager asked gently.

"Would you take me home?" Peter asked. He looked expectantly into Hager's face. "I have a letter from my mother."

Peter fished in his pocket and came out with a tightly folded manila envelope. He handed it to Hager, who unrolled it and brought out a hand-addressed green envelope. The return address was Tulare, a small valley town. The post office mark was a date six months before.

"You can read it," Peter said. Ray watched them both raptly, a quiet knowing smile directed toward Hager.

After the first sentence of the letter Hager stopped, embarrassed. "I am so glad you are happy," it read, "in your new home."

"Your mother is glad you are here," Hager said. "Don't you like it?"

"They help us learn to get along with other people and be independent livers," Peter said. Something strange was happening to him. His eyes were turning wild. At that moment, the classroom door opened and Mrs. Gilbert appeared. She paid Hager no attention but took Peter firmly by the shoulders, putting her eyes directly in front of his. He was nearly as big as she. "What are you doing here? Don't you make goo-goo eyes at me. You know better."

Hager said apologetically that Peter had escorted him to see her.

"Where are you supposed to be?" Mrs. Gilbert said to Peter with the same insistence.

"I'm taking Ray to the bathroom."

"Then you go and do that right now and don't stop to talk." Peter reached out and took his letter from Hager's hand, then went off without looking back. Ray trailed him, apparently undisturbed by the whole transaction. He took one last elfin glance at Hager as he went.

When they had gone, Hager said, "I'm sorry. I asked them where you were."

She dismissed it. "No, they know where they're supposed to be. They're not allowed to talk to strangers. They have to learn." She looked over Hager as though she might send him off too. "Well. You made it. Come on in."

The children were more obviously wrong when all together. A few might have passed for normal, but others flailed their limbs, or had folded-in eyes like Ray's. They sat at ordinary school desks, except for a handful who sat or lay on mats because they could not hold themselves steady enough for a desk. When Mrs. Gilbert told the class he was Robbie's father, they applauded. She had them sing a song for him. Those who could not sing beat time with tamborines. Then she set them to coloring with thick wax crayons and had a volunteer mother watch them while she took Hager to the main house.

In the teacher's lounge she offered Hager a styrofoam cup of coffee. The room was a small scuffed cubbyhole with a multicolored carpet patched together from rug samples.

"Cute kids," Hager said.

"Lambs," she said. "This is the Lambs School. Isn't that idiotic? If they were lambs they would only need grass. We could put them out to pasture." She snorted a laugh. "People should never be called after animals."

Her face was heavily lined and sun-beaten. "What's the matter?" she asked. "The way you look you might have lost four more kids today."

"Nothing," he said softly. "I was just thinking about Robbie."

"He was a sweet kid," she offered, and they were both silent for a few moments. "You do love them," she said in a choked voice. "No one understands that."

"Well," she said in a let's-get-down-to-business tone, "you wanted to talk to me."

He told her about his decision to discover the truth. "At the funeral," he said, "you got me thinking about the sheriff's department. So I'm trying to do a little poking around of my own. I thought I couldn't do any worse than the sheriffs. I wondered if you could give me some general background on the school, the kind of people who work here, any problems you might face."

She looked at him curiously, trying to see what was behind his words. "You're sure you want to do this?" she asked. "It doesn't seem like you, Frank."

"You were the one who brought it up in the first place."

She laughed. "Oh, I blow off steam. But all right, let's go."

She fished in her purse and got a cigarette. "I'll help however I can. What is it you want to know?"

Hager said slowly, "I'm trying to understand who gets involved with retarded kids. Like our boys. Did they have any enemies? Did they get into fights?"

She laughed again, lighting her cigarette. "Yes, Frank, they get into fights, just like other kids. If you think about any bunch of kids and the way they act, you'll have a good idea of the way these kids behave. They're intellectually impaired, but emotionally they're just like anybody else. More so. It's the most extraordinary thing to be around this place. You see all of human nature undisguised.

"Donnie and the other three had a lot less impairment. I mean, think of Robbie driving a car. Those kids in my class are not going to drive a car. Granted that you must have worked at it an incredible amount, still, he did it. Those four were our stars. They were making it. Our goal is to help our children fit into society, and they were on their way. I think Donnie would have been able to hold a job. He couldn't drive, but if he lived in a city he would have been able to ride the bus. We don't want these kids to spend the rest of their lives in institutions."

She began to talk about the school's program, and after a few minutes Hager realized that she might talk all morning. He broke in.

"Is there anybody who shows an unhealthy interest in these kids?"

"You mean like perverts?" She laughed and ground out her cigarette, which had burned to the end. "Not that I ever heard of. I suppose it could happen. I'm smiling because when you said 'unhealthy interest' I immediately thought of parents. Some parents try to clean up the mess by sending junior away to the state hospital. That's what everybody wants you to do. But the ones who come here are always wanting to clean up the mess too. You can't imagine the bake sales we've had. Stupendous.

"Usually it's one parent. You don't usually see them both. The mother. She does everything. She goes to all the meetings. She tries to know more than the doctors know. Which sometimes isn't that hard. And the father doesn't do it.

He considers it hopeless. Or he just thinks they're exaggerating how bad Junior is. He wants to get on with life. So his wife considers him an uncaring jerk, and he proves that she's right by moving out, or else she throws him out. The siblings catch a lot of extra unwelcome attention in all this too. They get so much responsibility. It's hard on the families."

She stared past Hager, her face hard and troubled. "That's me. Raymond left when Donnie was five. He'd had enough. I don't totally blame him now. Of course, then I called him every name in the book." She shook her head and laughed.

"We started here in 1953," she said. "In those days if you were so unfortunate as to have a retarded child, the doctors, the ministers, all the wise men told you in their most solemn tones that the best thing, the kindest thing for the whole family, was to give him up. You remember? Send him to Napa. If you didn't want to do that, people treated you like you'd tracked doggie-do into the house. You were supposed to keep them out of sight. That was the only sociably acceptable thing to do. Keep them in a closet.

"So some of the parents got together. You weren't around then, were you? But you know how it is. We were near to desperation. We didn't know what to do, but we thought we could do something. Mrs. Boyden lived here, and at first we met in her living room, two hours a day. We had crafts. Sometimes we had a sock hop. Then we talked the National Guard into dragging that Quonset hut in here. Gradually it turned into a school. When Mrs. Boyden died, she willed the place to the school. She wanted it called The Lambs School. We had the whole house, so we took in some boarders. You see, there was nothing. For some people it was too far to drive every day. So we took them in during the week."

She began talking about the legal situation, throwing acronyms around. Hager gathered that the school would be changing. The county was taking over responsibility. Boarding would soon be unnecessary. They were hoping for new facilities.

He asked her about Peter's letter.

"Pathetic, isn't it?" she said. "I don't know when that letter business got started, but there are several kids who pull it.

Even though most of their parents are incredibly responsible. Look at me. I'm typical. I never gave a minute's thought to retardation before Donnie was born. Now it's my life." She gave her head an astonished shake.

"After all," she added, "Peter's parents could just send him to Napa. No more trouble then. Everybody would be so pleased. They would all say what a wise thing they did, it was really too much strain on the whole family."

Mrs. Gilbert lit another cigarette. "It's rough for a mother, you know. You can't help loving them. They're so helpless when they're born. Just like any baby. But then you can't fix them. Everybody knows what to do, and they all disagree. The pediatrician told me to treat him just like a normal child, expect everything out of him you would any other kid. Then he put him on drugs so he couldn't see straight. I took him to a psychiatrist, and he told me that Donnie was under too much stress, that he was withdrawing because of all the demands." She began to laugh at the memory. Mrs. Gilbert blew out smoke and gave her head that little shake. Hager saw that there were tears in her eyes again.

He wanted to go. He did not like to talk about these things. There was no use dwelling on such painful subjects.

"You never had any other children?" he asked.

"No. We never had the courage."

"That helped Carrie," he said. "She snapped out of it when Stephen was born."

"Yeah. Another kid proves you're normal," Mrs. Gilbert said. "Truthfully, though, Frank, you didn't have it hard compared to some of these parents. Robbie was a sweet kid. You asked if they had enemies. I can't imagine him having an enemy. They got in fights, sure, but that was with their friends. The other kids looked up to Robbie."

"That's why I was asking about perverts. It would take somebody sick."

"The only sick people around here are the parents." She laughed. "All day long: 'What can I do with my little girl? What's wrong with her?'" Mrs. Gilbert smiled at Hager. "It's natural," she said. "I don't blame them. I was the same way."

"The four boys stuck together a lot, didn't they?"

"They were always together. Nobody else could squeeze into that circle."

"Were any of the teachers particularly involved with them?"

"Well, of course, Robbie had a thing with Mary Ann. You probably knew about that."

"Really? No, I didn't. A thing? She's my son Stephen's girlfriend. I think that's how she learned about the job here, in fact. I knew Robbie liked her."

Mrs. Gilbert snorted. "He more than liked her. He was embarrassing." She saw the confusion on Hager's face and added, "He was slow, but he wasn't castrated, you know. They have the regular drives."

It made Hager squirm. "What did he do?" he asked.

"Oh, nothing," she scoffed. "He was very jealous. He didn't like her talking to anybody else. Wanted to hold her hand. Hung on her if she let him. Kid stuff." She stood up abruptly. "They're just like other kids, only more so. They don't know how to pretend."

"Mary Ann has gone," he said. "Stephen said she's moved."

"Yes, very suddenly," Mrs. Gilbert said. "I didn't expect her to stay. A nice girl but strange. And she has a life to live."

CHAPTER

15

Hager's mind kept returning to Margaret Gilbert's distasteful words—"He was slow, but he wasn't castrated." Of course Hager had always known that Robbie was a sexual creature, but he had thought very little about what that meant, practically. Hager had, in fact, kidded Robbie about looking over pretty girls and laughed at the way he would squirm and grin when teased. Hager wasn't amused by the thought of Robbie's hanging on Mary Ann, however, trying to squeeze her. That sounded ludicrous and gross. Hager was glad Mary Ann was gone, glad that she had disappeared from the lives of both of his boys.

He stopped at his office and greeted his secretary, who was there alone reading a magazine.

"More messages," she said. "Van Brocklin says he can't start those forms until he talks to you."

"Oh, yeah," Hager mumbled while leafing through the phone book for Mary Ann's home phone. He did not feel like talking to her, but she might know something. "So tell him that he won't get paid, either. I don't have time to hold his hand." He dialed the number. "Don't you have some bookkeeping to do?" he asked while the phone rang.

A man answered. Hager had never met Mary Ann's father, Mr. Kurtz. He understood from Stephen that Kurtz was retired and ran a Swap and Shop secondhand store in Three Streams.

When Hager identified himself, the man's voice suddenly doubled in volume; Hager had to ask him to repeat himself. "It's about time you called," the man said angrily. "One more week and you'd be talking to my lawyers."

"What? Why?" Hager asked.

"You know what I'm talking about. My daughter and your son."

"No," Hager said. "I really don't know what you're talking about."

"Don't be cute with me."

"I'm not being cute. I don't know what you're talking about." Hager was nettled.

"Did you read my letter?"

"No. What letter?"

"I sent you a letter two weeks ago. I sent a copy a week ago. You have not responded until now."

"I'm not responding now. I never got any letters."

"I sent them to your home."

"Well, you better check your address. I never got them. Why don't you tell me about it."

Mr. Kurtz grumbled; he said he thought these things were best conveyed in letters. "Your son is every bit as responsible as my daughter, and since she is determined to have this baby, I am determined that you share the expenses."

Hager looked over at his secretary; she was filing her nails. "Just a minute," he said to Kurtz, then, "Lila, will you go get a cup of coffee?"

She looked up surprised. "For you?"

"No, for you. I need a little privacy for this phone call. I'm sorry."

"Okay," she said with a shrug and got her coat. She was sturdily built and moved heavily. It seemed to be a very long time before she had found her way out the door and Hager felt free to talk.

"Mr. Kurtz," he said, his voice trembling slightly, "I don't know anything about a baby. Are you telling me that Mary Ann is pregnant?"

"Well why on earth do you think she's left town?"

"I thought she just wanted to get away. I never thought."

"Well, she's gone up there to have the baby. She was insistent. I told her that was the last thing she should do, and I wasn't going to have a baby born here in this house. So she found this place in Madera. Or maybe your boy found it for her, I don't know. I'm not having anything more to do with that. I told her he's responsible and he owes his fair share."

Kurtz calmed down when he realized that Hager intended to cooperate. Kurtz said he had contacted the head of the home and found out how much it cost. That was the information he had sent to Hager. He wanted to make free with his anger, but Hager said Kurtz could rest assured money would not be a problem. He would have said anything to get the man off the phone.

He had written down Mary Ann's number, and when he hung up he stuck the note in his pocket. He could not call her now. He was too upset. He walked down to the coffee shop and found Lila reading her magazine. She looked at him with wide-open, curious eyes, but all he said was, "All through. Sorry about that. Tell Van Brocklin that he'll just have to do the best he can. I'm tied up."

She left and he took her seat, waving at the waitress for a cup of coffee. When it came, he drank it mechanically. He felt he could sit there drinking coffee all day. He wished to stop thinking.

He finally lugged his body out of the seat. When he got out the door, he realized he had not paid; he stopped in his tracks, looked down at the cracked sidewalk, then went on across the parking lot in front of the professional building. He could pay some other time. Or not at all; it was just a cup of coffee. Who cared?

At home he found Carrie on her hands and knees in the bedroom; she had the contents of a dresser drawer on the floor all around her. She barely looked up; she was concentrating on the job. For a moment he watched her, wondering how the news he possessed would affect her.

"Who's been getting the mail?" he asked.

"Why?" She looked up, knowing from his tone that something was wrong.

"I talked to a man on the phone who said he's been sending me some papers, but I haven't received them."

"Are you sure he really sent them?" Carrie said slowly. "Stephen usually brings in the mail when he comes home from school. He leaves it on the kitchen counter. I can't imagine Lizzie getting into it."

"Doesn't it sometimes come before Steve gets home?"

She said that it did. Sometimes she got it, but anything for him was put on the kitchen counter.

"Stephen's in trouble," he said finally and told her. Carrie said nothing. She picked up some of the clothes she was refolding and held them for a moment, as though trying to remember where they belonged, and then she put her head down into her lap. Hager went to hold her, but there was nothing to hold. She was curled tightly on her hands and knees and did not open to him. He rubbed her back softly.

"I wish I could cry," he said. "I'm all cried out."

"My poor baby," she sobbed. "Now I understand the way he's been."

"Poor baby, my foot," Hager said, his hand stopping its motion on her back. "The poor baby is the one who's going to be born."

She sat up and dabbed at her eyes with a shirt. "It could happen to anybody, Frank. It could have happened to us when we were young."

"That doesn't change anything," Hager said. "Poor baby. His brother is dying and he's quietly sending his girlfriend off somewhere to have his kid."

She turned to Hager, pleadingly. "Frank, they don't need blame. If you blame him, he might turn away forever."

"Well, that's just fine," Hager said. "His girlfriend is pregnant, he steals our mail, and I'm supposed to treat him like the Prodigal Son."

"Yes," she said fiercely. "That's the idea. Like the Prodigal Son."

"Okay," he said, "but first I'd like to hear his lines. Remember? 'Father, I have sinned . . .' You can't forgive somebody who doesn't feel sorry."

She looked at him with eyes brimming full of tears. "Please, Frank," she said. "You're too angry. Be careful."

Hager tried to heed those words when Stephen came home. He started off fine, asking about the mail and then whether what Mr. Kurtz had told him was true, but within a minute his control had popped loose and he was shouting. Stephen shouted back. Carrie was crying. Stephen and he stood face-to-face shouting at each other simultaneously, neither hearing, both ready to hit.

In the middle of this they heard the front door slam. Carrie hissed and said, "Lizzie." And in an instant they were quiet, still tensed, still at each other, and then Stephen walked out, down the hall to his room and slammed the door.

Lizzie came in with a load of schoolbooks that she dumped on a chair. "What's going on?" she asked.

Carrie pointed at the books. "Those do not belong in here. You know that." Lizzie sighed, said okay, and took the books off toward her room. Hager and Carrie were quiet, nor did they move until they heard her door close.

"What are we going to tell her?" Hager asked.

Carrie came to him, put her arms around him and her head on his shoulder. "I don't know, Frank. I don't know."

The sound of breaking glass interrupted them. For just a moment Hager stood still, listening, then he trotted down the hall. He threw open Lizzie's door; she was standing there looking astonished. "Sorry," he said, and left her.

Outside Stephen's door he hesitated. "Are you okay?" he shouted, and waited a moment before pushing the door open. Stephen had a tennis racket in his hand, and he was breathing heavily. For a second Hager flinched, thinking that Stephen would hit him with the racket. Then Hager saw blood on Stephen's hands and for a horrible fraction of a second thought that he had slit his wrists. Then he saw the aquarium. The front wall was gone, there were jagged pieces of glass on the floor, and water everywhere, and small, wriggling shapes dancing on the rug.

"Oh my goodness," Hager said. "Can we save them?"

Stephen said nothing, and Hager knelt, grabbing at one of

the fish. It slipped out of his fingers, and he jumped forward, cupping his hand on top of it.

"Don't touch the turkey fish," Stephen said. "It's poison."

Carrie and Lizzie were standing in the door. "Run some water in the bath," Hager shouted to them. "And get a bowl or something to catch these in." They went off, and Hager tried to catch another fish while holding down the first one. "Which one is the turkey?" he asked.

"I don't know," Stephen said. "Let them die."

Hager heard the bath running and cupped his two slippery, wriggling fish in his fists. He hurried out of the room with them.

"They're saltwater fish," Stephen said after him. "You can't save them."

Hager put the two fish in the bath anyway. The turbulence from the rushing tap bowled them over end over end and they did not seem to try to swim. Hager told Lizzie that was enough water and walked slowly back to Stephen's room. Stephen had not moved; he was still holding his tennis racket. His breathing had slowed. Hager went over and wordlessly took his arm, looking for the source of the blood. It was a long, shallow cut up his forearm, bleeding profusely.

"You'd better get something on that," Hager said.

Later on, after they had bandaged the arm and cleaned up the room, Hager felt the full impact of what had happened. He stopped blaming Stephen and turned his anger on himself. He lay back in his recliner, his thoughts a heavy weight pressing him down into the chair. Nobody wanted to talk to him. Lizzie had come and asked him what was wrong, and when he said he would explain later even she had left. Stephen had stayed in his room, and Carrie was there with him—comforting him, Hager guessed.

Carrie was right; this did explain Stephen's moods. He had seemed affected by Robbie's disappearance, terribly quiet and withdrawn, occasionally very touchy, occasionally unusually sweet. They had thought it was Robbie because it matched how they felt. But this had been going on too. In fact, Hager thought, Stephen's strangeness had begun before Robbie's disappearance.

Carrie came in. "He wants to talk to you, Frank."

Hager sat up. "What does he want?"

"Just go and talk, Frank. Don't yell at him. Just talk. He's your son."

He found Stephen's curtains drawn. Stephen was lying on his bed, staring toward the ceiling.

"Your mom said that you wanted to talk," Hager said guardedly.

"Yeah." Stephen cleared his throat. "Dad, I would have told you but I didn't want to burden you. I thought Robbie was all you could bear." He paused for a moment. "I knew how you'd feel."

"But didn't it happen before Robbie disappeared?" Hager asked.

"Yeah. It did. It was hard to know how to tell you, but I was going to, and then Robbie. It just seemed too much."

Hager could not help being moved. Once again he had mistaken his son's motives. Always he was too hard on him.

"And I guess I haven't been very easy to communicate with," Hager said. "I knew something was bothering you, but I just thought it was Robbie."

"That was part of it, Dad. It was just everything. I didn't want to bother you, Dad. I knew how you were feeling."

Hager pulled out Stephen's desk chair and sat down. He waited—heard the minute flip over on Stephen's clock radio. "I'm sorry I overreacted, Steve. Maybe you were right not to tell me."

They were quiet together for a few more healing moments.

"No, I should have, Dad. I just couldn't see how to tell you. But you had to find out. It was inevitable. I'm sorry about the mail."

Hager decided to let the mail go. "I told Mary Ann's dad that I would help pay the medical bills and whatever. I need to go and see her anyway. That's why I called him in the first place."

"You need to see her?"

"Yeah. Why? Shouldn't I?"

Stephen had half sat up; now he lay back down again. "It's just not necessary," he said. "I'm not going to marry her. The best thing is to make a clean break."

"I don't want to talk to her about you," Hager said. "I want to talk about Robbie. I went to see Mrs. Gilbert today, and she said Mary Ann was close to him. I thought she might be able to give me some information."

"They weren't close, Dad. Just leave her out of it, please." Stephen sat up again. "I don't want to think about her."

Hager shrugged.

"I need to make a clean break from her," Stephen continued. "It's for her good too. I don't want it to be messy."

"It's already messy," Hager said. He got up quietly from the chair and stood for a moment rolling his sleeves. "Did you sleep together a lot, Steve?"

Stephen took a long time to answer. He had his knees tucked up under his chin. "Not really," he said. "She said she was using birth control."

"And she wasn't?" Hager felt horribly confused and embarrassed talking about this to his son. He wanted to get out of the room. But he wanted to know too.

"How could she get pregnant if she was using birth control?" Stephen said.

"Oh," Hager said. "Lots of things can happen in life." He put his hand lightly onto Stephen's shoulder. "As I guess you're learning."

CHAPTER
16

Hager decided to get some chicken for supper. "Do you mind?" he asked Carrie. "I think we're all too confused and upset to have a regular meal." He did not say nor did he even like to think his real message: that he could not bear facing them all around the table. It was easier to deal with his family individually, in glancing blows, than in one massed silence.

Carrie hardly looked up. She was kneeling with the piles of clothes again, laying them out carefully, her face glazed and sorrowful as though she were preparing a body for burial. She said fine, and he left her.

Passing through the den he found Lizzie sprawled in a chair, watching a TV show. His heart went out to her as soon as he saw her, thin, gawky in a body she had not grown into.

"Come on with me, Lizzie, would you? I'm going to the Colonel's for some chicken. Keep me company."

"Okay." She got up and stretched

"Turn off the TV," he reminded. She did so. He put an arm around her shoulders and squeezed. "Thanks for going with me."

They drove down the hill in silence, reaching the main highway and turning toward town without a word. The quiet was unbearable to Hager; he thought his heart would burst from loneliness. *Everything that could go wrong in a man's life has gone wrong*, he thought. "Thanks for coming with me," he said again. "I need you right now."

"Daddy, what was Stephen so mad about?" Lizzie's question was quiet, seemingly unstudied.

Hager realized that they had not decided what to tell her. He wanted to tell her everything but he was not sure. He wanted to ask Carrie first.

"I don't think he was mad, exactly, just upset. It was a lot of things," he said.

"Well what was he upset about? I was scared."

"It scared you? I guess I was too, a little. I'm sorry, Lizzie. There wasn't anything to be scared about, really. It's just that when he gets so mad it's scary."

"I thought you said he wasn't mad."

He decided that he would tell her. It would be a relief to talk. "Lizzie, Mary Ann is going to have a baby. Mom and I just found out. Stephen didn't want us to know. That's why he was so upset. I think it's why he's been acting so negative."

"Boy, everybody in this family has been negative," Lizzie said.

Hager was surprised that she did not ask for more details. *Maybe she is afraid*, he thought. He volunteered, "Stephen and Mary Ann don't want to get married, so Mary Ann has gone to a place in the valley where she can have the baby."

"Is she going to let someone adopt the baby?" Lizzie asked.

"I suppose so. What else could she do?"

"She could have an abortion."

"She wouldn't be in this place if she wanted to do that, Lizzie."

They had entered the business section, a strip of gaudy lights for drugstores, hamburger joints, liquor stores. The parking lots were merely a continuation of the highway's asphalt—no curbs—so cars could roll on or off anywhere they chose.

"Do you ever squint your eyes to look at these lights?" Lizzie asked, out of the blue. "They're beautiful."

Hager reached out for her hand on the seat beside him. "I remember when Grandpa was alive that sometimes he would take his glasses off when we drove at night. He said it was more restful."

They pulled into Kentucky Fried Chicken and said very little while standing in the cramped, box-like interior. Hager gave Lizzie a hug again; he felt his body relaxing and realized that he had been tense the entire day. He was tired. Back in the car, the smell of fried food filled up the interior.

"Lizzie, do you remember the trip to New York we took? When you were really little?"

"I don't think I really remember it, Dad. I've seen the pictures so many times that it seems like I can remember, but I don't think I really can."

"You must have been three or four then. That's pretty young to remember," Hager said. "That was a happy time. Robbie was just eleven, I think. We stayed in motels and went to all the souvenir stands. Carlsbad Caverns. The boys loved that place." The memory, to his surprise, brought tears to his eyes. That time seemed so far off, so impossible ever to regain.

"I never got to go on family vacations," Lizzie said, with a note of resentment. "You always went hiking."

"I guess that's true," Hager said slowly. "It wasn't as easy once the boys got bigger." He reached out his hand and found Lizzie's again. "I'm sorry, Lizzie. I really am."

He realized that she was weeping, silently. "What's the matter, Lizzie? Why are you crying?" His own chest felt blocked; it was hard to breathe. She was so dear to him. "Please tell me."

"I don't know," she said. "It just doesn't seem like anything is going right. Our whole family is falling apart." She was choking on her sobs now. "Nobody ever talks to me. Everybody is so busy."

Hager had to overcome his own emotions to talk on, to try to reassure her that things would soon be normal again, to tell her that he would try to be with her more. She had calmed down by the time they reached home.

Hager loved Carrie's body. They slept like spoons, nesting together and turning unconsciously from side to side. Sometimes when both were awake at night, they would turn to each other and wordlessly make love. Their daily communion of body, of warmth and skin, was the most continuous comfort in Hager's life, seeming to draw poison from the day.

When things were not right between them, he could sense it in her body. That had been the case for weeks. Though they held each other at night, had even once or twice made love, the harmony was missing.

Hager had not thought about it; it seemed a natural function of the disjunctures of their lives. Robbie missing, Stephen angry, Carrie weeping, each of them grieving separately: How could they find each other across such a wasteland? There was ordinarily a rhythm to their sexuality: sometimes long stretches when they were bodily ignorant of each other, then, with hunger heightened by abstinence, the care and the giving. Hager hoped that, as so often before, they would discover themselves as one again.

That night, as he was brushing his teeth in front of the mirror, Carrie stood beside him and put her arms around him. "We haven't made love in a long time," she said softly.

He looked at her with a grin, his mouth full of foam. "You want a kiss?" he asked.

"Sure," she said, leaning against him. Hager felt his own weariness but he was glad for this.

"Just a minute," he said, and spit, then rinsed. "Now I'm ready," he said, and held her, kissing her. He was tired, very tired, body and soul; he knew that if they made love, he would sleep deeply. "I love you," he said, running his hands up and down her back.

When they were in bed, she lay back in the darkness while he stroked her. He could tell she had begun to think of something else; her body seemed disconnected. He was not surprised when she spoke. "I want you to stop playing detective, Frank."

His hand stopped where it was, then proceeded, softly, slowly. "Why?"

"We need to let it go, Frank. It's tearing our family apart. We need a chance to heal, to just be together."

"Why can't we do that now?"

Her tone became angry, desperate. "We can't catch up

with what's happened while you're out stirring things up, asking questions."

He took his hand back and propped himself up on his elbow. They would have to talk, he could see. "Carrie, are you sorry that I found out about Stephen?"

"In a way." She sounded frustrated, aggrieved. "I'm sure it had to come out sometime. But I would have rather let Stephen tell us when he was ready."

"I don't think he would ever have told us."

"Yes he would," she said. "You don't know him. You really don't."

Hager rolled over onto his back, stung by the remark, thinking what to say, what to do. He wanted to make love; he was aroused. He turned back toward her. "Let's not talk about this now," he said and moved to her. He kissed her and felt her relax her body against his. He pulled her tighter. He felt the warmth of her skin against his down the line of her body. He thought he did not ever want this to end; let the darkness and the warmth continue forever.

She pulled away. "Promise me you'll stop," she said.

"Can we talk about this later?"

"Just promise," she said. "I need to know that you'll leave it alone."

He did not know what to say. He wanted her, tried to pull her to him, but she resisted.

"Why?" he asked. "How does it help anybody that I stop? I feel that I owe it to Robbie. Are you asking this for Stephen? Because he wants to make a clean break with Mary Ann? I can't see that it hurts anything if I go talk to her."

"It's not that, Frank. It's the whole thing. You don't know how to let it go."

That got him. He was fed up with her tone. "I don't want to let it go. Don't you understand that? I love Robbie. He may be dead but we don't know that. Until we know that I don't want to let it go." He reached out and turned on the light beside the bed. She was on her back, looking straight up at the ceiling. Hager went on. "Even if we do know that Robbie is dead I don't want to give it up. I want to find out who killed him. I am not happy just letting it go. And I'm surprised you are."

Carrie looked angry, distant. She had pulled the covers up to her shoulders. Hager felt how much he wanted her. He had always liked to see her angry; she looked imperial. It was strange how passion and anger could coexist.

"I am so sick of hearing how you loved Robbie," she said. "You didn't know him. You made him up. You lived with the Robbie of your imagination. Sweetness and light."

Hager was shocked, stunned. He felt almost afraid to go on; he had never seen her so mean. It was a low blow, unfair, unprecedented. "What do you mean?" he demanded. "I spent a lot of time with Robbie. More than you."

"Sure, joy-riding around. But who cleaned up after him? Who took him to school every day? Who settled the fights around here? Do you even know that they had fights? Did you ever see Robbie's mean side?"

It seemed to Hager that everything was snapping, timbers were falling down on his head, his house was collapsing. He looked at Carrie, unable to believe her hardness.

"No," Hager said. "I never saw Robbie's mean side. I'm seeing yours, though."

That enraged her. He saw it in her eyes and the way her body began to tremble. He could even feel it in the bed, an earthquake from her body traveling through the mattress.

"You think that teasing in Fresno was unprovoked, don't you? You think those kids were just mean. I've let you think that. But Robbie Hager started that. Yes, Robbie Hager. He would steal their things and hide them. He would keep them and not let them go. And he was bigger than they were, remember. Once he threw a boy's magazine in the ditch. So they didn't want him around, naturally. But he wouldn't leave them alone. That's how the hazing began. It was Robbie."

"How do you know this?"

She hesitated. "Stephen told me. He took the worst of it."

"And why didn't I know?"

"Stephen didn't want to spoil your idea of Robbie. He made me promise not to tell. He only told me after we moved."

Suddenly her fury turned to weeping, gales of weeping,

sobs, and she put her arms around Hager and draped herself on him, heavy as though her skeleton had been removed. "Oh, I'm sorry, I'm sorry," she kept saying. But Hager lay passively, nursing feelings that seemed as though they never, ever, could stop hurting. So not just today but for years they had been separate from him, had kept secrets from him.

"Frank," she said, her face on his shoulder and soaking him with tears, "I just want it to stop. I feel so guilty. When Robbie disappeared, do you know what I felt? I felt relief. Oh, yes, relief. I'm so ashamed."

He felt the sobs jerk her body, like a fish on the end of a line. She had lost control, and he wanted, in his mind, to comfort, to console, to touch and hold and even make love in the dark—to forget all this, to put it out of mind forever. But he was not going to do that. So he lay there, holding her but saying nothing, his anger making his body stiff and tight.

Her sobs lessened. Her body still clung heavily to him. He realized finally she was asleep. Her breathing was soft. He shifted his body to make it comfortable and pushed her weight over, off him. She was completely asleep, dead to him. He could not sleep, so he got up and made himself hot chocolate and watched Carson until he dozed off in his chair.

CHAPTER
17

The front porch was overgrown with wisteria, an untrimmed profusion of bare, viny branches that in weeks would flourish in lavender. The old frame house was faded, its paint unfresh. Tufts of crabgrass patched the clumpy grass on the front lawn.

A blue plastic baby rattle lay on the sidewalk. Hager picked it up and carried it to the front door. Over the lintel was a cardboard sign hand-stenciled to say, "Thou didst form my inward parts; thou didst weave me in my mother's womb. Psalm 139:13."

Hager had to wait a long time for an answer to his ring. His face had a grim set. He had made up his mind to do this no matter what the results. Finally a fiftyish woman with a rust-colored permanent opened up. She had a baby in her arms whom she was trying to feed from a bottle, and she paid more attention to the child than to Hager. She led him into a living room and said, "You can wait here." Then she called up the stairs: "Mary Ann! Somebody here to see you!"

Two girls, maybe fifteen or sixteen years old, were playing checkers; they sat on the floor with the checkerboard between them on a coffee table. Glancing at Hager, they kept playing. He took a seat in an overstuffed chair with an orange-red throw over it. One of the girls, heavy anyway, had a huge pregnant stomach. They talked to each other in low, intimate voices.

Hager put the baby rattle softly on a lamp table. The room needed dusting, the furniture was worn, and over the fireplace was a large hand-lettered Scripture verse done in blue marking pen on yellow construction paper: "Trust in the Lord with all thy heart, and lean not on thine own understanding—Proverbs 3:5."

Mary Ann came down. She stood a little away from him, smiling. Her hair was greasy and unkempt, and her face seemed flushed. She had on old jeans and a hand-knitted purple sweater; her feet were in gray sneakers.

"Has something gone wrong?" she asked.

"No," Hager said. "Everything's okay. I just found out about the baby. Yesterday." He sounded severe because he was nervous, uncertain what to say. You didn't congratulate her, certainly. Seeing Mary Ann, seeing this untidy place, he felt his original dismay that Stephen had become involved with her. She had disrupted their lives; her own was a steady stream of confusion.

"Well, you're the first to visit," Mary Ann said. The two girls glanced at him idly. "It's okay, though. There are plenty of people to talk to. I kind of like it here. I've been reading. Don't look so mournful." The last sentence she said with a strange, fond smile, or perhaps with amusement. He remembered that Mary Ann talked like that, volunteering whatever came to her mind.

Hager asked whether there was any place they could be alone. Mary Ann said they could go into the kitchen but that wasn't too private. Or else they could go on the front porch.

"Isn't it too cold outside for you?"

"Oh, no. I'm hot all the time."

They sat on a sagging gold velvet sofa in the sun. The weather in the valley had warmed up into a tolerably warm March spring. The porch had a cement floor mottled with a worn brick-red stain. Mary Ann took off her shoes and put her feet flat on the floor; the cold felt good, she said. Her feet tended to swell.

"You're seeing a doctor?" Hager asked. On the drive down he had suddenly realized that this strange girl was carrying his grandchild. He had originally intended to talk about Robbie, nothing else, but a good many other concerns were involved now whether he liked them or not. If he was going to pay for this place, he at least wanted to know for certain what he was getting.

She smiled. "It's sweet of you to ask. We all go to the same doctor. He's very nice."

"And is there any trouble with the money?" he asked.

"So far so good," she said. "I'm still not quite sure but I think it's going to be fine. Bethel House takes you in whether you can pay or not. They're going to send a bill to my father, which should be interesting."

"I talked to him," Hager said. "We've worked that out. I'm going to pay."

Very quickly and very firmly she answered, "No, that wouldn't be right. I'm here because I want to be here. You don't have to feel responsible."

That touched off his temper. "I don't really care who feels responsible. Stephen is responsible. He gets at least half the credit for this."

"No," she said quietly and stubbornly. "We worked that out. Stephen wanted me to have an abortion, and I said no. I took the decision, so it's my responsibility. He has nothing more to do with it."

"Oh, for heaven's sake."

"What?"

"You can't just divvy up responsibility for a baby."

A mockingbird was tearing through its repertoire. Hager looked until he found it, cocking its tail on top of a telephone pole across the street.

"How did you find this place?" Hager asked.

"Stephen found it for me. My father said I couldn't stay at home. So I just came. I came on the Greyhound, and they took me in."

"I thought you said Stephen wasn't responsible," Hager said.

"Well, he's not from now on." She smiled. "I think he wanted me to be out of town before I began to show."

She went on. "But I was glad he found me a place. I like it here. Most of the girls are younger. They got kicked out of

high school or would have been. So they have special classes."
She looked over at Hager with the same amused, contented
smile she had used before. It was almost as though she was
patronizing him. "I really don't have much to do. They don't
want me to work because it wouldn't be good for the baby. I
read, and we girls talk a lot. I'm learning to knit. I'm knitting a
sweater for the baby. Do you want to see it?"

She got up before he could stop her and soon came back
with a small, shapeless scrap of would-be sweater tied to a ball
of pink wool yarn with two knitting needles run through it. He
had never noticed how lightly she moved; she tucked one leg
trimly underneath her as she came back to the sofa. Hager
held the material up and put it down and listened to her talk
about the other girls. She talked to him as though he and she
were friends catching up on the news. One of the girls, she
said, had come home from the hospital yesterday with her
baby. Another, Laura, was due at any moment. Mary Ann said
they were all holding their breath. She was thinking about
giving her sweater to Laura's baby if it was a girl.

She went on, describing the baby that had just come
home. The adoption agencies would come any day, and
Suzanne, the mother, would not stop crying. The whole house
was stirred up because of it.

"I bet," Hager said dryly. "Why is she crying?"

"Because she loves little Brian. Mrs. Nabors says it's
sometimes better not to look at the baby when it's born,
because you can't help loving it. Mrs. Nabors tries to talk to
Suzanne, but she just cries any time Brian is near her and then
Brian starts crying too. I hope I won't feel that way."

"But it's best for the baby," Hager said.

Mary Ann's eyes stared at the porch floor. One shoulder
shrugged. "Yes, I think she knows that. But everybody says it's
hard. Mrs. Nabors says Suzanne isn't handling it very well,
though. She says you need to think about the baby when he's
grown up and the kind of life he'll have, not look at him as a
little, tiny, helpless baby."

Mary Ann went on, spinning out the girls' names,
mentioning months and weight gains and then talking about
baby names. Sometimes, she said, the new parents kept the

name you gave. Hager felt that he was listening to a conversation in code; he was not sure what was at stake, though evidently it had captured Mary Ann's undivided attention. He grew more and more edgy as she talked.

Mary Ann eventually sensed that. Stretching her arms, she resumed a quiet, happy look. "Now," she said. "I've talked too much."

It was a little while before Hager realized she was inviting him to talk, and another while before he was able to remember his questions. For a few minutes he had forgotten about Robbie.

"I really came to talk about Robbie," he said. "That's how I found out you were here. I went to talk with Mrs. Gilbert at the school. She told me that you and Robbie had been close. That's when I called your father to get your number, and he told me about the baby."

"I thought so. I knew Stephen would never tell you," she said with an affectionate smile. "I told him I didn't think you were so bad."

Suddenly she seized his hand in both of hers and said feverishly, "I felt a kick." She put his hand on her abdomen, which was tight like a cucumber. "Right there," she said in a stage whisper. "Isn't that amazing? Somebody is really in there."

After a decent interval he took his hand away. "Did you feel it?" she asked.

"No," he said. "But I've felt babies kick before."

"Oh, I'm sorry," she said. "It's just so exciting. Now please go ahead. I know you have something you want to talk about."

"Yeah," he said. He was beginning to feel chilly despite the brilliant streaming sunshine. "I'm just on a fishing expedition, really, trying to learn anything at all about Robbie and his friends, who knew them, who they might have had for enemies. Did you ever think anybody ever had a strange interest in him? Like a pervert, maybe. Or just anybody who seemed involved in an unusual way."

She thought about it a minute, her head lowered, and then said simply, "No."

"You were close to him? Mrs. Gilbert said he had a thing for you."

She seemed troubled by that, glancing at Hager suspiciously, then looking down before speaking. "Oh, poor Robbie. Yes. He was so sweet. He called me his girlfriend. Do you know what he tried to give me for my birthday? He wanted to give me his quarter collection. You know what a thing he had about quarters."

"Yeah, I know, but how did you know? That was supposed to be a family secret."

"Stephen told me when I said what Robbie had given me. He said I should give them back."

"And you did?"

"Oh, of course."

So that explained Robbie's quarters. Hager puzzled over it for a moment but could not see that it led anywhere. He continued his questions with a growing sense that Carrie had been right, that playing detective was leading to nothing, only prolonging their misery. He asked the questions he had rehearsed but had no more conviction that he would learn anything from her answers.

"Knowing Robbie as you do, could you think of anybody who might want to hurt him?"

She shook her head definitely. "He could be a pest but not half as much as most of those kids." She smiled at the memory. "You know, I miss them. That was the hardest thing about coming here. I didn't even go in to say good-bye because I couldn't answer any questions." Her thin, angular face suddenly carried a look of sadness. "It was partly Robbie who made me realize I had to keep this child. When Stephen was trying to get me to have an abortion, he said retardation might run in your family. But when I thought of Robbie, that made just the opposite effect on me. I thought about what a wonderful person he was. I realized that every life is holy."

"Holy," Hager repeated.

"Do you know what it really means?" she asked ardently. "I read it in a book they have here. It means something is distinctly different, set apart to be specially used by God. I had been thinking that but didn't know that was the word. Don't you think Robbie was like that?"

"Yes," he said miserably. Sadness was flooding him in a way it had not for days. "Yes, for me he was."

"Because of God," she said.

"Yes, I suppose so," Hager replied, remembering his question to Robbie: Why did God make you slow?

Mary Ann was looking at him as though in eagerness, expecting the conversation to go on. She had a leg up on the sofa between them and she was leaning forward toward him, her slim arms wrapped around her torso. He could see better why Stephen had been attracted for so long.

He wondered whether to keep quiet about Stephen but after a moment's hesitation decided to ask. She was not a girl who made you afraid of saying the wrong thing. "Will you and Stephen be together again? I mean, after all this is over?"

She pressed her lips together, speaking with melancholy certainty. "No, Stephen has to go on. He's going to go to Stanford, and that will be a new life for him."

"I'm sorry it had to end this way," Hager said.

"It was my fault," she said. "I talked him into it."

"That's what he said."

"Did he?" She smiled that fond, wistful smile. "Well, I did. I really love him, Mr. Hager. My father says I'm a fool, but I don't know. You make mistakes when you love someone, don't you?"

Hager heard a catch in her voice. He wanted for a moment to put out a hand and catch hers, but before he did she straightened up and took a deep breath. "It's working out for the best, anyway. Really, it had to happen. I wouldn't have seen it any other way. I didn't want to see it. Stephen needs to be free, and he couldn't be free as long as I was there. I don't think he loved me. He said he did, but I think you're the only one he really loves."

"Me?" Hager almost laughed.

"Well, he does. He looks up to you, and that's the same as love for Stephen." She gave her head a little shake. "He doesn't look up to me. So he has to go on. Sometimes, Mr.

Hager, you have to let it go. Let it drop and let the wind carry it away. Let God take care of it."

"I think at this stage of his life he only cares about himself," Hager said.

She nodded. "Yes, maybe. At any rate, he has to go on." She said it very confidently; he realized that she talked like a much older person, like a woman who had achieved distance from the world. It was somehow alarming in someone so young. Perhaps that was what Stephen felt.

Hager tried to draw his thoughts back to Robbie. "You said, I think, that Robbie called you his girlfriend. Was that common? I mean, did he ever talk about anyone else that way?"

She laughed, suddenly happy again at the memory. "I don't think so. Mr. Hager, he was just so in love. It was sweet. Kinda sad too. Very jealous."

Hager stood up. A breeze had sprung up, and he suddenly was too cold. "Robbie would have wanted me to take care of you then," he said. "And Stephen should, even if he doesn't care."

"Oh, he does care, Mr. Hager. I told him not to come."

"Well, I want to pay the expenses and help any way I can." He paused, wondering whether to say what was in his mind. "That's my grandson you've got in there, you know." He smiled crookedly.

"Could be a granddaughter," she said, her hands automatically stationing themselves on the sides of her swelling stomach.

"Yes," he said. "Either way."

CHAPTER
18

JUNE

Waking, Hager heard a patter of drops on the tent fly. He listened to be sure of the sound, then rolled over in his sleeping bag and looked at the glow of his watch. The time was 3:30. Lying still, he tuned his ears to the soft whiffle of Stephen's breath, and the random static of rain pipping the tent.

It was their first night in the mountains. The morning would be dreadful if rain continued. Not that he minded the discomfort so much himself, but that he had eight inexperienced kids along on this hike. Ever since Robbie had reached junior high age, Hager had been taking groups from the church on fifty-mile hikes across the Sierra. Rain had never come at night.

It is a good thing, Hager thought, *that Stephen's along to help*.

Hager took a certain amount of consolation from knowing that Stephen was competent. He remembered what Mary Ann had told him, that Stephen looked up to him, that respect was the same as love for Stephen. That, at least, made it easier to live with him, to ignore his indifferent attitude. You can put up with almost anything from someone who respects you.

They were close here, close enough to hear each other's breathing. Hager knew he could reach out a hand and touch his son's sleeping form.

As he had time and again, Hager let his thoughts drift to that conversation with Mary Ann. He had never gone to see her again. He received the doctor bills as he had arranged with Bethel House, so he knew that his grandchild was still growing toward birth in Madera. He thought sometimes that he would go see Mary Ann when that day came if he could make it there before an adoption was arranged.

He had learned something from her: to let things go, to stop clinging to the past. Carrie had tried to tell him that, but somehow in a way he had been unable to accept. For Mary Ann it was an act of faith: to let God have his way. Hager could not quite share so hopeful a view, but at least her words had helped him to give up playing detective, to go back to Carrie and tell her he was sorry, to try to see that there was a future. Even this hike. He hoped that it might be a chance for him and Stephen to go beyond their truce. It was the first time ever they had been in the mountains together without Robbie.

The drops grew sparser and then quit. Hager drifted back to sleep. When he woke again, the tent was filled with a soft, gray light. He could see the outline of the tent poles. No rain was falling, but he heard another sound, a faint, irregular scratching. Thinking it might be a mouse, he heaved up on one elbow, making a terrific rustle in his nylon sleeping bag. It could not be a mouse; the noise would have scared it away. Besides, the sound continued in soft flurries of two or three strokes. Hager listened carefully, trying to locate it, straining his eyes into the gray to see. Then he remembered where he had heard that sound before. It was Stephen's eyelashes blinking against the nylon of his sleeping bag.

"You awake?" Hager asked.

"Yeah."

Hager almost asked what Stephen had been thinking about but checked himself. Questions seemed to send Stephen further into the distance, not bring him closer. Carrie said to stop trying so hard.

Instead Hager asked, "Did you hear the rain?"

"No. When?"

"Just a little, in the night. Let's hope it's moved through."

Hager struggled to find his clothes in the darkness and to

dress while propped on his elbows. When he had everything on but his boots, he unzipped the tent and stuck his feet out the door. Chill, moist air flooded in. The breeze felt like rain. He tied his stiff boots, tugging hard on the laces, and then stamped around to make the leather take its shape around his toes. It was too early to see anything in the sky, but the granite cliffs behind their camp were dull, lacking the glow of impending sunrise. He judged that clouds covered everything.

The rain began again when they were well on the trail. A wind gusted up the steep, dry canyon they were ascending, and drops buried themselves in the dust. Hager was with Zachary, lagging behind the main group. Zack had long, lank hair that hung over his eyes and down his collar. His limbs lacked muscle, looking like cooked asparagus. Hager had made certain Zack carried the bare minimum of weight. The brown square of Zack's backpack rode high over him like the sail of an old square-rigged sailing ship. A strong wind might blow him over.

Zack stopped, wheeled to one side of the trail, and clumsily slumped against a boulder. From behind, Hager had been watching a pack with two legs underneath. Now that he could see Zack's face, he felt a small alarm. The kid was exhausted already. Zack sat with his mouth open.

"Feel pretty tired, huh?" Hager asked. He wanted to keep it light. "It's a steep son-of-a-gun. The first day is always tough, but you'll make it. I personally guarantee it, Zack. Just try to pace yourself. You'll get a second wind sometime soon."

"Are we almost there?" Zack asked.

"Well, we're getting there. We've still got some climbing to do, Zack. We have to get up to the pass. After that it's all downhill."

Zack's face was absolutely slack, drawn, pale. Swinging his own pack off, Hager unzipped a side pocket and pulled out a bag of raisins and peanuts. He got Zack to eat some, watching him carefully. Sometimes Zack would slack off chewing in the middle of a bite as though he lacked the stamina to swallow.

"Come on, Zack, eat," he said. "You need some energy in

your system. Get some of that stuff down your throat. Do your feet hurt?" He was thinking about blisters.

Zack said his whole body hurt.

"Well, the first day is always the worst, Zack. You get through this and you can get through anything."

Hager had to do some talking to get Zack up again. He staggered under the pack's top-heavy weight, caught his foot on a rock, and nearly fell. He was breathing hard before he had taken a step. Hager looked at him helplessly. "Okay, Zack, let's roll," he said. "Nice and slow. The trick is not to stop. Take a breath after every step if you need to. But keep putting one foot in front of the other, and we'll get there."

They met a party coming down in a hurry, wet and bedraggled. Hager grunted a hello but did not stop them to ask about conditions. It would surely be worse on the pass, but Zack wouldn't need to know that.

"Zack, we better go on," Hager said. Zack did not move. His hair hung into his eyes. He had sunk onto a rock by a lead-gray lake.

The canyon had opened into a wide gray basin guarded by granite ridges. At this altitude the trees were reduced to head-high, windbeaten shrubs, wedging their roots into granite. The rain was a steady drizzle.

Hager had never learned to like the barren country above the tree line. He preferred the fecund lower altitudes to this territory of fractured rock and sickly pink snow. The snow was pink because an algae grew on it; lichens and a few hardy flowers persevered among the rocks. Little else. Here by the lake a fringe of wiry grass survived no more than ten feet from the water; after that, rocks and sand. The rain merely ran off; there was no soil to soak it in. Tiny streams ran underfoot in the cream-colored granite sand. Hager's boots were already wet through.

"Zack, time to go. The longer you sit, the stiffer you get. Let's roll." Zack's face had sunk down so that all Hager could see was the top of his sopping wet fishing hat. He still made no response.

"Zack, we can't stay here." Hager tried to put some

authority in his voice. "Zack, I know how you feel." He crouched down and put his face near the boy's, trying to talk in the voice of parents and teachers. Slowly Zack got to his feet and, when Hager gestured toward the way, slumped forward into motion. He stopped after several steps to gasp for breath.

Out of the lake basin their trail followed the rock-strewn course of a small, swollen stream, which petered out in a few crude acres of dark rocks. The clouds had descended to their level, so that everything was obscured except this jagged pavement; they might be on top of the world.

Out of the mist appeared the dark bulk of the ridge looking as steep as a wall. Hager felt a sudden sharp stinging on his face, and the sound of the rain on his poncho pitched instantly higher. He saw richochets off the rocks, little frozen pinpricks. Zachary stopped. He negotiated a slow pirouette and moved his face close to Hager's ear. Hager did not understand him at first; it was hard to hear in the din of the hail on their nylon covered heads. He yelled to Zack to say it again and moved the hood back from his ear. This time he got the words. "Are we going up that mountain?"

Hager leaned back and nodded his head, watching Zack's eyes. He thought he had never seen a more miserable face.

Zack leaned forward again. "I can't."

"Sure you can," Hager said with a firmness he did not feel. "Just put one foot in front of the other. Don't think about it." He pushed Zack gently ahead. In the blue folds of his poncho sleeve a slurry of ice and water had begun to collect.

They heard shouts. An orange dot was moving sideways on the ridge above them, coming fast. By silent consent they stopped and watched. The dot grew into a human figure. It was Stephen. When he reached them, he was grinning like a coyote.

"Some day, huh?" Stephen said. "Wait until you get to the top. You could get blown right off the edge. It's really something." Stephen had seen them struggling and had raced down the mountain to get Zack's pack.

At the pass, the trail ran a few yards along the blade of a long ridge and then descended in switchbacks down the other side. For the moment the rain had quit, but the wind ripped at their rain gear. Clouds rushed up the ridge and streamed over the edge into space. They could not talk for the noise.

Hager felt unnerved by the chaos and wanted to hurry on, but Stephen, still with a smile, seemed to want to linger. He had stowed his pack a few yards down the back side of the pass, and they talked a little as he got out some M & M's. He had sent the other boys ahead. He said they were doing all right. They would wait at the lake.

"There's not much shelter there," Stephen said. "But they may be too tired to go down into the canyon. We'll have to see. I think some of them may have wet sleeping bags."

"You think this is fun, don't you?" Hager asked.

"I guess so." Stephen smiled crookedly. "It's wild. I like it when you get up out of the trees."

The rain fell more heavily on the western side of the pass, and the weather was even colder. After a stumbling jog down the ridge they came into a rock-studded bowl. A tiny guitar-shaped lake lay at its base; trees were no taller than waist high. They found the seven boys hunkered down behind boulders, their teeth chattering, their foreheads gleaming with the rain. When asked a question, they answered but were too cold to think. They were done for the day.

There were few spots flat and clear enough for their small tents. Hager stumbled around looking for sites and whenever he found one he shouted for one of the boys to come. He showed them how to dig trenches, clawing into the gravelly soil with a stick or a sharp rock. The trenches filled quickly with icy water. Tents were soon flapping up all over.

Hager discovered Zack standing in the rain, his head down. "Zack, what are you doing? Get your tent up."

Zack was shaking. His shivering teeth were hitting like stones.

"Zack, answer me. Where's your tent?"

"I can't find a place." The words rattled out between his bouncing teeth.

"Oh, gosh, Zack. We've got to get you warm. You can't stay out here in the rain." He remembered that Zack had not brought a real tent but a tarp to be tied between trees. The wind would whip through it unmercifully, assuming they could find trees tall enough to tie it to.

Stephen came up while Hager tried to reason with Zack. Hager was glad to have him, to gain the implied strength of his frame standing near and blocking the wind. All day he had barely kept Zack from quitting and now he could not move him.

"Why don't you put him in our tent?" Stephen suggested. "I'll put his up while you get him warm." When Hager hesitated, Stephen said, "He really needs to warm up. And get some food too."

Stephen led them to the tent, which he had wedged into a depression behind a circle of stunted trees. Hager unzipped the fly and maneuvered Zack in; Zack sat in the doorway, dripping, with his feet outside while Hager pulled off Zack's boots and stuck them inside, into the corners of the tent. They would never dry but at least they would not freeze. The heavy wool socks came off, soaked and cold. Zack's feet were marbled red and cream.

Stephen said, "He needs to get all those clothes off, Dad, and climb into my sleeping bag. He's soaked to the skin." Zack's fingers were too numb to cope with his buttons, so Hager undressed him down to his underwear. He rolled the wet clothes into a ball and stuffed them into the corner with Zack's boots. Zack still sat with his arms wrapped around himself, shaking. Hager coaxed him into Stephen's sleeping bag and covered his head with the hood. He tightened the drawstring until all he could see of Zack were his nose and eyes and a thatch of wet hair. Then he got up and talked to Stephen, who had found a spot to sit and was eating raisins, his back to the stinging rain.

"Why don't you go and get Zack's tent up now? It's going to get dark early. You ought to get out of those wet things, yourself."

"Okay, Dad. What about dinner?"

Hager looked at his watch. "We still have a couple of hours of light. I don't think we can build a fire tonight, though. Not unless it clears up dramatically."

"There's no wood here anyway," Stephen said.

"Yeah, that's true. At least we made it here. Thanks for all you did."

Hager wanted to say more. After Stephen left, he climbed backward into the tent, unpeeled his soggy boots and socks and pants, and wiggled into his own sleeping bag. There was no sound except the violent flapping of the fly, beaten by the wind. He rolled over to check Zack and found that he had gone to sleep.

Something's been happening with Stephen, he thought. Somehow they were in touch today. The thought filled his chest. That would make the whole stinking day worthwhile.

"Dad, can you get up? I want you to see something."

Hager awoke, surprised to find day still dimly with them. Stephen's body filled the tent door. He had a hand on Hager's shoulder.

"What's up?" Hager asked.

"The weather's changing. Come and see."

He emerged from the tent and needed a moment before he could see what Stephen meant. The rain had stopped, and clouds had lifted off the surrounding ridges; they stood under a smooth, dark sky. Steve pointed to a patch of rosy light, clearing in the west. As they watched, it grew larger. The clearness slid silently across the entire western border of the sky, slowly flowing toward them. It took perhaps twenty soundless minutes. Then the sky was clear, a dim, purplish blue. Wisps of mist boiled up under the peaks. The wind did not abate.

Stephen was smiling. "Do you realize how cold it will be tonight?" he asked.

Hager nodded. "We better check everybody to see if they're dry."

"They are, pretty much. I went around and gave them all some food. I told them to stay put until the morning."

"Right," Hager said, turning slowly to examine the lightened horizon from west to east and west again. "Thanks, Steve. I was just too tired."

"It's great weather, isn't it?" Stephen said. "Wild."

"Do you think we should move Zachary now?" Hager asked.

"Why don't we leave him there, Dad? I'll sleep in his tent tonight. His bag got a little wet."

"Are you sure?"

"Yeah, sure. He doesn't need to freeze after the day he's had."

It was a relief to think that he could leave Zack in slumber. "Stephen, that's really nice of you."

Stephen said nothing in response; he seemed lost in contemplation of the last haze of light on the peaks around them.

The mind loses its bearings at night; thoughts wander like a lost child. Frank Hager was cold in his sleeping bag; he listened to the wind rattle the tent, heard Zack's sleeping snorts, and relived the day. If there was rain in the morning, he decided, they would have to go back out.

One image returned several times: the unplanned and unanticipated minutes when he and Stephen had stood at the top of the pass in the snapping wind, Stephen grinning. It came to him how much he loved the boy. Why, all these years, had Robbie's problems figured and not Stephen's? He was sorry for all he had missed with him. Even after Robbie died, he had mattered more than the kid who was living.

Hager contemplated the top of the pass, the clouds washing over them, the shoving wind. He did not think there had ever been a moment like that before. Where had it come from? It was like the patch of clear sky that had appeared at dusk: Let it spread, let it cover the earth. Let it remove all I have done wrong.

The first light came like a trick, the barest hint of gray light. The bowl seemed more vast and beautiful: quite still and empty, except for their insignificant tents scattered across the side of the hill. Hager inspected the ice on the puddles. It had frozen all the way through the thin pools under his tent; in a deeper puddle he snapped off a triangle a quarter of an inch thick and held it in his shivering hands. He set this plate on end against a rock, to shine and melt when the sun came over the horizon. Meanwhile he would build a fire.

It was evident that no one had recently camped in this place, for though the trees were small, Hager found plenty of loose branches and twigs. He took the thinnest, driest ones and balanced them into a teepee. When he tried to light it, he found that he could not hold the match steady. His hands were so numb that he dropped the match repeatedly. Just before he gave up, a tiny curl of yellow flame caught a twig. He nursed it into a blaze.

Stephen joined him. Hager remembered his vows of last night, but as they stood over the fire, warming themselves and willing the flame to grow, he found that he had lost the words he had planned to say.

"It's great to see the sun," Hager said because he could think of nothing else.

"Yeah. Do you think we can stay around camp today to let everyone get dried out?"

"Sure," Hager said. "Good idea. They deserve a break. They did pretty well, even Zack. But you were great, Steve. I mean it. I don't know how we could have made it without you. I was proud to be working with you."

Hager thought this might lead to something, but Stephen did not acknowledge the compliment. They stood by the fire, and part of the time Hager thought that it was good for them to stand together, side by side, even without speaking. But part of the time they seemed to be falling back into the old pattern: he, speechless and gloomy, ignorant of what was in Stephen's mind, and Stephen not even caring to try to talk. The boys began to get up and join them. They chattered about the cold and the rain the night before. They broke ice off the puddles and smashed it on rocks, throwing it into the fire to watch it melt until Hager had to tell them to stop. The sun marched down the bowl and finally splashed over them. Stephen moved away, and the day began.

CHAPTER
19

Late in the morning they set off, following a stream flowing out of the lake and down the side of a steep canyon. The water broke over fat slabs of granite; soon, at a lower altitude, the trail was hemmed in by tall, straight trees and tiny hillside meadows. It was a different and closer world. They found a substantial river roaring above its banks at the bottom of the canyon, and they turned south to follow it downstream. In a dense, still forest they camped for the night.

The next morning they continued down the river for several miles until, on a wooden bridge, they crossed a large tributary stream. The trail turned to the southeast and began to ascend a narrow valley overhung with steep talus slopes. Occasionally now they broke out into the sunshine, usually where winter avalanches had smashed flat deltas of trees.

By an unspoken division of labor, Stephen stayed at the head of the pack while Hager lagged behind with Zachary. They saw each other only at lunch time, when Stephen offered apologetically to trade roles. Hager said no, thanks, he was happy to take it slow with Zack.

Twice on the second day Hager had lost Zack. When he went back to look for him the first time, he found the boy completely panicked on the other side of a small stream he could nearly jump over. Zack had no sense of balance for picking his way across over rocks or logs. Hager got him to take his boots and socks off, roll up his pants, and wade the streams.

But that didn't help. The water was so cold that it hurt his feet, and the rocks underfoot cut. Zack would lunge around until he fell. Hager had to stay right with him to carry his pack across for him and offer a hand or a shoulder for balance. He worried that Zack would really hurt himself.

Hager had done enough hiking so that the performance was routine, but he did it for the kids, not himself. He never liked feeling exposed, unable ever to shut out the sky. He was just as happy to lag behind with Zachary for whom he felt genuine pity. Zack wanted to be anywhere but here, but here he had to be, by the laws of adolescence. No one was allowed to be afraid at thirteen.

In late morning Hager and Zack caught up with three of the boys who always clowned together. They acted stunned and confused when they saw Hager. By the stream, about fifty yards farther up, a truck-sized anvil-shaped rock lowered its head into the rushing water. Sunning on it were four stripped bodies, two belonging to young women. They either did not know they were being watched or did not care.

Before Hager thought of what to say, Zachary spoke. "Oh, gross!" he said.

The threesome were lifted from their stupor. "Gross? Oh, sure, Zack." "We're looking at the girls. Which ones are you looking at?" "Zack, do you know what those are? Those are girls, man." "Zack, one of them is waving for you to come over." And the like.

Hager shooed them all up the trail, and they did not resist though they kept wisecracking long after the vision had disappeared behind the trees. Later on, when they all were resting, four hikers came up the trail and passed them. The boys fell into a hush until the four were well past, and then the jokes broke out. "Jim, what were you staring at?" "I'm sure I'm going to sleep in the same tent with you tonight!" "Did you see what I saw? They must have lost their bras back on that rock." "Hey, then why don't you go back and find them for them?" "Oh, I'm sure. I bet you'd like to cuddle up with it in your sleeping bag tonight."

That evening when the boys had come back from fishing, everyone lay around the fire and watched the cooking. The

Handsome Threesome—so Hager called the three whom he and Zack had overhauled—were in charge, and he could tune in or out of what they said to each other as he chose. Some of their insults were funny; there was energy if not sense in every word, as though, like babies, they made noise for the sheer joy of society. Zack wanted to talk about a huge fish he had seen in the lake, and the Handsome Threesome tried to make him shut up. "You probably just saw your nose," one of them said, and they laughed as though it had been hilarious.

Two other boys played chess on a miniature magnetized set. The rest were just tired, said little, and were slow to respond to a question or an order. They had climbed up out of the trees again, to a lake cupped under a ring of high peaks. The sun had disappeared very early, and the day's warmth was being sucked quickly into space. The air was still, the lake black. The sky seemed far away, held above them by the mountains' thick fingers.

When they had eaten and the light on the peaks had died and grown darker than the star-crusted sky, they fell into fire-watching. Their conversations lowered to grunts. They turned to warm their backs, then their fronts again. In the fire they saw scarlet and white castles, pathways, mountains. White-hot worms coiled and uncoiled themselves.

Zachary screamed. "Shoot! Shoot! Shoot!" He leaped from the fire, seemingly dancing, twisting as though something had hold of his foot. He sat down hard and pried at his shoe, then leaped to his feet again, running full tilt for the lakeside, splashing in, staggering and luckily not falling, stopping only when he stood shin-deep in water.

'What on earth was that, Zachary?" Hager asked. The boys were already laughing, jeering, and shouting.

"My shoe caught on fire," Zack said, his voice high and desperate.

The boys laughed harder, but Hager went over to help him out of the water. When the boot was off and Hager saw Zack's foot by the light of a flashlight, it was obvious that Zack would suffer. He had a large blister on two toes. The boot seemed all right, though you could see that the rubber sole had bubbled. Stephen put salve on the wound, and Hager fitted

Zack into a pair of his own oversize tennis shoes. Zack was whimpering.

"Zack, don't be such a baby," one of the boys said.

"Lay off," Hager said. "Or I'll stick your foot in the fire and see how you like it."

Hager had to tell them several times to shut up. Eventually Zack stopped making the high moan in his throat, and the talk stopped. The boys were cold and made a mass decision to go to bed. Stephen sat on a stone; Hager stretched long legs beside the fire and propped himself on one elbow.

"Could be rough for Zack tomorrow," Hager said. "The worst thing you can do is hurt your feet."

"He'll be all right in your tennis shoes, Dad."

"I don't know," Hager said. "We'll be in snow a bit, I think. The footing is tricky too. You remember?"

"I remember," Stephen said. "I love this pass."

"I can't say I love it. Remember when we came over it before? With Robbie?"

"Sure. He did fine, Dad. He never got scared."

"No, you're right. He did fine. It was me who was going nuts, worrying about him." Hager kicked a stick into the embers. His face was creased with the pleasure of the thought. "I don't think he knew enough to be scared of the mountains. So long as I went first, he'd go anywhere."

"He was something special."

"Special kids," Hager said, remembering Margaret Gilbert. The phrase was another that she scorned. Then he wondered whether there was irony in Stephen's comment. "Look, Steve, I don't know how you meant that, but Robbie was special. He couldn't do the things you can do, and sometimes I think I bent too far over backward to let him know I loved him. I love you too. And your sister. Anyway . . ." His thoughts petered out.

"You really did love him, Dad. I don't think it was bending over backward."

"No. I didn't mean that. I meant that maybe I tried so hard with Robbie that I didn't leave time enough for you."

Hager waited anxiously for a response. He watched the fire, not his son's face.

"I never thought you were trying so hard with Robbie," Stephen said at last. "It always seemed to come naturally."

"No. No, it wasn't hard. What I meant was that I . . ."

"You meant it was hard with me."

"No, I just didn't take the time." He looked at Stephen now, though Stephen was looking away into the night. "You always seemed to be doing so well. I overlooked you. And I'm sorry."

The fire was glowing on his handsome son's face. Hager wished he could read that face. It was so unlike Robbie's, which showed his internal weather as abruptly as the shadow of a cloud.

"It's okay, Dad," Stephen said, glancing over at him as though in shyness. "That's all done now. We're starting over. I feel as though I'm starting a whole new life."

"Why is that?" Hager asked.

"Robbie's gone. Mary Ann's gone. I'm going off to college."

"I'm glad you feel that way." Hager looked back into the fire and kicked the coals. "In a way, I think that's how your mother feels. Now that Robbie's gone she has a life of her own, for the first time in twenty years."

"But you aren't very happy about it, Dad."

"I'm happy for her. I wish I could feel that way. I guess I'm still trying to get out of reliving the past. It's hard."

"You and Mom aren't getting along?"

Hager could not read the tone behind that question. Was it disapproval? Worry? "Oh, it's hard to explain, Stephen. We get along fine. I mean, we've been married a long time. We just seem to be thinking along different lines right now. It'll straighten itself out. It's nothing to worry about."

A few minutes of silence passed. Hager said, "Well. Let's go to bed. Steve, don't worry about me and your mom. When you're married someday, you'll understand. You go through these periods when you don't communicate. It's just a stage. I wouldn't have told you if I thought you would worry."

"I'm not worried, Dad," Stephen said, standing up and moving next to the small glow of the fire. "I don't understand it but I'm not worried."

"What don't you understand?" Hager too got to his feet. The bowl of sky above them was huge, cold, black.

"I don't understand how you love someone when you can't communicate."

The comment troubled Hager, but he did not know how to respond. "I don't know either," he said. "But you do. You just do."

CHAPTER
20

The suspension bridge crossed the small river where rock banks forced it into a narrow chasm. The bridge was too high to wash out, and in its particular situation no avalanche could smash it. But the winter had dealt with it more simply, piling on tons of snow and ice until one of the steel cables had snapped. The remaining cable held the bridge spavined, its floor vertical at the side they looked from, and thirty degrees from the horizontal on the opposite side.

Their packs were lighter, their bodies stronger, and having crossed miles of snow fields and dozens of swollen creeks, the boys were cocky. You would think they had been out six months rather than six days, the way they talked. Since the morning, they had been shouting about what they wanted to eat when they reached civilization. But the sight of the bridge silenced them; they nervously had a quiet lunch on the rock shelf leading to the edge. Hager and Stephen had gone up and down the river, looking for another way over.

Then they sat with the maps, talking quietly about alternatives. They would have to backtrack and come out by another exit trail. It would take at least an extra day, for which they had no supplies. No one would be there to meet them, either; they would be many miles from the cars.

Unfortunately, no one had a rope.

"It can't be that hard," Hager said. "I'll bet you can almost reach from one cable to the next." Stephen did not disagree but he did not agree, either.

Hager got up to try it. He stood for a time where the bridge leaped from the rock into the air, then pulled his lanky body onto it, balancing by holding one of the cables. He was not terrifically agile. The side of the bridge's floor that he would balance on was a bolt-studded steel strip four inches wide. Every five feet a supporting cable stretched straight up from that floor to the single remaining overhead cable.

Hager edged out from the first supporting cable, holding it with one hand, and reaching into the air with the other, measuring the distance to the next cable. His long upper arms opened and extended themselves. He could reach within a few inches of the other cable, but there his hand waved helplessly for a moment before he pulled himself back and looked the situation over again.

Once more he pushed out his right leg, planting it firmly but not so far out this time. Several times he flexed it as though he were about to leap. Then he poised himself and easily stepped forward, grabbing the next cable and guiding himself in close to it, swinging his body around it.

He shouted something to them, hanging there by one hand. The roar of the water drowned his voice.

Carefully but more quickly he crossed over two more gaps. He had reached the center of the span, where the floor of the bridge had begun to twist back closer to its original horizontal. The strip of metal underfoot twisted as well, so that Hager stood on the corner. High water raged far below. Hager tested his balance there for some time, but when he leaned forward, letting his weight release from one cable and almost fall toward the other, it went as smoothly as before. In a few more moments he was standing on the other bank, waving his hands to them and smiling, shouting something. Then he came back, more quickly, by the same method. Their eyes stayed on him the whole way, and no one said much.

"Nothing to it!" Hager shouted when he reached them. He took a deep breath. "Nobody is going to have any trouble. A piece of cake!" He told them that the most important thing was to relax and not hold on for too long to the cable they were leaving. "And don't look at the river. Just pretend you're balancing on a curb. It's actually not nearly as hard as that because you have those cables to hang on to for all but a split second."

Hager had them leave their packs behind; he would carry them over since his arms were the longest. Stephen was the first to go. Hager was surprised to see that his legs were trembling. No one else noticed; Stephen's face was impassive, and he did not hesitate as he jumped nimbly up to the bridge. Hager watched his face, however, and saw terrible, close concentration. It moved him. He knew Stephen would be all right but still he watched intently as Stephen's hand reached into that gap.

As he leaned into space, he lost his balance, lunging and for an instant sawing the air with his hand in search of something to hold. Then a moment later he was safe; his hand grasped the cable and he hung on, clutching the cable too closely as though staggered by what he had done. Hager wanted to shout encouragement, but his voice was stuck and his heart hammered. Stephen went on grimly until he reached the rock abutment on the other side and sat down as though stunned.

The others followed. Hager watched them closely, trying to show no emotion, all the time wondering whether it was crazy. Surprisingly, they had less difficulty than Stephen had.

No one had said anything, but Zack was the obvious weak link. As the boys crossed one by one, Hager felt his tension growing. Then he and Zack were alone. On the other side of the creek the boys sat in the sun watching—a little braver now that they had made it, but still too scared to make any fun. Zack, with Hager's helping hand, got up on the bridge. He looked shaky, hooked to the cable like a potato vine. Trying to shift his grip, he lost his balance and swung around the cable, from one side of the bridge to the other, until he regained control and hung on to the cable with both arms.

He was still over the rock, and in no danger; Hager stood beneath him, telling him it was all right, urging him to go forward. Finally he put a hand on his boot and pushed it out, along the edge. "Now reach," he said. "Just reach out and lean into the next cable." Zack leaned forward cautiously but pulled back, clinging to the cable. Hager grasped his boot again and pushed it forward. "Don't think, Zack. Just stretch out there and go."

When Zack would not try, Hager pulled himself up behind Zack. Holding Zack's trailing arm, he pushed Zack's body into the gap. "Don't worry, Zack. I'll hold you. It's easy, you'll see." Zack swayed, hung on for life, and finally with Hager's prodding released his grip and staggered into space. He seized the next cable and hung on. The boys cheered and laughed.

But Zack's face was white. "Keep going, Zack," Hager said. "Just go. Don't think." But Zack stuck fast. "Come on, Zachary, you jerk," Hager said, and then immediately was sorry.

Hager looked across, saw Stephen sitting, watching, and thought that perhaps he could help. They needed to move Zack quickly. He waved for Stephen to come over, signaled for him to put out a hand to Zack. Stephen got to his feet but seemed to hesitate. Hager wondered whether he was asking too much. He assumed Stephen's fearlessness and had momentarily forgotten what he had seen when Stephen crossed. He was about to wave Stephen back when Stephen came, not hesitating, moving quickly from cable to cable.

Now Stephen was leaning toward Zachary, offering his hand. Seemingly he intended to pull Zack across. But Zack did not move. "Move!" Hager called over the roar of the water. It seemed to arouse Zack. He leaned forward toward Stephen. His arm stretched out. His hand grasped Stephen's. Hager thought he would go. But violently, as though bitten, he pulled back. He hung on to his cable with both arms, and he did not appear to be looking toward Stephen but down into the water.

Hager felt his stomach sway. He had made a mistake trying to do this. Now something had to move quickly. Zack was not far out but far enough to kill himself if he fell. The longer he stayed, the more the risk grew. As Hager began to lean toward Zachary, he felt the bridge shudder and he raised his eyes for a flash to see Zack swing helplessly in a circle around his cable. He did not risk looking any longer. His self-preservation meant minding his own business until he clutched with both hands to the rusted metal strands of the cable Zack was on.

When he reached it and got his balance and looked, Zack's eyes were pointed blindly up into the sky. Hager felt Zack's legs hammering like a sewing machine.

"Zack," Hager said quietly, his mouth next to Zack's ear. Zack lowered his eyes for an instant to catch his; then, as if stung, he tore them away.

"Zack, listen to me for a second. It's not hard to make it. You can manage it. The longer you stick here, the more difficult it becomes."

Zack made no answer; he looked upward as though God would stick a hand down from heaven and take him off the bridge. Hager looked over at Stephen, who made a despairing gesture, a shrug.

Hager put his foot next to Zack's, urging it across the metal side of the bridge. He put a hand on Zack's hand and tried to pry it off the cable. "Zack, listen to me," he said. "Just reach out. I've got you. You can't fall."

Once again Zachary's eyes flashed at him desperately. Those eyes scared Hager; Zack could pull him right off this bridge. But the eyes looked away, as though to hide.

"Zack!" he shouted. "Get out there! Don't waste my time." Part of him was wishing, oh, please, don't do it. But part of him was angry and wanted to shake Zack loose from his grip.

Those eyes again. "I can't. I can't. Leave me alone."

"Zack. Listen to me. There is no helicopter. You have to do it. Listen to me. You have no choice."

But Zack did not look or listen any more. He hung on to the cable as though he were a bat clinging to a dead limb, as though he had died.

Hager heard a shout and looked up to see that Stephen was waving him back, away from Zack. He could not hear his words, but he did as Stephen wanted. He leaned out away from Zack, stepping across to the next cable to safety.

When he turned, Stephen was already on Zack's cable. He had his hand on Zack's hand, prying his fingers off their grip.

He was pushing with his body. Zack was shouting, crying out, and Stephen was shouting too, though the roar from the river drowned out them both. Then Stephen had Zack's hand loose from the cable; he was holding his wrist fiercely and still pushing, kneeing Zack out into space. Hager felt himself trembling. They could both fall.

Stephen was kicking at one of Zack's feet, trying to break him away from the cable; it looked almost as though he wanted Zack to fall. He got Zack partly loose; Zack's weight twisted away from the cable while he shrieked so loudly that the sound carried over the water's noise; in an instant Stephen had moved his body around the cable, between Zack and his last, one-handed purchase. Stephen was looking at Hager now, shouting, and Hager realized suddenly what he must do: reach out for Zack, give him some hope of being held before he fell. He moved out quickly, put out a hand, saw Zack's dehumanized eyes. They might all fall. But Zack saw his hand, grabbed it, and in an instant lunged toward him. Hager had just time to grasp his wrist, to brace himself against the cable and swing Zack down, under the bridge and onto the edge of the rock below. Zack fell in a heap.

For a moment Hager thought Zack was hurt. He jumped down and squatted beside Zack, crying, "Are you all right? Are you all right?" Zack did not answer; he was shaking. Hager looked him over, sat him up, concluded that he was not hurt. Stephen joined him, looking at Zack in a businesslike way.

"That was close," Stephen said.

After a few minutes Zack picked himself up slowly and moved away from the edge of the chasm. He sat still, cradling his head in his arms, saying nothing.

CHAPTER
21

"Zachary, my friend, we're in a mess." Hager's low voice was answered only by the soft hush of wind in the high pine boughs. The two were sitting on a spongy pad of forest humus, Hager tracing with his finger on the large, green Geological Survey topographic map. It was still morning, but Zachary lay exhausted, his T-shirt soaked with sweat. Hager glanced at him, making an assessment, then went back to his map. "It looks, Zachary old buddy, as though our best chance is to climb back up the way we came, and follow along the side of this ridge until we get a few miles farther down the canyon. That way should be easy."

They were on a steep, forested hillside, slippery with a carpet of needles. In pursuing a way down to the river they had found the going increasingly steep until finally Zachary panicked and clung to a tree. Hager did not want to go through that again.

Yesterday, after near-disaster on the bridge, Stephen had gone ahead with the other boys; they would squeeze into the van and leave the car. Hager would take Zack out across country, following the river down until they reached another bridge.

Miles downriver from the chasm, Hager and Zack had camped on a piece of level ground showing no sign of human presence—no blackened fire circles, no patches worn bare by tents. Under the thick forest canopy the ground was littered with firewood; the river roared nearby. Zachary refused to eat or come close to the fire; he crawled into the tent at the moment Hager finished putting it up. Piling the fire high, deliberately squandering wood, Hager hadn't had much of an appetite himself. He felt tired and frustrated, and vexed with himself for the hardness of his heart toward Zack. No doubt the kid was humiliated as well as frightened. Why did his incompetence bring out such scorn when Robbie, for instance, had generated such a different reaction?

Robbie, Hager thought, *had always been willing to trust him*. It made a vast difference when someone was willing to try.

But then Hager reminded himself that Zack had been willing to try. He had gotten onto the bridge. He had crossed one gap. Who could really know another person's fear?

Thinking of Zack, Hager's mind went back to that instant when Stephen's panic had been visible in his legs and his face just as he got up onto the bridge. Hager felt thankful for Stephen; someone might have been hurt had it not been for his help. Probably Stephen's fear had been nothing like Zack's, but it was fear nevertheless, and he had not given in; he had helped. Afterward, Hager had thanked him, formally, awkwardly, though Stephen barely acknowledged his little speech. They had talked mostly of what to do to get the boys out of the wilderness, both of them thinking hard, speaking quickly, not wasting time with sentiment. Yet perhaps in those moments something new had been born. Nothing was spoken aloud, but perhaps it was a beginning of partnership. Hager felt some hope for it.

Watching the fire that night, not wanting to go into the tent and lie next to Zack, Hager fell into a strange mood. He felt detached from his body as though his soul had shifted a few inches out of his corpus, which he could feel and see as animated, heavy flesh. His thoughts shifted strangely to Robbie and his death.

Tomorrow when he and Zack climbed the ridge across the river, they would be only a few miles from the cabin where he had found the Gilbert boy. Thinking of what had happened there, Hager felt that his thoughts took on a momentum of their own, moving with an unnaturally frictionless speed.

What he thought, what had seemed awfully clear, was that whoever had killed those boys had known them.

Someone had wanted them to die, it was no accident. And since there was no obvious reason, it must be a perverse and personal reason hidden from others.

Not only that. Why would they walk so far into the snow? Only someone with an equally hidden influence over them could get them to do it. Such power, such motive, pointed to someone who knew them well, who mattered to them. Hager had been quite sure of it by the fire.

With the morning light the strange mood was gone and so was the certainty. Waking, Hager rolled over and took a few seconds to remember where he was, then jogged Zack's shoulder and told him to rise and shine. Zack did not move, and it flitted through Hager's mind that Zack was dead. But it was not so; Zack groaned and sat up though he still did not speak.

When he remembered his thoughts of the previous night, Hager decided ruefully that he must still be grieving. All through the hike, Robbie had been at the back of his mind. There was no point in thinking about these things.

Hager got Zack to eat some nuts and raisins, and they hefted their packs. It proved impossible to stay too close to the river, however, as it entered a gully choked with boulders and brush. The terrain pushed them farther and farther away and above the river until they found themselves unable to get down because of the cliffs.

"It's tough, isn't it?" Hager said as he stopped to pant. Now he too was sweat-soaked. Zack still was not answering, and Hager felt a flash of annoyance. Hager wished he could squeeze out some pity for the kid. He spoke cheerily to him, but it was forced.

They were still far from the river, and the side of the hill was so steep they often had to double back before they found a way across. They were descending a north slope, and snow still lingered in deep masses that wound through the trees like headless snakes. Some mounds were shoulder high, forcing them to scramble up one side and down the other. It added to the work, but Hager was merciless. He wanted to get out of these woods as soon as humanly possible.

They finally came out into the clear. From a rock outcrop over the valley Hager could see the river far below. Rushing water spilled into a pool, a silvery bush shivering in the blue. The valley was steep, shelved with granite the color of concrete. Hiking through would not be easy. *There are reasons,* Hager thought, *for the routes that trails follow.*

A long slope of rock debris started in front of them, sweeping down at the angle of repose into a grove of miniature aspens, knocked silly by repeated avalanches. You could not say the saplings stood; rather, they survived, poking their flimsy limbs out of the rocks at all attitudes. Hager saw that they could follow the talus down and meet the valley floor among them.

Poor Zack did not even have the curiosity to see where he was. He had collapsed, sitting with his head down on a ledge of the rock.

"C'mon, Zack," Hager said.

They half slid, half walked down the steep sand and scree at the top of the slope. Then the gravel tongued into piles of rock, first the size of potatoes, painful and shifty underfoot, then rocks the size of cats, packed unsteadily. Then, lower, bigger rocks that grew to fullsize, over-your-head boulders, rocks that took wit and breath to scramble through. Zack inched painfully among these, leaving Hager plenty of time to hop to high points and plot their route. Finally they came into thickets of tough, red-stemmed manzanita, and Hager knew they were down.

On the valley floor he was glad to walk on solid, unshifting bedrock, cutting their way toward the riverbed. Near the water, Hager dumped his pack against a rock, took his and Zachary's plastic water bottles and descended a shelf to the river. Without the pack he felt so light that his feet might lift from the ground.

Squatting, Hager plunged his hands in the water up to the wrists, letting them soak and feel the drag of the current. Then cupping them, he threw a bowl of water into his mouth and face and rubbed the numbing water into his forehead. Just across the river a rib of snow channeled down a wide rock crack right into the water. It could not be more than a few degrees above freezing.

He had intended to hike on, but a few minutes without motion made him aware of how tired he was. Perhaps they should camp here.

Above where he squatted, the river fell over the end of a granite bench. It was a beautiful, chilly spot. Hager's eyes caught the sight of something moving in the water. A *fish*, he thought at first. He stood up and walked closer. Something was there, all right, near the rock where a snowbank met the water. It moved rhythmically with the current, too steadily to be a fish. It might be a green branch, trapped under water. He climbed over a few rocks to get a closer view but was stopped where the snowbank and its protecting rock bulwark dived into the stream. Putting a boot edge up on a nubbin of rock, Hager stood a foot higher. What was waving in the current, quite clearly, was a gray human arm and hand issuing from the snowbank.

Panic came, the need to act, the instinct to rescue, and he thought madly about swimming in the water and pulling out whoever it was. But the person must have died long before. Even from a distance the skin looked like hide. Hager sat for a moment and quieted his heart. He looked again to see if he had been mistaken. When he balanced again on the nubbin of rock, the sight of the hand was unmistakable.

Someone must have drowned, he thought, *perhaps some distance upstream, perhaps even at the bridge where Zachary had balked*. Then he realized that a drowned person cannot find his way to the bottom of a snowbank. He looked again. The arm did, indeed, come from the snow. There had been only one missing person in the mountains that winter. With a wild surge of blood to his head, Hager realized that he had found his son.

CHAPTER

22

"Zachary," Hager said quietly. The boy had not moved, and the sound of Hager's voice did not budge his head from staring in its exhausted downward track. What a wonder it was that while Hager's world had turned over, Zachary had not felt the movement. Hager wished violently that he were alone. To have to put such a thing in words, to be sane and informative, when he wanted to wail.

"Zachary, I found my son's body. It's by the river."

Zachary did look up at him, though his face was blank and stupid, registering no understanding.

"You remember," Hager continued, "he was lost last winter?"

Still Zack's face showed nothing.

"It's my son," Hager shouted. "You could say something."

Zachary just stared, and Hager turned away. He looked around for something to throw and jerked up a large rock and dashed it down. It cracked into two pieces; Hager pounced on it and threw one half into the brush. Then he stopped, trembling.

When Zachary finally spoke, Hager could hear that he was on the verge of crying. His words were drowning in his throat.

"Mr. Hager," he said, "I just couldn't do it. I was so frightened. You'll never know how frightened I was. I will never come into the mountains again, I promise."

"What are you talking about?" Hager asked.

"Without me you could have gone the other way."

Zack thought Hager was angry with him about the bridge. Hager almost laughed, and he calmed down. No one could penetrate what he felt. Zack lacked the social graces to offer sympathy—but everyone had to be the same, unable to see from any angle but his own. No one knew anything about the sins and griefs of others; they only knew their own. Hager drew a breath. He could not say he was sorry for shouting at Zack but he said, "Zack, let's go down there. I need your help."

About six feet above the swift, deep water, seated on a rock, Hager surveyed the situation and wondered how Robbie could have got there. He might have drowned and been washed up when the water was higher and then later covered with snow. Another possibility was that when the snow was deep and strong enough to bridge the water, Robbie had crossed over and dug a snow cave there and died waiting to be rescued. Or someone might have killed him and put him there.

In any case Robbie, or someone—it had crossed Hager's mind it might be the murderer, instead, or even someone completely unknown—was there. The arm, which could be seen very distinctly from above, was in a gray quilted parka, sometimes lifted partly out of the water by the current. The river must have melted away the part of the snow that held the arm. In a few days it might melt the rest and sweep him away. They should get him to a more secure spot.

There was no way down to the level of the body; the bank of snow ran nearly straight down to the water. What they would have to do, Hager decided, was to dig down from the top. The snow was packed hard, almost to the quality of ice, so it would take time. He scrounged in their packs for implements: spoons, tent stakes, poles.

With these it was excruciatingly slow. Beneath the top inches of crumbled slush, the gravelly crystals could only be scraped away a fraction of an inch at a time. Soon his hands were red from the unbearable cold of handling the ice. It was already late afternoon, and Hager saw that if they did not find a better way, they would need most of the next day to get to the bottom. He considered cutting steps down the snowbank to the edge of the water and digging directly in to get the body out. But if they lost their balance and fell into the river, they might easily drown; and without a rope, how would they get the body up?

You can quarry ice, he thought, *almost like rock.* He tried taking a tent pole and hammering it into the snow with a rock. It went in a few inches, and then the bludgeoning rock began to hammer flat the soft aluminum tip of the pole. The pole bent slowly toward a J, and he saw that it would not do. But he had his idea.

Zachary, still silent, was doggedly digging in the snow with his spoon. His hands were red. Hager told him to forget the spoon—to go and gather sticks as straight and strong as possible, about one inch thick and two feet long. With a fish knife they sharpened the ends and then used a rock to drive them into the snow in a line. When that was done, all they had was a line of holes into the snow—no leverage. But that was easily solved. Starting within a foot of the edge, Hager hammered a line of holes and then broke off the foot-thick chunk of ice. It fell to the water and was rushed away.

After that they only had to work. The sticks broke, and Zack took the job of looking for new ones and sharpening them while Hager held rocks and smashed the blunted, vibrating sticks into the hardened snow. His hands were soon raw where he held the rock, and his arms ached from the vibration. But piece by piece the ice fell away into the river. He worked as fast as he could, desperately, because the sun was near to going down.

Before they reached the body, the sun disappeared behind the high ridges over the valley. Zack climbed down—still silent, and by now Hager was grateful for that—and helped dig the last bit. Ice had bonded with the clothing, so it took a long time before they could clear the body enough to see it distinctly. They worked silently, close to each other in the narrow slot they had dug.

The body lay on its face, with one hand under the head and the other arm stretched out—now into the water, surely then in snow. Hager began to cry, at first silently and then noisily. Zachary still said nothing.

Hager stopped digging and noticed that they were on a rock shelf a few inches above the level of the river. There had been no hurry to dig the body out, after all; it would stay put unless the river rose. That answered part of the question of how Robbie had gotten there. He would not have washed down in the stream, for the water would rarely be higher than it was now, in melt. Robbie must have come all this way, must have built a snow cave, must have taken every survival measure. Hager had always told Robbie that if he were lost and could not simply wait to be rescued, he should follow a river downstream.

They dug with their spoons around and under the perimeter of the body. Then Hager took it under the arms and lifted. One sharp pull and he was able to turn the heavy, stiff corpse over. The sky overhead was pink, the light fading. Hager clenched his teeth to look at the face. The skin was shrunk and discolored, rubbery. But it was Robbie's. He felt no shock of familiarity, but the features were clear. The clothes were also Robbie's except for the jacket. Hager remembered that they had found Robbie's jacket on the Aranian boy.

Hager was suddenly aware of Zachary's watching him. "It's Robbie all right," Hager said. "My son."

"Mr. Hager, I'm not feeling well. Could I go up and sit down?"

"Sure." Hager looked at Zachary's face and saw that he was exhausted. No wonder. They had hiked all morning and dug all afternoon. "Zack, maybe when you catch your breath, you can look around for a place to camp."

"You don't want to hike out?" Zack's eyebrows rose, his mouth opened in relief.

Hager laughed softly and patted Zack on the shoulder. "No way, Zack. There's no hurry now."

When Zack had scrambled up and disappeared, Hager wondered what he ought to do. It would be right to pray, or do something solemn, but instead he felt a little giddy. He decided to lay out the body and cover it with snow.

Lifting it again from under the arms, he felt something hard in the jacket pocket. It was zipped shut, and he forced the iced zipper open. Inside, in a single icy ball, he found at least fifty quarters. He looked them over, he turned them, he hefted their weight. Why on earth were they there? The quarters triggered something deep inside him. They were completely Robbie, more than the face of shriveled skin. They made him know, really know, that this was Robbie, his Robbie, who greedily treasured quarters more than anything else. Hager leaned against the snow for a moment, very still in body and mind. *So this is where it ends*, he thought, and found it very hard, though the light was gone and he knew he must, to climb up and find Zack.

He moved with effort while they ate uncooked food, threw their sleeping bags out under the open sky, and built a fire. Hager felt his mind stuffed with thoughts. Neither he nor Zack spoke until he told Zack goodnight and left the firelight to crawl into his bag.

He lay on his back, his eyes trained on the soft banks of numberless stars. Under their calm spell his thoughts began to separate themselves. He knew he was exhausted but also that he was far from sleep. Images paraded in front of him: thoughts of Carrie and how she would respond to this final blow; memories of the television crews he had talked to on the day Robbie had disappeared (would they come back now?); the insistent question of how Robbie had died in this place. A shapeless dread fell over him. He was half convinced someone was moving near their camp. He heard noises; the glow and snapping of the fire seemed intentional, demonic. He nearly called out to Zack, to hear his own voice, to hear Zack's. He closed his jaws and listened, and heard nothing that could not be explained. He mastered himself and lay still, wishing to sleep.

Then his mind returned to the body and to the lump of quarters. They brought him fond thoughts of Robbie. The quarters were a mark distinctively his.

Then, while he thought of them, the quarters' meaning changed. Perhaps they did not mean merely that Robbie had begun that day with his ordinary greedy delight. For quarters could make Robbie do things. Perhaps someone had used them to make him do—what?

He remembered when he had first used them to get

Robbie to pick up his room. You held them out, Robbie would inspect them like a jeweler, then like magic he would do whatever you wanted. He loved those quarters.

Something had made Robbie leave the car, go off into the snow. Quarters? Quarters had always been a fond family thing; nobody had ever tried to get Robbie to do something he shouldn't. They had talked about that; they had joked that Robbie would do anything for them.

It was at that moment that the thought crept in unwelcome. Who knew about the quarters anyway? Only their family, as far as Hager knew. And Mary Ann, he remembered. Who had seen Robbie last on that day?

As soon as the thought came in, he could not get it out. It clung to his mind like an eel in a hole. Stephen had known about those quarters. Stephen had seen Robbie last.

CHAPTER

23

For the last hour Hager and Zachary had been passing day hikers on the trail: families with young children, couples holding hands, people dressed in bright shorts and white tennis shoes. Hager's eyes bored a hole straight ahead on the trail. After hiking since daybreak, they had reached the disappointing, dusty border of the wilderness.

Hager opened the trunk to the Chrysler, and they threw their packs into its deep mouth. As they had expected, the van was gone from the parking lot. Hager smelled his own bitter, nervous sweat. His hands were stinging from small cuts and scrapes. He wondered where Zachary had found the strength to keep up—they had practically run the trail.

Zack dumped himself down right in the dirt behind the car. His shoulders sagged forward; his hands touched the ground as though for balance. He had not complained all day.

The parking lot was a narrow strip bulldozed out of the hill just below the dam. Above, overlooking the lake, was a log-cabin store, selling salmon eggs, fishing tackle, ice, barbecue, potato chips, pocket knives, ammunition, and souvenir ashtrays. Ordinarily, Hager liked to end a trip by buying an ice cream sandwich and sitting on the bench outside. Instead, he got into the car, which smelled of hot vinyl. He stretched on the soft cushions, then stuck the key in the ignition.

The car started hard, coughing and stuttering, dying every time he jerked it into drive. It had been sitting for a week, and the carburetor setting was wrong for the thin air. Hager gave up trying to drive away immediately and let the car roar and splutter, warming up. He glanced over at Zack, who had slumped in beside him and was leaning slightly forward, his mouth open and his eyes exhausted, stark. *Zack will never forget this day*, he thought.

There is no real hurry, Hager said to himself. Robbie's body isn't going anywhere. But immediately he felt the urgent sick sensation he had carried all day. Over and over, helplessly, he had seen Robbie's gray skin, had handled the lump of quarters, had watched the chunks of ice falling into the stream to rush away with the current. He had to see Stephen. He had to know. He pushed the stick into gear and nosed the pedal down. The car hesitated, jerked, and then gave a startling rush of acceleration.

It took nearly two hours to wrench the car down the narrow, twisted road to the first telephone at Hunter Lake. He used an ancient booth on the porch of the Hunter's Lodge, a sagging clapboard rectangle where dances were held in the summer, where he had first danced with Carrie when they were kids. He called the sheriff's department. It was late Saturday afternoon. The dispatcher listened to his story and said she would have to call him back. He told her where he was and said they would find him at home as soon as he could get there. Then he called the Forest Service. He knew they would be involved in bringing the body out. He was halfway through his story when the man on the other end interrupted and asked whether he was the person who had been lost.

"Not exactly lost," Hager said. "We had a problem getting over the bridge at Pewter Creek. It's out, you know. So we went across country."

"But you're out okay."

"Yeah, we're okay. Somebody reported us?"

"Less than half an hour ago. Somebody named Stephen Hager. Is that any relation to you?"

"He's my son. Did he say where he was?"

"He didn't say. He gave me a telephone number." He read off the numbers of the Hager's home phone. "Oh, right. I see that's the same number you gave me."

Hager hung up and hustled to the car. If Stephen had called from this same phone and wasted any time, Hager might catch him on the road.

They came into sight of the van on a long, gentle curve. Even when they were still far behind, Hager began honking the horn. His entire concentration had been on driving, and he had no plan for what he would do and say to Stephen.

The van was poking along, and in a minute they had come up behind and could see heads in the back window. Hager kept honking. He opened his window and put a hand out and up over the car roof, pointing to the side of the road. The air rushed over his hand, warm with valley heat. As they approached a turnout, he took his foot off the gas, anticipating a stop. But the van kept going.

"Oh, for heaven's sake," he muttered. Then to Zack he shouted, "The trouble is, I used to play a trick. I'd get Stephen to pull over and then I'd sail by and beat him home."

He hit the horn again, two sustained notes, and the van honked cheerfully back. "See, he thinks it's a joke," Hager said. Three heads were in the back window, waving and making faces. "Look, Zack," Hager said. "We're coming up on a long straightaway. I'm going to pull alongside. You roll down the window and tell Steve to pull over." Hager began to accelerate even before they came out of the sharp, downward turn. His wheels squealed slightly and he got a good jump. Otherwise he would not have caught up so easily, for Stephen seemed to have accelerated as well.

They came alongside, flying. The trees streaked by. Zachary rolled the window down, leaned out and yelled something. The boys in the van had their heads to the side windows. Hager could see their mouths move; they were yelling and laughing. Stephen was smiling too. He rolled down his window, and Zack shouted to him to pull over. Hager wondered whether he heard.

The van slid forward a few feet as Hager began to let off the gas; then he punched the accelerator and came alongside again. "Tell him we found Robbie," Hager shouted.

Zack yelled, cupping his hands. Inside the van it looked

like pandemonium. The kids were wild. The wind made Zack practically inaudible to Hager. Had Stephen heard?

Just ahead, the road curved blindly around the mountain to the right. Hager began to slow, letting the van slide ahead.

But he heard the van's tires squeal and found himself hurtling up alongside the van again. He put the brakes on harder. This time he was far enough behind to see Stephen's brake lights come on. The van slid dangerously back toward them, and over, across the yellow line toward Hager's front fender, very close. They were to the turn. Zack was shouting, "What are you doing? What are you doing?" Both cars drifted along slowly for a moment; then Hager punched his accelerator, and the Chrysler spurted ahead. A second later Stephen must have done the same to the van, for the Dodge stopped sinking behind them, but hung alongside, a few feet back, coming left, pushing Hager out. They were only inches apart as they went hurtling into the curve.

An RV was suddenly in Hager's vision. Tires screamed; Hager shouted; he pulled the steering wheel hard to the right and slammed the Chrysler into the side of the van. They were thrown sideways, spinning. The tires seemed to scream forever, the RV shot by; somehow by miracle Hager heard no sound from the collision. Then they were still and stopped. Incongruously Hager heard the distant, lazy sound of an airplane buzzing in the distance. He sat, stiff and pale, clasping the steering wheel. Zack was sobbing quietly.

"Are you okay?" Hager asked.

The van was stopped ahead of them, turned backward so that it pointed up the hill on the wrong side of the road, a back wheel off the shoulder. The RV was gone. Somehow, they had missed. Hager started up his engine, for it had stalled in the spin. He pulled alongside the van. "Zack," he said, "ask if everybody's okay."

Zack leaned out. The boy in the passenger seat wanted to babble, but Hager said vehemently, "Zack, find out if anybody is hurt. We've got to get off this curve."

CHAPTER

24

The sun was down when Hager's dented Chrysler swung into his driveway, grinding rock under its wheels. Hager got out, weary, stretching. He had received a double body slam: uncovering the cadaver of one son, having the other try to hurt him. Yet, for the moment, he felt nothing terribly momentous: only the flat, colorless aftermath of grief.

He went around and opened the door on the passenger side of the car. "Come on, Zack, you can't sit there all day. Go inside and call your parents, tell them you're home."

Hager had his first chance to examine the side of the car where it had smashed against the van. He ran a finger along a seam where the metal had buckled, the paint split and peeled. Actually, the evidence was unspectacular, not immediately obvious from a distance, hardly matching the violence he had felt in that collision. How often it had been that way in the last six months: terrible certainties straining inside him but the world unimpressively degrading, rusting rather than exploding. Even today, when the end had come, what did he have to show? A body, shriveled and rubbery, and a dented car.

"What happened?" Carrie had come out so quietly that he was startled by her voice.

"A little accident," he said. "Stephen ran me off the road."

"What?"

He hated having to explain it to her. At least with Stephen he would be driving at something: Let's know the truth. But to talk to Carrie was to let a knife slice him open like a fish's belly, to let his guts slide into public view. He was afraid that she would see this as more fantasy, more obsessional guesswork and amateur sleuthing.

She knew already that he had found Robbie; the sheriff had called. Hager led her into the kitchen, her zone. "Carrie," he said, and heaved a deep breath. "Carrie, I don't know. But I think Stephen must have had something to do with Robbie's death."

The moment he said it, tears filled up her eyes. She squeaked out from her screwed-up face the question of how he could say such a thing. He told her about the quarters. It seemed so flimsy when he said it. He told her about the near-accident on the drive down the mountain, but already she had begun to speculate on who else the quarters might implicate, or whether there might be another reason why Robbie had hung on to them.

"I don't see it," she said in a scolding, parental voice that nonetheless trembled with emotion. "Robbie might have simply had them. Mary Ann told you he had given her the quarters. Maybe he wanted to give them again. You don't know."

Hager heard the sounds echo and reverberate but he could not attend. He held out his arms and went to hold her. She did not become pliable. She was thinking, driving at a means to vindicate her son. She took this as another sign of his lack of love, Hager thought, as he tried to cradle her. He was so willing to believe the worst.

She stopped crying and got herself a Coke out of the refrigerator and poured it into a tall blue aluminum tumbler. Hager watched the beading of moisture on the glass and then noticed that Carrie's hands were shifting, splotching the dew. Did her hands ordinarily fuss?

"You're right," he said, his voice worn. "The quarters don't prove anything. But how do you explain that he tried to kill me?"

Carrie put her finger to her lips, thinking of Lizzie. Hager frowned in annoyance. "It doesn't matter," he said. "That's the smallest of our worries."

"Don't say what you don't know," she burst out harshly and broke into tears again. "You haven't even talked to him," she added feebly. "You're not always right."

"Why is this?" Hager asked, throwing up his hand. "Why do we have to fight? I only want to know. If I'm wrong, I'll be glad."

She spoke more calmly, sipping her Coke. "I always loved this in you. You didn't care whether it was in your interest or not. You wanted to know the truth. If it was zoning or whatever. But then it didn't concern me. It's different now."

Hager had just gotten out of the shower when he heard the van pull in. He stepped back into the tub, clutching a towel around him and slid the glass window open. He could see the driveway.

The boys piled out of the van, shouting and pushing, happy to be back. They had already forgotten the accident. Stephen sat for a moment behind the steering wheel, as though gathering himself, then got out and opened the van's rear doors. He pulled out the packs and stood them against the garage door.

Balzeti was suddenly there too, sidling over to Stephen. Hager felt a shock. He had not heard the car; Balzeti must have parked down the drive.

Hager could not hear what Balzeti and Stephen said. He saw Stephen give his head a little shake and leave to go inside.

"Hi, Steve," Hager said gravely. "You got home." He had put on a blue bathrobe and hurried out of the bathroom without taking time to comb his wet hair. Stephen had his pack slung on one shoulder.

"Yeah. Everybody is okay."

"Where are they all?"

"They're outside, waiting for their parents. I got Mom to call."

"Steve." Hager spoke slowly. He felt as though a great weight dragged on his voice. "Steve, I need to talk to you."

"Dad, I don't know what got into me. It was like I was just

joking and it wasn't a good joke. I just lost it." Stephen did not look directly at him.

For a moment there was a nervous silence. "Well, okay," Hager said. "I need to tell you about finding Robbie's body too."

Stephen shrugged, looking away. "I don't know if I want to hear about that, Dad."

"You need to hear it, Steve."

"Maybe. Can I take a shower right now?"

Hager let him go past him. Dressing, Hager wondered how they would talk, how the issue could be forced. Then he went outside to talk to the sheriff's deputies.

Ramirez was leaning against the car with Balzeti, watching the kids' parents drive up and collect their gear. Hager shook hands with everybody, telling the parents what a great hike they'd had and trying to seem jovial. The parents did not dally; their cars wheeled, backed, and departed, shining pale yellow beams on the trees sheltering the drive.

Zack was the last to go. For a few minutes Hager stood with him, waiting for his mother. He did not know what to say, though he felt he ought to say something. Finally Zack's mother swung up the drive. Zack hesitated and then spoke with deadly seriousness. "Mr. Hager, I'm sorry about all the trouble."

Hager smiled and shook his head. "No trouble, Zack. Just a little adventure. Did you have a good time?"

Zack nodded, and Hager clapped him on the back and told his mother that Zack had done some remarkable hiking in the last two days. "He really showed his stuff," Hager said.

After Zack had gone, Balzeti came over. He acted tender and solicitous as he made arrangements for Hager to go in by helicopter to collect the body. He suggested avoiding the press. "There's no need to contact them. That just feeds them."

Hager had a thought. "Would there be room on the helicopter for one more?" he asked. "I was wondering if my son could go." When Balzeti didn't answer, Hager added, "It would mean a lot to me. If there's any way."

Balzeti seemed to sniff the question all over before answering. "I don't see why not," he said slowly.

Hager tried his best to look directly at Balzeti, as though completely naturally. "It's his brother," he said. "I'd just like him to see where he died."

"Oh, sure," Balzeti said, sounding relieved. "We'll be on the big bird. There's room. He can help identify."

CHAPTER

25

Hager waited for dinner anxiously, avoiding Carrie, avoiding thinking. His instinct was to be out in the car, driving around, but as much as he could not stand to be in the house he could not face being away from it. Stephen was in his room, like a bear in his cave. Hager could not go in to him but could not go off and leave him either.

He went behind the house and shot baskets. The night was still and warm, and the sound of the ball bouncing on concrete rebounded from the stucco of the house with a high, metallic noise. He made himself push, made himself sweat, trying not to think, but his mind kept turning over. He had a terrible taste in his mouth, like the smell of mildewed newspapers, and he swallowed constantly.

Finally he made up his mind to do what had to be done. He went in the back to avoid Carrie, slipping quietly down the hall to Stephen's door. He knocked. After a moment of silence Stephen asked, "Who is it?" and Hager went in.

Stephen was reading, lying on his side on the bed. Hager wordlessly sat down in the desk chair, draping his hands over the plastic armrests.

"Would you sit up, Stephen?" Hager's voice was parental and irritable; he spoke too quickly.

Stephen did what his father said, leaning against the wall and wrapping his arms around his knees. He looked at Hager as though daring him: a look that was simultaneously hostile and disinterested.

"All right." Hager took a breath. "Steve, this is harder for me to say than you will ever know." He gulped another mouth of saliva. "I found the quarters."

Stephen did not change his expression.

"They were in Robbie's pocket. Frozen in a big lump."

"What quarters?"

"Robbie's quarters. From his bank."

"I didn't know they were missing."

Hager let out a sigh. "I'm not playing around."

Stephen made no answer. He continued to look at Hager as though from a great distance.

"Do I have to spell it out, Steve? I know. I know."

A flicker of disgust passed over Stephen's face. "What do you know? Tell me what you know."

Hager looked imploringly into Stephen's soft, handsome brown eyes. "Stephen, who else knew about those quarters? Nobody knew but you and me and your mom and Lizzie. Nobody knew. All that time we couldn't understand what got those boys to go into the snow."

"So now you know? Do you, Dad? Then why are you talking to me about it?"

Hager lowered his eyes and was silent for a few beats. He took another swallow. "I love you, Steve. I can't bear doing this."

"Oh. Thank you for doing it despite yourself."

Hager stood up, stopped short for a moment, and then reached and ripped a poster off the wall. It was the girl in the see-through T-shirt. Pure oxygen-fed adrenaline surged in his chest. He wadded the poster into a ball. He threw the wadded paper at the window. "Stephen!" he shouted. "You're killing me!" Then he seized Stephen's arm, putting his nose an inch from his face. "I've lost one son." His voice was trembling. "I don't want to lose another."

"I think," Stephen said, his eyes flicking away, "you should have thought of that long ago."

"What do you mean by that?" They were so close that their faces almost touched.

"I mean it's a little late to be telling me you love me. Of course you love me. I'm what's left."

Hager let go of Stephen's arm. Grief filled him heavily like sickness. "Is that really what you think? It's not right, Stephen. I've always loved you."

"Then where were you?"

"Where was I?"

"When you were out with Robbie, did you just forget me?" Stephen's lips barely split open to say it.

"Stephen, Robbie needed me. You don't have to put yourself in competition with a retarded kid."

"I don't appreciate your coming in here like my best friend."

Hager's anger lit again. He leaned forward. "Well, get this. I'm not here trying to be your best friend. I came to find out why you killed your brother."

Stephen's voice rose louder than Hager's. "I didn't kill my brother! He died of the cold!"

"Oh, sure. After you sent him there."

"How did I send him? You're crazy."

"With those quarters! He'd do anything for those quarters!"

A light of horrified recognition struck Stephen's face even as he shouted an answer. "I didn't!"

Then they were quiet. "Your mother will hear us," Hager said softly.

"She doesn't know what you're thinking?"

"She doesn't know I'm talking to you."

Stephen sat back against the wall, drew his knees up to his chin, and seemed to withdraw from the world.

What do you do now? Hager asked himself. Stephen seemed to diminish, drawing away. Hager shook his head to make the hallucination stop.

Stephen was right. He was too late.

"I know I haven't been a good father to you, Steve." It was so difficult to push the words out. "It was never intended. I was just . . . thoughtless. But Robbie's gone now. I love you. I want to start over. But I can't just act as though nothing went on."

"Why not?" Stephen said, his voice slow, low, almost lazy. "You're not going to get Robbie back."

Hager's misery rose out of the background again, spreading over him. "Because I have to know," he said, stubbornly holding on to that one certainty. "I have to know so I can deal with it."

"Dad, I'm going to college. You don't have to deal with it. Just let it pass."

Hager remembered saying things to his father like that. He remembered saying them in the cool, lace-doily-speckled parlor. He could remember the dead weight of his father's concerns and his own desire to shed them, to get out, to go.

"It's not that simple, Stephen. You have to deal with me." He meant that no one ever sheds his father's concerns like he thinks he can, but when the words came out, he realized that they sounded threatening, and he almost took them back. Yet he was unsure that he could. There was another question. He would have to decide what to tell Balzeti, if anything. He wanted to say to Stephen that it would be just between them, but how could it be? This was murder.

Stephen took Hager's words the wrong way, as a threat. "If you knew anything, I would deal with you," he said. "But you don't know anything."

Stephen's face, however, belied his tough words. He looked pale, slight, uncertain, stunned. He looked as though he might have been hit at the base of his spine with a ballpeen hammer. Hager knew he had the kid, but he could not go on. His rage had left him. He averted his eyes and then, after a time, he began to weep.

CHAPTER

26

Hager stooped, burying his head into his shoulders as he trotted to the helicopter. He couldn't help it—the wash of the prop over his head was so near. Balzeti, following him, tried to keep his shoulders straight, but he, too, let them slump down, tensed for the blow that could pop his head off. And then Stephen came. Hager watched him walk as erectly as he would if he were strolling into the hardware store.

In the orange and black dawn there were no clouds. Far away, the straight black horizon was broken by a row of palm trees, their shaggy heads dancing like musical notes above the bass line of the earth. Still, cool air carried the musky smell of the fields. This was the best time in a Fresno summer day. The air still held the chill of the desert night, but the silent, even flow of orange into the sky promised heat.

The pilot looked over the banks of dials and switches, occasionally adjusting something with a quick girlish touch. The sun came up. For just these few minutes they could see the mountains clearly, a sawblade silhouette of surprising height. They would disappear in the day's haze.

The helicopter lifted, and in seconds they were looking down on the toy, rectangled farmland with lone trees casting hundred-foot shadows. They headed into the sun. Soon straight lines began to fold into rounded contours, and then lines disappeared altogether as the farmland failed and they crossed the dry, white-yellow foothills.

The mountains looked barren, the peaks pimply; their particular beauties were invisible from above. Leaning over the map so he could guide the co-pilot, Hager found himself speechless, recognizing terrain only after the co-pilot pointed to it on the map. Even when they found the rock-choked valley and he saw the blue-and-orange postage stamps of the ponchos they had left to mark the place, he could hardly believe it was the spot. As the helicopter hovered down, the valley seemed to come out of disguise.

Hager knew that the rock was flat enough for landing, but they did not trust his judgment. The paramedic threw a rope out the doorway and lowered himself to the ground. A few minutes later he waved for the helicopter to descend. The noise of the engine pounded up from the ground. Hager watched the prop wind whip his orange poncho. It was weighted with rocks, but one end came free and the poncho rolled and writhed to the bushes, where it hung up. Then they bumped the ground, settled, bumped again, and were down. The pilot killed the engine and the rotor swished into silence.

Hager led them to the bank of the river and pointed out the lump of snow where Robbie's body lay. It was undisturbed though already clothes showed through where the snow was melting. Balzeti scrambled down, then called for the co-pilot. Stephen stood with his hands in his pockets, showing nothing. Hager thought that if he were in that position he would be burning, splintering into fragments, but Stephen showed nothing. Balzeti was gesturing, calling him down. They must have cleared the face. Stephen descended slowly, then stooped over the body.

Hager had hoped to force something but saw that he had been foolish. Stephen was too strong. He would reveal nothing.

Hager walked away and sat on the bed of rock near the helicopter. The sun had not come up from behind the ridge, and the granite under his hand was cold. He wondered whether he should have left the body here, never telling anyone. Robbie might have stayed a secret for a hundred years.

It still lay in his hands. One word to Balzeti and it would

be beyond his control, but here and now, in this chilly mountain canyon, where his first-born son lay by the surging river, where his second-born looked cooly at the face of the brother he must have killed, somehow here and now the knowledge had not escaped and it could remain locked up still.

Only it was not locked up now. It was out and loose between him and Stephen. And Carrie too.

And then Hager thought, *It has never been locked up. It has been in Stephen's mind.* Hager did not know how a person could live with such facts.

Balzeti and the co-pilot staggered toward the helicopter with the black, zipped body bag. They lashed it to the skids. Hager watched the sunlight slowly creep across the valley floor toward him. Stephen stood by himself. Balzeti came over and Hager jumped to his feet.

"Time to go?" he asked.

"Not just yet," Balzeti answered. "I need to make a thorough search of the area. I don't expect to come back." He pulled a zipped plastic bag out of his jacket pocket. "Does this mean anything to you?" The bag was full of quarters.

Hager did his best to smile calmly. "Yeah. I found those too. In his pocket, right? Robbie had a thing about quarters. He just loved them."

"Did he usually carry this many around?"

For just a moment Hager wanted to spill his misery, to open up all that he knew and feared. He teetered on the edge of that abyss for an instant, then pulled back. He was not ready, he could not see what result would come.

"Not usually," he said, taking a deep breath, "as far as I know. He usually kept a lot in a bank in his room. He just liked them." He wondered whether he should mention Mary Ann but kept his peace. The less Balzeti went around asking questions, the more likely nothing would disturb them.

"Do you know if he was planning on buying anything?"

Hager thought. "Not that I know of."

"Where did he get them?"

"Well, I would give them to him. Or my wife. It was kind of a family joke. Robbie always wanted quarters."

The sun broke on them, and immediately warmth penetrated the thin cold. Balzeti looked at the quarters, shrugged, and put them away. "Do you think they could have anything to do with the murder?"

Hager saw that Stephen was, despite himself, watching, listening from the spot where he stood with his hands in his pockets. Seeing Stephen's taut, attentive face erased any remaining doubt. Hager felt as though he were dying, every living cell in his body surrendering to the sorrow.

Struggling, though, he kept up appearances. "Not that I can think of," Hager said. "I hope you're a better detective than I am." It sounded false, but evidently Balzeti was unsuspicious.

As Balzeti walked away back toward the river, Hager glanced at Stephen, hoping their eyes would meet, hoping for some sign of gratitude. But Stephen had turned away and was flipping stones into the bushes.

CHAPTER

27

In the night, the Mono wind came up. Hager heard it soughing softly in the pines in front of the house and then leaning its steady, hot weight down the canyon. The bedroom grew stuffy, so he threw off his covers and lay in his short pajamas. Carrie slept quietly, curled on her edge of the bed. Hager thought of how he had sometimes wakened Robbie when he was a baby, just to play with him.

He got up, slid into a bathrobe, and padded down the dark hall. He had halfway hoped that Stephen's light might be on, but there was no glow from under his door. Did he sleep under these circumstances?

They had driven home in silence. A dozen times Hager had begun to speak but then remembered Stephen's quiet, contained posture as he stood with his hands in his pockets overhearing Hager deny that he knew what the quarters meant. Every time he remembered, Hager felt such a sense of revulsion he was afraid to speak. When he spoke, it would be terrible, trembling, annihilating.

Hager poured a glassful of milk, then dumped it into a saucepan on the stove. Turning it on low, he stirred the milk with a teaspoon until bubbles formed around the edge; then he poured it carefully back into the glass. He added chocolate powder and slurped down the sweet mixture.

The milk coated his teeth, and he could taste mildew underneath the chocolate. He was full of fatigue, yet nervous with energy. He would never get to sleep. It was too late to find anything on TV. He did not want to read. He would have to think about Stephen despite a powerful desire to escape those thoughts.

Let's face it, he told himself, trying to be objective, *I have not been a good father to Stephen.* Stephen felt neglected. He said so. Maybe he had said so to kick a little guilt away from himself and toward Hager. Motives aside, it was a terrible thing to say. It was a terrible thing to do, neglecting a son.

But why did Hager feel, nevertheless, that *he* had been mistreated?

He made a fist of his large right hand and squeezed it until the fingers turned the color of plums, then he banged it softly on the plastic top of the kitchen table. He was the one who had been hurt by this boy with the sullen, accusing attitude, who always acted as if help were unwanted. His attitude must be a defense mechanism, because every son wants his father's approval, so they said. But what did that help?

Hager would have loved to cry—Carrie would have. Stephen felt unloved? Well, join the human race.

He put his head into his hands, leaning forward over the table. The key question, the one he had to decide soon, was what to tell Balzeti, if anything.

Would he go down and sit at Balzeti's cluttered desk? What would he say?

The near-accident would mean nothing. The quarters, Hager was sure, meant something, but they proved nothing. Balzeti might write it all down and do nothing. But more likely he would want to know more. He would want to talk to Stephen, of course. Stephen would admit nothing.

It would be even more shameful—to go and accuse your son and not be believed.

What did the quarters prove? Could they have made Robbie walk all those miles in the snow? Why, if he already had them? If he had them in his pocket, their power was gone. Unless someone had been with him and had given them to him much later—after he had done the walking. But then it could not have been Stephen. Stephen had been in bed.

Yet he had seen Stephen's face. Stephen knew. He was not imagining that. But knew what?

Hager listened to the wind blowing. In the back of the house something fell—perhaps a branch knocked off by the wind. Hager wanted to sleep, to forget.

He got up, carefully rinsing his glass in the sink, and then did something that he had not planned. It seemed to come to him spontaneously as though he were sleepwalking. He went down the hall. He paused in front of Lizzie's door. His heart was hammering. He opened the door slightly, felt around the inside doorknob and pushed in the lock. It made a small noise: *thunk*. He quietly pulled the door shut, and when he reached the kitchen again his adrenaline surged and he was almost dizzy with fear and excitement.

Until that moment fear had not occurred to him. He had not thought that Stephen was dangerous, that in this night they were sleeping with a killer.

No, he thought, *we cannot go on. It cannot be endured.*

Moments later Hager heard a door open down the hall. For a time he could not discern any further sound; then he recognized quiet footsteps. Stephen came into the doorway, fully clothed, squinting in the light, his hair disheveled. Automatically Hager sat up rigid, ready for anything. Then he was ashamed of his fear, and he made himself sit back.

"Can't sleep?" Hager asked, acting innocent, and pulled out a chair.

Stephen sat down softly. "You locked Lizzie's door," he said. "I heard you." His face was hostile, implacable. "I'm not the monster you think I am."

"How am I supposed to know what you are?" Hager said. "You won't talk to me."

"I am your son," Stephen said. "Your flesh and blood. That might count for something."

"I can't help it, Steve. I don't know what you did, and I don't know what you'll do next. What should I think? Why don't you just tell me what happened?" Hager's voice had a pleading tone; he wondered how he came to this loss of dignity. He wanted to fall on Stephen's neck with tears like the father of the Prodigal Son, but Stephen's neck was rigid and his look warned Hager away.

"Because I don't know whether I can trust you."

"You want me to trust you, but you don't want to trust me? It won't work that way, Steve. You can't have it both ways."

"You threatened to turn me in to the police."

"Oh, Stephen." Hager's voice was exasperated, but he still heard himself pleading; he could not stop it. "I don't remember saying anything like that. All I want is to know what happened."

Stephen spoke softly. "I'll tell you, Dad. I'm ready to tell you. Just listen. Please listen." When he had said it, he stopped short as though he could not catch his breath. He groaned.

"What did you say?" Hager asked.

"Nothing, nothing. Let me tell."

"Wait," Hager said. He stood up. "Let me wake up your mom." He put a hand softly on Stephen's shoulder. "You don't want to have to tell this twice," Hager said.

He walked softly to their room and stood over Carrie a moment before shaking her awake. Ruefully he thought, *So this is my triumph.* "Carrie," he said softly. "Come out to the kitchen. Stephen wants to talk with us."

She seemed to understand though she did not answer; she got out of bed. Hager did not wait while she put on a robe but went out quickly to Stephen, feeling a mixture of anxiety and horror and excitement. Stephen was staring ahead and did not look at him. "Mom's coming," Hager said. "Can I get you anything to drink?"

Carrie shuffled out in her bathrobe and slippers, stopped to try to open her eyes, seeming to say by her expression, Why are we doing this? She scowled and sat down, pulling the chair away from the table, equidistant from the two of them. "I'm listening," she said.

Stephen still looked ahead into space, absorbed in some invisible drama. His lips were parted, but no sound came. He seemed to hang, poised on the brink of confession.

Finally he blurted out something. "Robbie hated me," he said, as though he had been waiting to say it all his life. He spoke violently, accusingly, addressing Hager. "You thought Robbie was incapable of that. You thought you knew Robbie so well, but there was a lot you didn't know. He was deceitful. With you, most of all. He hated me. You'll never believe that."

"I don't know." Hager answered slowly, as though the words were dragged up out of his throat with a hook. "I could believe almost anything. Tell me."

"He was jealous. You'll never know how much he wanted to be normal. He wanted to be like me. He loved Mary Ann. He wanted her. He would always hug her, and it wasn't platonic. Robbie wanted to be normal, in a really pathetic way; he wanted a wife and a family; he wanted a regular job that he drove to in a station wagon every day. He wanted a house."

Hager gave a quick, miniature shake to his head, like a spooked horse. He was puzzled and uncertain where this would lead.

"I made a big mistake one time," Stephen said. "I told Robbie that you loved him more than me. Which you will have to admit is true, but I should never have told him. To Robbie there was no such thing as your subjective opinion. You were God. If you loved him more, he was better. Or . . ." Stephen searched for the right word. "He thought I should feel that stick in my throat for the rest of my life. For once he had beaten me." Stephen flicked his eyes to his father. "You didn't know that side of Robbie, did you, Dad? He was jealous."

Hager stirred himself and asked as though to himself, "How can a retarded kid be jealous?"

"But he didn't think of himself that way," Stephen said. "He was trying to get his just like anybody else."

The sound of the wind was still beating the trees. Hager glanced at Carrie but her face was absolutely neutral, impassive.

"Where does this lead us, Stephen?" Hager asked.

"Just wait. Just listen. You'll see." Stephen sounded almost eager, now that his words were pouring out. "There's another part you never knew about. When we lived in Fresno and we had to move? A lot of that was me. Robbie had some reasons to hate me."

Hager leaned forward, his big shoulders leading the rest of his body. "What? A lot of what was you?"

"The fooling around. The hazing, I guess you call it."

"Yeah, I know. Your mom told me." He glanced again at Carrie.

"Not just me. All the kids in the neighborhood. Robbie wouldn't let us alone. He was always bugging us. He would destroy my things. The other kids didn't want to play with him, they called him the vegetable. And I was supposed to defend him. I always had to take his side."

"Why?" Carrie said. "Who said?"

"Because of him!" Stephen said, enraged, pointing at Hager. "He set such an example. We all had to live our lives like it was church!"

Hager half rose in his chair, shooting back. "So you tormented him? When you knew what it was doing to him?"

"Yeah." Stephen spoke more softly, sitting back. He was not willing to face up to Hager; he seemed suddenly not proud. "It got out of hand, and I didn't know how to stop it. I was just a kid."

"You could have told me."

"Yeah. But I was afraid."

"Afraid of what?"

For a couple of beats there was silence. Then, "Afraid you would hate me."

"Hate you?" Hager stood up, walked across the kitchen to the refrigerator, opened it, looked in, shut it, and came back again. Stephen's eyes tracked him carefully.

"I think I get the picture," Hager said. "You and your brother were rivals." He paused and shook his head. "So you just lost control? You got angry and ran him off the road?" He glanced up at Stephen, a look like nausea on his lips.

"No, no. Dad. Please listen." Stephen's anger had vanished. He hesitated, looking intently at his father, then seemed to give it up. He stood up from his chair. "Maybe this is a waste of time."

Hager did not say anything.

"No," Carrie said, firmly, her voice coming up from some

dim wasteland. "Sit down, Stephen. You've started. Now finish."

Stephen sat back down.

"Robbie found out," Stephen said slowly. "He knew about Mary Ann."

CHAPTER
28

On Saturday afternoon Mary Ann told Stephen that she was pregnant. It came out of the blue, thoroughly shocking him, so he could barely speak. The next morning, in church, he was nearly hallucinating, imagining that everyone knew, that the pastor would point him out and accuse him. He began to scream self-pitying phrases at himself, like "It's not fair!" but of course it was fair; hadn't he been the one to sleep with her? It was perfectly logical, and nothing stood out as disturbing the organization of the universe, yet it threatened to throw him into the unpredictable, the uncontrollable.

He kept imagining that it would stop, just vanish, but every time he came around a corner it was there again just the same. All that week large bright shapes moved in front of Stephen's eyes, voices spoke, even his own voice sounded as though it came from someone else. None of it seemed to touch him.

On Monday after school he saw Mary Ann and told her she had to get an abortion. She looked at him sweetly, like a mother. Mary Ann seemed untroubled, almost pleased by the pregnancy. *She is living in a dream*, he thought; she always had, but he had liked it before. She said gently that she wouldn't consider taking the life of a *living* thing.

"I'm a living thing," he said. "You're a living thing. That is a *fetus*."

"It has a heartbeat. The doctor said I could hear it in eight more weeks."

"We can make a thousand more of those. Anytime. We cannot make up for what we do to ourselves."

That was his first brush with rage, the urge to catch her and make sweetness disappear. He trembled. He frightened himself, but not, apparently, her. She was full of the living thing. He told her she could ruin her life, but his urgent words appeared not to connect to her attention. She moved and spoke from another country.

By Tuesday Robbie knew. Stephen was lying on his bed, reading, when Robbie barged in like a bull, talking in the deep, blunt voice he used when he wanted to be annoying. "How's your penis?" he asked. "Does it feel powerful?"

Stephen somehow kept the surprise and alarm out of his face. "What are you talking about?" he asked. You never could give an inch to Robbie. He would take it as an advantage.

"How many times did you do it? You can get her pregnant in just one time, you know."

Stephen did not give in, did not open up a crack. But Robbie knew. If he had been in any doubt, he would have shown it, but he was all bumptious energy, envying Stephen's sexual potency, demanding to know details, and jubilant at being in on the secret. He loved to know something he wasn't supposed to know, especially something about Stephen.

Until that moment Stephen had still hoped that somehow the damage could be contained. Now she was telling people.

Robbie would not quit parading around the room asking questions. Stephen treated him cautiously because if provoked he would cry or bellow and their father would be there. The realization that this was what he cared about, this was what caused his fear, made Stephen dizzy with hatred. He wanted so much to tell his father to take a leap.

"He guessed it, Stephen," Mary Ann said the next day. "Isn't that amazing? I think they have other senses, maybe that we all have but haven't developed. Like blind people learn to hear better? He just came up at school and put his hand on my stomach and said, 'Are you going to have a baby?' I was so surprised. I just said, 'How did you know?' and he smiled so proudly."

"He was thinking about how he'd like to sleep with you. That's all. It was his way of asking if you were having sex with me. He was jealous. You were dumb to answer him."

That disappointed her. "Oh, is that it?" she asked sadly. "I suppose you're right. Why was he thinking about such a thing?"

"He's a human being. They didn't castrate him."

She said nothing, only kept her small, wan smile, with one hand draped across her stomach as though waiting for a signal. Stephen left abruptly so as not to shout at her.

After that, the window through which he saw the world seemed to grow smaller. He could hardly pay attention to what went on outside when inside his own shouting thoughts gained weight and color. Stephen drove around, submitting to these thoughts, not knowing where he was going. He was startled to find toward the end of the week that he was nearly out of gas. Where had he gone to burn so much fuel?

Robbie would not quit. Robbie hated to be sealed off. He grew louder and more insistent that Stephen share the secret with him. At one point Stephen seriously considered telling him the truth, or something close to the truth. But that would never work. When Robbie knew a secret, he was so full of it he spilled over. Besides, his interest was more than curiosity; the more advantage he had the more he would press it.

So, without knocking, Stephen went into Robbie's room on Thursday and took his bank down from the shelf. Robbie was seated at his desk, his transistor radio next to his ear, writing down KYNO's top forty as they were announced. He did this every week.

"What are you doing?" he asked. Stephen never came into his room.

"In a minute," Stephen said, opening the back of the bank with a screwdriver and pouring the quarters into a plastic bag. He put the bank back on the shelf and tied the end of the plastic bag in an overhand knot. Robbie was frantic, asking questions, grabbing at the bag, but Stephen calmly fended him off. He put the bag in his jacket pocket.

"I'm going to keep your quarters," he said. "I'm not going to spend them, and I'm not going to lose them. I'm going to keep them for you, just to make sure that you don't talk to anybody about Mary Ann. Not one word. Not even to me. Every time you think of her, just think of these quarters."

Stephen went to his room to wait and see whether his gamble would work. Robbie might have bellowed and gone immediately to his father and then everything would have come out. Instead, he followed Stephen into his room. He tried to take the quarters back, but Stephen handled him just by slapping his hands away. He did not want to hurt him. He said nothing except, "Just remember. Not one word. The quarters are safe so long as you keep completely quiet."

Finally Robbie stopped grabbing and looked at Stephen with his big, dumb blue eyes full of astonishment. "You're mean," he said.

"If you say so."

"You're not allowed to touch my quarters."

"I'll worry about that," Stephen said. "I'm not going to lose them if you keep quiet."

That evening, at the dinner table, their father asked Stephen whether he would take Mary Ann to the game on Friday, and Robbie smirked broadly. Later on that evening, Stephen went into Robbie's room and told him to follow. They went into the backyard, to a concrete pad where a well had been abandoned years before when they got city water. Stephen took the plastic bag of quarters, opened it, extracted one, and dropped it into the unsealed casing. They heard it zinging down, then splashing a hundred feet below. "That's for making a face at dinner," Stephen said and walked back into the house. When Robbie cried out, he turned and said, "Do you want to lose some more right now?"

For that night and the next day, Stephen felt that he was regaining control. Chaos could be matched with intelligence and persistence and some luck. But then, at the basketball game, his design unraveled.

The gym was packed, warm and busy with basketball. The yellow floor and the banks of lights shone like poured honey; people murmured and mingled as in a hive. Stephen loved basketball for the sound of a ball bouncing on wood, for the silent, breath-held instant when a sphere hung in the air above the net. He was able to forget about his troubles a little until Paul's bellowing began.

Stephen was responsible by habit. He found the boys and extricated them, threading through the crowd and out into the cold, wet air, keeping them away from Harris and his drunken shouting, steering them into the chicken place. He paid for a bucket just to pacify them.

They sat crowded into a booth in the deserted restaurant: Paul, with his little pig eyes and stubby white mustache, rocking his body to an unheard beat; Pete and his thick shoulders and heavy head leaning over the table as he gnawed the chicken; Donnie's long red hair and his pianist's hands running thoughtlessly through it; Robbie, his melon-shaped blond head dominated by a frown; and Mary Ann, quietly squeezed between the bigger, thicker bodies. The four ate chicken as fast as they could, grabbing a new piece while there were still shreds of meat on the last one, throwing chicken bones back into the box.

Robbie pointed at Mary Ann with a chicken wing. "What are you going to do with her now?" he asked Stephen. He took the wing and rubbed it lewdly against his finger.

"Shut up, Robbie," Stephen said.

"He thinks he's the boss of everyone," said Robbie.

"Remember what I have," Stephen said. Robbie glowered at him, lowering his head like a bull, but he said nothing. The others raised their eyes from the chicken as though they heard a far-off trumpet. They wanted to know what Stephen had.

"Never mind," Stephen said. "It's between me and Robbie."

"You're not allowed to take them," Robbie said. "You're going to be in trouble."

"Will you shut up?" Stephen said, feeling the pent-up pressure in his arms, wanting to rise, to strike.

Mary Ann put her hand on Stephen's arm. "What is he talking about?" she asked.

"Have some chicken," Stephen said grimly.

"Stephen and Mary Ann sitting in a tree, K-I-S-S-I-N-G,"

sang Robbie. He had a mean, sly look, a slight crooked smile on his lips.

"What does he have? What does he have?" Paul asked.

"I can't tell you, but he's going to be sorry he has them."

"Come on, tell me."

"Robbie," Stephen warned. "You're going to lose them. Let's change the subject right now."

When they left the chicken place, the first flurries of snow were falling. Stephen pulled Robbie into a corner behind the door. "You've got to shut up," he said. "I'll give you the quarters if you'll promise to be quiet." Normally, looking at Robbie's face, he could see a problem working its way to an answer as plainly as an Etch-a-Sketch. But in the corner it was too dark.

"Okay," Robbie said belligerently. "Give me."

"Do you promise?"

"Yeah, I promise."

Stephen took out the bag and untied it, then poured the quarters into Robbie's hand, waited for him to put the first handful in his pocket, and poured some more. "Remember you promised," he said when they were all stowed away.

Robbie didn't respond.

"Zip up your pocket," Stephen said.

While Stephen drove Mary Ann home, she talked with her hand looped softly around his arm on the steering wheel, but he could not take in what she said. He was glad for her hand; he felt that he was losing contact with the human world and that she was a last remnant of warmth.

Robbie would tell. They had joked in the family about what he would do for quarters, and probably their father had genuinely wondered and worried about it, but now Stephen knew that quarters had only limited power.

"If only you hadn't told him," he said vehemently.

"Why does that worry you so much?" she said. "Nobody cares about the boy."

He did not respond, but he thought, *it's true. Nobody cares. People talk, but they forget.*

Then, on his way home after leaving Mary Ann, he came on Robbie's car. The lights were out and both left wheels were on the road, so he might easily have hit it. The right rear wheel was flat. The four were standing around with pieces of the jack in their hands. Already a glazing of snow coated the road, and huge misshapen flakes were lumbering down. Peter was whimpering because he was cold. No one knew how to put the jack together. Stephen grabbed it from their hands.

Peter said something he did not hear, and the others laughed.

"What was that?" Stephen asked. But Peter did not respond; he looked at the others and smirked.

Stephen fitted the jack's pieces together and set it under the bumper. The metal was cold. He took the tire iron and stuck the sharp end into the jack's bracket, then ratcheted it up to the bumper.

"He pumps pretty good," Peter said ummistakably. When Stephen looked over at him, he was pumping away with his groin. The others were laughing.

"Shut up," Stephen shouted, and they laughed at him. Paul was rocking back and forth with silent laughter; Stephen could see his silhouette against the car lights. The glare magnifying the blundering flakes, blinded Stephen from seeing anything more. But he did not need to see. He could hear. Robbie had told them. He must have.

The four were watching him from a little distance, as though to elude his reach. Stephen wanted to smash Robbie. He wanted to smash him and then give up, stop his efforts to keep the secret. He would submit to chaos.

"Was she easy, Steve?" That was Donnie's earnest voice. They were genuinely curious, not hostile.

"Yeah, Steve, like did she touch you on that secret spot?" They all laughed like fourth graders.

Stephen continued to jack up the car, to lift the pancaked tire slowly off the pavement. He was not in the habit of surrender; he did not know how. There were no more jibes, only silence as he pulled off the tire, set the spare into place, and tightened the lug nuts.

Robbie spoke again. "Was she good for you like she was

for me, Steve?" And he laughed. Of course he would want the others to think he had done as much as Stephen had.

Stephen finished, and the car sagged to its ordinary posture. He stuck the flat in the trunk with the jack and walked over to Robbie.

"You told!" Stephen said softly, urgently. "What did you tell them for? You had no right." He punched Robbie, once, in the stomach. Robbie bowed over in silence and for a long moment stayed that way. When he straightened up, Stephen saw his look of fear—just for a moment it showed in the car lights—and then Robbie turned slightly and his face was invisible.

"You hit me!" Robbie said. He was still gulping breath.

"You told them. You promised."

"You're not allowed to touch my quarters! I'm telling Dad as soon as I get home."

"Give the quarters back to me."

Robbie began to back up onto the road. Just then Stephen heard the sound of an approaching car and before he knew what he was doing, leaped forward, grabbing Robbie and pulling him forcefully off the pavement, though Robbie struggled artlessly to get away. A pickup swished by, leaving dark tracks in the skin of snow. Robbie was still struggling to escape Stephen's bear hug, and Stephen let him go.

"I'm not going to hurt you, you retard," he said in disgust. "Didn't you see that truck?"

The falling snow was audible, registering slight scratches as it sifted through the trees overhead.

"We've got to go," Stephen said. "Your spare is almost bald. I want you to follow me very closely so you don't get stuck. And look, Robbie, I gave you the quarters back. Be fair. You shouldn't have told. Now you tell your buddies to keep quiet about it. It's not a joke." He said it desperately, knowing that it would do no good.

CHAPTER

29

The snow was not dangerous, not yet. It was heavy and wet, almost melting, and their tires cut through it easily. Stephen drove slowly, and Robbie, who had little experience driving in snow, stayed locked on his tail. With everything blanketed in white, Stephen could not see the edge of the road, and the flakes shot at him out of the darkness like white tracers.

Tamarack Road came into his vision suddenly, and he took it on an impulse, without a plan. He merely held the wheel straight and was on it, and soon they were climbing uphill. Robbie would not know where they were. He would not know that they had left the road. The germ of a plan came to Stephen. Let him become confused. Let him get scared. He needs a scare. The quarters were not enough.

Stephen was not really worried about the snow; they had plenty of traction still, and anyway there were chains. The road was tricky in spots, and he enjoyed driving it, even slowly with Robbie's lights filling his mirror. He went a little faster to make Robbie feel his limits, and when he saw Robbie slip sideways through a turn, he laughed out loud. Oh, yes, he would scare him. He wondered if Robbie had realized yet that he was lost.

When they went up the long grade below the ridge, gaining altitude, the snow turned a degree colder, and Stephen began to lose traction, spinning his wheels. They could not go much farther without chains. He let up on the gas and slowed to a stop. The snow was beginning to pile up on the edges of the windshield.

He got out of the car and walked back, knocked on Robbie's window. Robbie rolled it down. Stephen slowly leaned over, feeling his heart slamming blood into his head.

"Do you know where we are?" he asked softly.

Robbie hesitated and then remained silent.

"You're lost," Stephen said. "You're lost in a snowstorm. You need help, lots of help, Robbie." He reached into the car, turned off the ignition and pulled out the keys. He held them up, jingled them, then turned, and with all his might threw them down the hill. They disappeared into the dark without a sound. Stephen grasped Robbie's arm. "If you don't keep promises, you can lose more than quarters. Think about it," he said and turned to stride quickly to his car. Hurrying, excited, frightened, he slammed the door, stuck the car in gear, wheeled forward and back and forward again to turn around, and drove down the road. He passed Robbie's car already covered with a glazing of flakes so heavy that he could not see inside. Stephen lumbered down the hill as fast as he could.

The first tears seeped into the corners of his eyes as he drove down Tamarack Ridge, and then a tide of sobs tremored through his chest and he could not stop. He was scared to death. Barely able to see, he had to slow the car, and when he reached the junction with the main road he stopped altogether, turned off the lights, and tried to let his emotions go. People always said that it did you good to get it out. As soon as he tried, however, the tears stopped and he was left with a horrible, consuming fear. He would be swallowed up.

Almost immediately he turned the car around and started back up the hill. Stephen had a key to the Chrysler on his ring; he could hand it to Robbie and warn him never to say a word about Mary Ann again. It would not work. But he knew of nothing else to do.

The car was slipping. The snow was turning colder and falling faster. To get up the hill he might have to put on chains, which would take time. Against all his defenses fear was rising; he had done the wrong thing. He had acted on impulse, without a plan. Stupid. The differential spun one way and then the other. He threw the wheel back and forth. A mistake could put him in the ditch. Get stuck and, oh, then he would be royally screwed up.

Which he deserved. From start to finish he had been screwing up. He swore at Mary Ann. If she had only kept quiet. If she had only left him alone in the first place.

He came out of the last curve and built momentum for the hill. There must be four inches of snow; he was fishtailing but he could still control it. He felt a small kick of satisfaction as he realized that he would make it, that he could drive in these conditions. Finally Robbie's car came into his headlights, covered with snow like a white boulder. Stephen scrunched to a stop twenty feet behind and went striding forward, twisting the extra key eagerly off his key ring. The cold, wet air filled his lungs and stung his cheeks. He would have to help them get chains on.

He had to brush away snow to find the door handle. He jerked it open, expecting to see the four sitting mute and scared. The car was empty. A swell rolled through his body, like the feeling when somebody jumps out at you without warning. The overhead light showed the car interior shut in by the snow like a tiny cave. They had vanished.

Stephen called out into the darkness. "Robbie! Robbie! I'm here!" He reached into the car and blew the horn. The sound was muffled up in falling snow. His car's headlights barely broke through, and for a moment Stephen thought that he himself might be in danger. But no, he knew where he was and there was no immediate threat. It was not too cold. Someone could last a long time in this weather. They could not be far, either. How much time had passed since he left them? *Twenty minutes, maximum,* he thought.

He reached into the Chrysler and flicked on the headlights. They did not seem to shine at all, which puzzled him until he went forward and saw that the lamps were blanketed with snow. He brushed them off and a dim flare of light broke out into the road ahead. Looking along its path, he could see footprints nearly filled in by the snow but sharply visible because the light's angle set their depths in shadow. They had gone ahead. They must have decided to walk for it. Naturally, they had chosen the wrong way.

He ran back to his car, slammed the door, put it in gear. He had to rock his way into motion. Then he fishtailed, yawing slowly across the road until he got control and built a little speed forward. He wondered if he should put on chains. But now that he was moving he hated to stop; and they might be just ahead somewhere, huddled up. Could they be hiding from him? *No*, he thought. *They must have panicked.*

The car resolved his question about chains by edging into a sideways slide; suddenly he was turning 360 degrees slowly, soundlessly. His right rear tire hit something on the edge of the road, hard, and he stopped. The engine had quit. He started it again and everything seemed to be fine, but when he tried moving, his wheels spun helplessly.

Since he could not drive onto the chains, they had to be inched painstakingly under the tires. He had no flashlight, and his hands burned from the cold. He went from the driver's seat to the rear wheels dozens of times, nursing the clutch to nudge the wheels an inch or two, then tearing at the chains and snow with his fingers. Finally he got them on. Even then the wheels spun until he found rocks and jammed them under the left side and was able to rock the car up on top of them and move ahead.

By then the footprints were invisible. The clear pockmarks he had seen in the roadway fifteen minutes before were completely gone. He drove slowly up the road, his chains clinking, blowing the horn in long ear-punching bursts. Beyond the headlights he could see nothing, but he expected to come on them at any second, shielding their eyes from the glare. He drove on until he was sure he had gone farther than they could walk, and then he went on for another mile.

He turned back. Surely he had passed them. Surely they had been off the road and had come back when they heard the car. He leaned on the horn. They must hear it. Stephen began to swear at them. Where were they? Several times he thought he saw them at the periphery of his lights, but always a tree appeared, dressed in white. Then he came to the small white dome of Robbie's car, softened like a pillow by snow.

Thoroughly frightened, he got out and stuck his head into Robbie's car, thinking he had been mistaken, maybe this was all a nightmare. The light came on obediently, showing the interior undisturbed. Stephen even stuck his head over the front seat to see the floor in back, looking for what he did not know. Any hint of what to do.

He heard a yell. Stretched out over the front seat, he froze, and listened. It was not repeated. He pulled himself out of the car and cupped his hands around his mouth. "Robbie! Robbie!"

He heard the yell again. It came, not from the road, but from below, somewhere down the hill. It did not sound like a call so much as a shout of triumph. "I'm coming!" he shouted and began lowering himself down the embankment. The snow had piled up there, for the wind was blowing up the hill. As soon as his head was below the road, he could see absolutely nothing but slid and stumbled down, calling: "Robbie! Peter! Where are you? I'm coming!"

He heard no further response, but kept going until he came up against a log. Had he imagined it? He yelled again and got no answer, but letting his eyes grope the darkness he saw a tiny light. For a moment he thought it was a star, but it moved. "I see you," he yelled. "Who is that?" The light disappeared.

"What is this? You think this is a game? Come on, you guys." He was relieved to have found them, then angry. So it was hide-and-seek. He began feeling his way forward along the steep slope. He thought he saw the light go on again for an instant and he went straight toward it. A few yards along he heard a grunt, and as his eyes had grown accustomed to the darkness, he saw a figure on its hands and knees climbing up the slope. He reached up, grabbed a handful of jacket, and pulled.

"Let me go!" The voice was Peter's.

"Where's Robbie? Where are the others?"

"They're gone. You're too late."

Peter turned on his light. It was a tiny penlight, its

batteries weak. He had turned to face Stephen, who could just make out his big, dim, fleshy face.

"Gone?" Stephen demanded. "Why didn't they stay in the car?"

"You'd like to find them, huh?"

In his panic Stephen had almost forgotten how he had left them. Peter's gloating tone reminded him.

"They're gone, and your ass is cooked." Peter turned away and began climbing up the hill. Stephen grabbed his coat again.

"Where are you going?"

"I'm going home. Let go."

"How, you idiot?"

"I have the keys. I found them." He held them up, jingling them.

Stephen was flabbergasted. "You found them?"

"I'm not dumb. I wasn't going to walk around in this snow. I saw where you threw them." He turned away again and began to climb. "I'm going to tell everybody."

Stephen pulled him back roughly. "Tell what?" He grabbed Peter's hand and tried to wrestle the keys away. "Tell what?"

"I'm telling everything about you. We all are."

"What do you mean, 'We all are'?"

"We're going to tell the police you tried to kill us."

Stephen applied his thumb to the soft center of Peter's wrist, twisting and forcing his thumbnail into that groove until Peter dropped the keys. Then he jumped on top of Peter and forced his head down, pinning him face down into the snow. "You won't tell," he was shouting. Peter struggled, and struggled hard; he was strong. But Stephen would not let him up. He would never let him up. He smashed Peter's face down, into the snow, struggling with him and not realizing that at some point he was no longer struggling against the rigid muscles in Peter's back and neck but against the hard earth. Peter had stopped struggling.

"Oh, my God," Stephen said.

He checked for breath, for a pulse, and found nothing. Peter's body was a limp weight.

He had to get out, so he struggled his way up to the road, like a diver forcing his way to the surface for air. He got in his car and drove down the hill, chains jingling, and this time when he came to the intersection he kept going.

CHAPTER
30

Hager had been resting his head in his arms, looking into a corner of the kitchen while Stephen talked. Now he looked up, hearing the heaviness of the wind beating back the pine limbs.

"And why didn't you tell us?" Hager asked like a drugged man. "Make up a story, anything, but tell us they were out there?"

"Why didn't I tell you?" Stephen spoke sarcastically. "I had killed him, Dad. M-U-R-D-E-R. I figured I had killed them all. I never dreamed they could make it to the cabin. I didn't even remember that cabin."

"You figured," Hager snapped. He swung around toward Stephen, who flinched back as though he might be hit. "You figured a lot of things. We might have found them. Do you realize that?"

Carrie had begun working on the refrigerator with a sponge, scrubbing it clean. It was her way; she could rarely sit still in a conversation. She sighed, seemed about to speak, then closed her mouth and went back to cleaning.

"What are you trying to say?" Hager asked Stephen. "That it was all a miscalculation?" He got up and went pacing hard around the room, bumping into a kitchen chair and shoving it out of his way as he went. Stephen was following him with his eyes.

"Well?" Hager asked. He had thought it would be better to

know, but it was infinitely worse. "Is that it? Don't you have anything to say for yourself?"

"Nothing more," Stephen said.

"Then what was the point of talking all night?"

"I told you to listen, Dad. You didn't listen."

"I heard every word."

"No," Stephen said insistently. "You didn't listen."

"Well, I'm kind of dumb. Why don't you spell it out for me?"

"Dad, I didn't want to kill him, but he wanted to kill me. He wanted me gone."

"You think you can plead self-defense because a retarded kid wanted everybody to know that you knocked up your girlfriend? You're more self-centered than I thought."

"Dad, will you listen?" Stephen's voice had a high, thin edge to it. "I'm not pleading anything. I'm trying to explain why it happened."

"Regardless of why, the facts are the same."

Stephen shook his head angrily. "You can hate me, that's your right. But don't be so dumb about it."

Hager felt his heart accelerate, nervous, fast, pounding like a mistimed engine. "Steve," he said. "Hate? I wouldn't be talking to you if I hated you. I'm just sick. I was hoping that if we talked it would make it better, but it only makes it worse."

"Dad, don't you see? Robbie hated me."

"Even if I saw that, what could it possibly change?"

"Why do you think he walked all those miles through the snow?" Stephen spoke ferociously as though pounding home a well-rehearsed speech. "Haven't you realized what that meant? He was walking just so he could tell on me. Robbie knew to stay with the car. You had taught him that. He walked because he wanted to tell. He knew that I would come back, and he didn't want me to find him. He had such a great opportunity to get back at me for being normal."

Hager's response was long in coming. "I guess I'm just dumb, Steve, but I still don't see how that makes any difference. Even if it's true."

"Then you don't know what it's like to be hated. By your own father. By your own brother."

"I don't hate you," Hager said, heatedly. "I've never hated you. I've been preoccupied, but that's not the same as hate."

"It's just as bad," Stephen said quickly.

"No, it's not the same."

"Well, I'm sure you'll hate me now, Dad. You won't be able to stand being near me because I killed your precious son."

"No, Stephen. I could never hate you. You're just as much my son." But Hager's inner voice asked whether he spoke the truth.

"Stephen." Carrie spoke up. "Stephen," she said in a low, soft tone, "don't take the attention off what you've done."

Stephen looked at them both a long time as though trying to make up his mind whether to speak. Finally he said, "You want to know what's the point."

"Yes," Carrie said. "We've been talking all night."

Stephen hesitated again. "I want you to forgive me."

"Forgive you?" Hager asked. "Not turn you in, you mean?"

"I mean forgive," Stephen said. "Accept that I made a mistake, that I didn't mean it. Forgive me. You know what 'forgive' means."

They finally went back to bed, not expecting to sleep. It was too painful to continue rehearsing what had already been said. In the hallway Hager put an arm around Stephen's shoulder, awkwardly trying to convey love as they parted.

Stephen merely shrugged. He was not going to give Hager the satisfaction of warmth.

In the bedroom Hager found Carrie already curled beneath the covers. He turned out the light and threw his robe into the corner, then lay beside her, cradling her in his arms. He had not known that grief could hurt physically, like a bruise all over his body.

Carrie turned over, facing him. She locked her hands behind his head and kissed him. "Make love to me," she said. "Would you?"

He was never ordinarily in doubt how to answer that question, but he had to think a moment before he said, "All right." He stretched his arms around her and for a while they did nothing, merely held each other.

"I wish I could cry," Hager said to her.

"Why? It doesn't help."

"I thought it did," Hager said softly. "To get your feelings out."

"It doesn't help me."

Carrie's hands began to move, stroking his back and then his chest, raking her fingers through the silky hair there. Then she was gently kissing him on the neck. He was not sure, for a while, that he could respond; he lay distracted. Then he began to move his hands, then his mouth, and soon they were locked hard together, clinching as though to press out sorrow.

It was over too soon and they lay together with nothing different, except that they had been joined. "We haven't done that in a long time," he said.

"No," she said. "I've been missing you."

"Have I been gone?"

"Yes," she said. "For a long time. I'm not blaming you, though. You were right. I wanted you to stop looking, but you were right."

"Sure?" he asked. "Now we have to live with what we know. Poor Stephen. I never knew that he was so alone. He thinks I hate him."

"You don't, do you?"

"Part of me will, I think."

"What are you going to do now?"

"About Stephen? I'm going to do what he asked. Forgive him. Try, anyway. Make a new start."

"I don't think I can live with him, knowing," Carrie said in a sad and vacant voice.

"You've been living with him for the past five months."

"It's not the same. I don't know if I could sit down to breakfast with him every day. Do we talk about it? Do we ignore it? What do we say?"

"He'll be going away to college."

"Fine, but he'll come home too."

"What are you saying? That we should turn in our son?"

She did not answer.

"All I know is that I've let Stephen down for eighteen years. I'm not going to let him down again."

"You sound like it's your fault."

He threw up a hand. "I've failed somewhere." She did not answer him although he had hoped she would dispute his guilt.

"We can't throw him out," Hager said. "At least, I can't. I've neglected him too many times. I'm not going to betray him now."

"Neglect is not the same as murder," Carrie said.

"No," he said. "It's not."

"Do you think it would be good for Stephen?" she asked finally.

"I think it would be good for him to know his family is on his side," he answered quickly.

"Yes, but on his side in what way? He has to live with what he's done."

"The issue," Hager insisted, "is whether you love your son. If you love him, you have to stick by him. If he wants to confess to the police, fine. But he confessed to me. I have to keep that confidence. I can't betray him again, Carrie." His voice cracked. He was tired, too tired to think.

CHAPTER

31

The morning found Hager in his blue bathrobe, seated in a wicker chair on the back deck and nibbling blearily at a bowl of Cheerios. Carrie sat with him, her bowl, napkin, and placemat neatly arranged but undisturbed. The deck gave them a view up the hill into a forest of long-needle pines, oak, and poison oak, through which sunlight spilled.

They sat without speaking, not hearing the loud grawking of a jay until he flitted down to their table and cocked his head toward their cereal. Hager stuck his hand in the Cheerios box and threw a handful out over the edge of the deck.

"Don't encourage them," Carrie said. "They make a terrible mess."

"Yeah," he said. "Sorry."

Carrie sighed deeply. "What are you going to do?"

"About Stephen? I don't know," he said. "Nothing."

"I can't," she said. "I've thought about it. I can't live with him here. It's impossible to pretend that nothing happened."

"Is it pretending?" Hager asked. He felt washed out from lack of sleep, and his certainty about defending Stephen had vanished.

"I can't do it," she insisted. "I'm sorry. I can't sit here eating breakfast and talking about the weather with him as though we just go on from here."

"You want to turn him in?"

"I think he has to decide. I just know he can't stay here."

The screen door slid open, and Hager flinched, startled. Stephen came out dressed in sweats and sat down beside them. "I heard," he said. "Don't pretend."

Carrie got out of her chair and went to put her arms around his unresponding neck, and she clung there.

"Don't turn it around, Steve," Carrie said. "Don't do that. Don't spend your life blaming other people for something you did. You have done something truly terrible. It could hardly be worse. But it will be worse for you if you try to make out that you did it because your family didn't understand you, or something like that."

"But you don't understand," he said. "That's just a fact."

"No, I don't. I don't understand a lot of things. But I do understand that nothing can excuse killing your own brother."

Hager stood up, roused from his fatigue by alarm. "What your mother is trying to say is that we love you. We really, deeply love you. We don't know where to go from here."

"I don't see that it's for you to decide," Stephen said coldly. Last night's vulnerability had disappeared.

"What about Lizzie?" Carrie interjected softly. "Is she supposed to know? How am I going to live day by day keeping a secret from her?"

"I can't," Stephen whispered. "Don't make me." He had so suddenly shed his sullenness that for a moment Hager did not grasp the change. Stephen looked to his father, then his mother, then his father again.

"Nobody can make you," Hager said.

"I want to stay here," Stephen said. "With you."

"No, Stephen," Carrie said. "I can't."

At last Hager was able to cry. "I'll go with you," he said. "You won't be alone."

"Dad, I don't want to tell. Please don't make me."

Hager went to Stephen and put a hand on his shoulder, squeezing the softened deltoid. He would have liked to hug him. Stephen's face looked as delicate as a child's.

Stephen looked back and forth between Hager and Carrie. "You want me to tell, don't you?"

"I'll go with you," Hager said again.

CHAPTER

32

In the back of the courtroom, where wide oak doors opened onto a tiled corridor, Hager and Carrie and Lizzie paused, looking out. They were dressed up; even Lizzie wore a dress. Hager had his hand on Lizzie's red and purple floral-patterned shoulder; Carrie stood close enough for him to lean against.

Hager was looking down the hall, where the foyer opened up. Standing out from the courthouse's subdued greenish light were two figures, brilliantly illuminated, gleaming like angels. They were being filmed for TV.

Most of the courtroom had emptied out. It was a modern rectangle with theater seats and a low acoustic ceiling, a room with oak paneling and subdued recessed lighting and the character of a stockbroker's waiting room. Only the lawyers remained in it, shaking hands, packing up their briefcases. "Well," Hager said, looking ahead at the TV lights, "it's only one more time. Or two. They'll be back for the sentencing, I suppose."

"Mr. Hager." Balzeti hurried up on his little legs, wearing a sensitive pucker on his face. "Would you like to go out another way? You can avoid the reporters."

It was not in Hager's nature to avoid anything, but he felt a deep relief at the thought of escaping questions. "Sure," he said. "If it's no trouble." As they turned away from the door, following Balzeti, he glimpsed Carrie's face, tight with strain.

They exited by the same door that Stephen had been taken through and were immediately in a very different environment, a concrete corridor with shining aqua walls and light bulbs overhead, naked in little cages. They walked quickly for a hundred yards, then through a heavy, echoing door, up a flight of cement stairs, through a series of locked doors. They emerged into the large, busy room in the sheriff's annex where Hager had talked to Balzeti long ago. A few of the men clustered there glanced up.

"Now," Balzeti said, "we can get your car." He called Ramirez, who detached himself from a conversation. "Luis, could you go get the Hagers' car for them? Bring it into the garage downstairs. They really would rather not talk to reporters."

Hager gave up the keys and told Ramirez where he had parked. Balzeti pulled up chairs. "Is that comfortable?" he asked Carrie. "I'm sorry there's no private place where you can wait. It will only be a few minutes." He brought a chair for himself and sat with them, standing up twice to adjust the position. He was fussing like an overambitious host.

"You remember when you came here?" Balzeti asked. "To this very room." Hager nodded.

"You didn't think we would ever find out who had killed those boys, and I don't think we ever would have if he hadn't come forward."

Carrie and Hager looked ahead, self-consciously not replying.

"It took a lot of courage for him to do that," Balzeti said. "I don't think they're going to be too hard on him. It was really almost an accident."

Carrie had turned to look off in another direction, toward the window. Hager's face revealed his feelings. He knew that Balzeti mostly meant well.

"What penalty do you think he'll get?" Hager asked. It was painful even to say the words.

Balzeti stretched, cracking his fingers. "Well, for manslaughter it can vary a lot. Under the circumstances I think it will be pretty minimal. The prosecutor told me he would go easy on him. Maybe four years. Maybe three. He could be paroled in eighteen months."

Carrie continued to look out the window. Lizzie alone looked natural: She was turning her head to all sides, observing with interest. "Where will he go?" she asked.

Balzeti raised his eyebrows. "That's up to the judge. Probably the ranch. That's where the non-dangerous ones usually go. I don't think they would consider Stephen dangerous. Otherwise, off to one of the state prisons. I hope he doesn't get that."

Ramirez came in, jingling the keys. "All set," he said and accompanied them, along with Balzeti, down two flights of stairs and out some security doors into a dim underground garage. The Chrysler was parked in front of the doorway, with the motor running. The Hagers got in. The car seats were hot from being in the sun.

"Thanks," Hager said and then pushed the automatic window closed. They went up an incline and out an automatic gate, blinking in the bright sunshine. Hager flicked the air conditioning up to high.

"Shall we get some lunch?" he asked, stopping the car at the curb. "It's almost noon."

"I don't feel hungry," Carrie said.

"Are you crying?" he asked.

"Yes."

Hager glanced over his shoulder into the back seat. "What about you, honey? Are you hungry? Are you okay?"

"I'm fine," Lizzie said. "Let's just go home." She sounded exactly, down to the last inflection, like Carrie.

But Hager did not want to return home just yet. Swinging the car onto the baking streets, he began cruising. Not a pedestrian was in sight; the heat was ungodly. The gray concrete sidewalks and tan stucco buildings burned white like overexposed film. He crossed the mall, where Fresno's main street had been blocked off to cars in favor of trees and fountains. The stores on the cross street were empty, their dark reflecting windows pasted with vacancy signs.

The sidewalks had been busier when he was a boy, before the shopping centers; even on a day like this people would be out. The stores had been local, the merchants home-town figures. It was all gone. That world had vanished. *And very little lost,* he thought. There was not much reason for nostalgia, other than the fact that he had been young here.

"Eighteen months is a long time," Lizzie said from the back. "Does that mean we won't see Stephen for that long?"

"No, we'll see him," Carrie said. "We'll visit him as often as we can."

"A lot?"

"I guess that depends on where he goes."

Hager added, "We'll go as often as they let us. I don't know the rules, but I think nowadays they encourage visitors." He let out a long breath. "Even two years isn't so long. It'll go by quickly." He felt uneasy about Balzeti's prediction of lenience. Such a terrible crime, and in two years Stephen would be forgiven? Yet Hager found that he was already counting on it, greedily. He wanted his son back, on almost any terms.

And what then? Hager asked himself. A new beginning? Would Stephen be able to go on to college? Would Stanford take him again?

He could not quite envisage what it would be like to have Stephen return, how they would talk, how they would sit down to breakfast, as Carrie had put it. Two years was not so long, it would go by quickly.

Hager glanced over at Carrie. She was still staring into space, still apart from him.

"You know what was strange?" he said to her. "When they led Stephen out that door I felt as though he was gone into some other world. That door was like the way into hell. And then a few minutes later we were going through it, and where did it lead? To an office." He laughed to himself. He was driving slowly, looping around the eight block circuit surrounding the mall. He cut off and crossed it, going west toward the tracks. In a few blocks the buildings were boarded up and the vacant lots full of trash.

"Let's go home now," Carrie said, her voice flat.

"In a minute," he said.

"Why do you love this place? It's ugly."

He sighed. "Yeah, I suppose. It reminds me of when I was a kid." He turned abruptly toward Blackstone Avenue, six lanes of hamburgers and traffic lights that led toward home. In a few minutes the view had changed, old Fresno fell behind them, and the new was all around. The sky was deep and cloudless and flat as an iron.

The sky stays the same, he thought, *and the orchards are the same, and the vineyards, and the smell of water seeping down the irrigation channels—that would be the same today as in my grandfather's time. And brothers against brothers, and fathers against sons, these are the same also. Nothing has happened to me that my grandfather would have found astounding. Thank God that we get new chances, that we can, if not exactly start over, at least try again.*

"You were right," he said to Carrie.

"About what?" she asked.

"We couldn't have lived with him that way. Couldn't have had breakfast."

"And now we can?"

"We will," he said.

*   *   *

Cain said to the Lord, "My punishment is more than I can bear. Today you are driving me from the land, and I will be hidden from your presence; I will be a restless wanderer on the earth, and whoever finds me will kill me."

But the Lord said to him, "Not so."